OPAL EYE DEVIL

A Novel by:

John Hamilton Lewis

Published by:
Durban House Publishing Company, Inc.
7502 Greenville Avenue, Suite 500
Dallas, Texas 75231

ISBN 1-930754-01-9
$24.95

Publication Date October 1, 2000

Advertising and author tour.

Dedications

龍

OPAL EYE DEVIL

Prologue

ERIC GRADEK'S EYES OPENED AS THE CARGO ship heeled against the squall's force. Darkness surrounded him, and he could smell his sweat mingling with the stench from the bilge. How long he had been in the ship's hold he could not say. What he did know was that each heartbeat brought him closer to death. Probing his gut, Eric's fingers told him blood was everywhere.

Dominate the fear, he told himself. *Don't panic.*

Ragged thoughts, but somehow his body obeyed. Tearing off a piece of his shirt, Eric stuffed it into the wound, then lay motionless on his back. Distant echoes from the ship's boilers gave him a focal point to fight the fear. Then the rat came. It sniffed the wound, then moved up to his chest. The claws were random pinpricks through his shirt. Its nose touched Eric's chin.

Gathering his remaining strength, Eric stiffened his fingers and jabbed. A loud *screee*. Scratching sounds. Scurrying feet across the metal deck.

Eric closed his eyes, replacing the sounds of the boilers with an image of Alex Bartrum. Hatred blossomed like an ugly wet rose. It would keep him alive, get him through.

The ship heeled again, a dull dinning of its hull plates. But Eric did not feel it. He was focused on Bartrum.

*   *   *

EARLIER, Eric had gone up to the main deck. Dusk was approaching and a north wind tugged his hair. Cumulus lumbered across the sky and to the west an orange and amethyst sky cut a swath of rippling gold across the sea. He had just finished dinner and relished these moments of free time. Fatigued from eighteen hour work days, he leaned against the rail, letting spray and salt hit his face. The sea whispered, renewing him, lifting his spirit.

Tomorrow he would be landing in Shanghai. England now seemed a distant dream. "Shanghai." Even the word sounded exciting. Eric stared at the sea and infinity beyond. And, for a moment, felt himself rendered insignificant.

The wind freshened. Eric licked his finger and held it high in the way the old salts along the English docks had taught him.

Storm was in the air, its first hint burling around his finger-tip.

Eric nodded to the beefy Irishman who stepped up beside him. Both men had signed on as seaman, forfeiting wages for passage. Their ship was *Northern Star*, one of more than forty such cargo steamers belonging to Bartrum & Sons, Asia's largest trading company. Comfortable in their silence, Eric and the Irishman stared at the sea until laughter distracted them.

A group of men had gathered at the far end of the deck. Eric watched Alex Bartrum, a tall, swarthy Englishman with the kind of arrogant good looks attributed to the overindulged.

"Bloody hell would you look at that," the Irishman said. "Bartrum and his cronies have got themselves a new plaything."

The plaything was a Chinese dwarf. Bartrum clapped his hands in mock musical time. "Come on little man, let's see you dance a heathen jig."

When the dwarf failed to respond Bartrum shoved him into the center of the circle. The dwarf stared in fright at the giants surrounding him.

Bartrum gave him another shove. "Damn your yellow hide, I said dance."

A man next to Bartrum splashed brandy on the dwarf's face. "Let's see if a drink will wind him up --- eh, Alex?"

Laughter, followed by a flood of brandy. The dwarf scrambled on his knees trying to escape the ring of torment. One of the men jerked him up by his queue. "What kind of man are you, anyway?"

"A freak, that's what he is," said another. "A bloody afterthought of nature."

Another flood of brandy.

Bartrum kicked the dwarf. "I said dance. You think speaking the Queen's English makes you more than a godcursed heathen?"

Eric's anger roiled. The beatings he and his mother had suffered at the hands of his father surged like the sea. A scream snapped his head up. But it was not the dwarf crying for help --- it was his mother.

Bartrum's boot found the dwarf again. Another shriek. Eric

started across the deck. There would be a terrible price to pay, but anger sent him forward. He pushed through the circle of men and knelt beside the dwarf. Ignoring belligerent stares, he picked the bony bundle up and began walking back to where the Irishman was standing.

"Put the godrotten Chinaman down, now." Bartrum's voice cracked like a whip.

Northern Star heeled on a gathering wind.

Eric turned, green eyes flashing. "This man's done nothing wrong."

Bartrum turned to the giant, who was never far from his side. "Mr. Jones, this insolent sod doesn't know how to follow an order."

"I'll tend the sodding bastard, sir."

A knife appeared in the bodyguard's hand.

Eric retreated, but stumbled. Jones's blade slipped under the bony bundle to find its mark. Eric's insides turned to fire, the dwarf falling to the deck. Through the descending darkness, he saw Jones and Bartrum over him.

"Should I finish him now, Mr. Bartrum?"

"God's blood no, Mr. Jones. Nothing so easy for this sod. Throw him in the hold and let him bleed to death."

*   *   *

ERIC wrapped his arms around himself. He was in hell. A seventeen-year-old boy slowly dying with his dreams.

Why in God's name did I intervene? I knew I'd wind up in the muck, but to bleed to death in a stinking hold.....

His first time out of England. Was his life to end before having a chance to begin? The thought was beyond comprehension. His gut twisted against the bloody rags. Eric cursed Bartrum and swore before God and the devil he would have his revenge. He was passing into something deeper than sleep when a candle flared. Darkness pressed around him like purling velvet. The rag covering his wound was removed and replaced with a poultice.

Eric was unable to lift his head. "Who is it?"

"Do not move. I am Tong-Po --- the dwarf."

It was October 29, 1887.

SHANGHAI 1900

He hath out-villained villainy so far
that the rarity redeems him.

...Shakespeare...

One

THE WOMAN CARESSED THE BAG UNDER HER arm. her face, old beyond her years, had the patina of ancient ivory. Walking was difficult, for her back was bowed by years of working the rice fields in her native village.

She licked her lips, eyes constantly searching about her. Some hungry soul might try and steal her treasure. Inside the bag was an assortment of fresh vegetables she had gotten from kitchen duties at the Commerce Club. With proper management there would be three days of food.

It was ten p.m. when she approached the front gate of Havershire's godown, one of Shanghai's largest trading houses. The old woman was relieved at having reached the warehouse district. Her body ached, but there was no time to dally. Ahead lay the flickering oil lamps of home.

Five years ago, the old woman and her husband joined millions fleeing famine in the interior to find work in the city.

After surviving the tortuous journey, they were once again on the brink of starvation. Home was a one room hovel in the shantytown located on a stingy outcrop of land along the banks of the Huangpu River.

Oppressive heat had smothered the city for a fortnight and the old woman found it hard to breathe. She stopped in front of Havershire's. It was unusually quiet, only the endless beat of the surf against the sea wall. Then the stillness became alive. Sounds of stray dogs and other creatures rummaging the streets for food. Nearby, a dark form moaned.

The old woman pressed the vegetable bag closer to her frail chest and began walking. Several steps later, she stiffened then doubled over. Vegetables scattered as her gnarled fingers grasped the stanchions of the gate. She had previously suffered attacks of angina, but never so painfully suffocating as this. Minutes passed as the old woman waited in fear for her breath to return to normal. When the pain subsided she lowered herself to the ground and gathered up her vegetables. Once her bounty was safely back in the bag, she pulled herself up. Movement at the rear of the building. Was it her imagination or did a pair of shadows leap the rear fence? The ground began to shake. *Why,* she wondered, did the barbarian, Havershire, not have guards posted?

Whhuuump.

The old woman's eyes grew wide as the front of the warehouse ballooned outward in a blazing inferno. She stood silhouetted against flame.

Other explosions followed.

At the southern edge of the harbor, fireballs shot skyward as three British-owned kerosene depots erupted. Wind from the northwest carried the flames southward, along the harbor, toward the Bund and central business district.

Ancient hands clutched the vegetable bag as Shanghai's northern wharfage turned to cinder.

Civil defense sirens wailed. Thousands of people poured onto the streets. Children clung to their mothers. Along the pier, fire-fighters retreated to the next pump station. Army engineers dynamited warehouses, followed by volunteers hacking through the remains to clear fire lanes.

The old woman's eyes watched all this as fire and shadow played across her ivory skin.

*   *   *

ERIC Gradek raced from the Fire Marshall's office to his godown complex. He knew his warehouses, or a least many of them, would be lost. *No time for pity,* he told himself. This was joss. Take what the gods leave and fornicate the rest.

Crowds writhed and surged, but he paid them little notice. Steadying the burlap bag on his shoulder, Eric looked to the easement beside his warehouse. The canal was used to barge-load kerosene drums he manufactured exclusively for Trident Industries. He checked the wind, its force and direction. *Maybe enough width to hold ground.* But, explosions said otherwise. The fire was hungry, tongues of flame enveloping everything in its path.

Eric went inside. Employees were frantically packing books and records. Desks and chairs had been shoved to the side to fill the accounting rooms with file boxes. Tong-Po, his comprador, was on top of a wooden crate screaming out orders, his small arms flailing. Catching sight of Eric, the Chinese dwarf turned and shouted, "More men should be arriving any time, Taipan."

17

"Good." Eric pulled a handful of damp gauze mask from his pouch and handed one to Tong-Po. The rest he handed a clerk to pass around. Even with the mask, breathing was difficult as smoke thickened.

"Not much time, Tong-Po. How long before you can get the vital stuff out?"

"Watchman Choy took the most important documents to my house. Another ten minutes and I'll have the rest boxed and gone." Tong-Po coughed, racking his bulbous chest. He stared at Eric. "Most of Shanghai will burn. Shouldn't we break out the hoses and make a stand?"

"Forget it." Eric's voice was raw. "Hoses are no good against what's out there. Every breath of oxygen within fifty yards is being sucked up. No way we can hold it off."

Tong-Po's face was a rictus of fear in the flickering light. "By all gods, what then?"

"I'm going to dynamite the south warehouse. Shanghai will be lost or saved at the canal. With luck we might create enough of a break to cut access to the city. The Fire Marshall's sending every available man. Maybe the offices and north building will be spared."

"Dynamite the south warehouse? That's an entire season's worth of silk!"

"There's no other way." Eric grasped Tong-Po's shoulder. "Don't worry, old friend, we'll come out of it. You've got ten minutes to gather our people and get the hell away from here."

*   *   *

NEXT door breathing was almost impossible. Adair MacAlister, the company's general manager, was exhorting

---

about fifty bare-chested coolies to load silk bolts onto an awaiting barge.

Eric pulled the burly Scot aside. "Addie, we've only minutes left. How much can be salvaged?"

"With God's help, perhaps seventy to eighty percent." Sweat streamed down the Scot's face. "But we need more barges. I've sent word, but --- "

Eric bit his lip. "How much is left in the north building?"

"A few random bolts. I had the European inventory transferred here."

Eric was sick. For five years, he had controlled Shanghai's silk trade. He was the only Westerner allowed to deal with the *co-hong*, a guild of China's largest silk producers, a position arranged by his mentor Jing-Jiang that had made him one of Asia's most powerful taipan. Now more than ten thousand bolts were about to be turned to ash.

An entire season gone. Godrot it all. Every bit of cash tied up. Shanghai, or the silk? Which do I save?

Eric turned to MacAlister. "Addie, in ten minutes this warehouse is going to hell."

*   *   *

ON a distant warehouse roof, two men watched the orange glow above the docks. Both were dressed in black pantaloons and loose-fitting cotton tops. The shorter, more muscular, of the two was Dragon Mok, High Tiger of the Red Pang. Beside him was his lieutenant, Ting se-Bing.

Mok focused his binoculars. "The dragons of the dark realm have risen." He glanced at Ting. "By destroying three kerosene depots instead of two, the destruction will be great. Many will

---

die."

Ting watched the fire spread. No reason to tell Mok he had arranged for the third fuel depot to be detonated. So much better if the dragon incinerated every last big nose with a white face.

The orange glow brightened along with Ting's excitement. His position in the Red Pang had accorded him great wealth. And until recently, it never bothered him that his fortune was a result of working with foreigners to exploit China. The Red Pang and rival Green Pang, headed by Formidable Fung Xio-Ling, maintained alliances with the barbarians. If workers rebelled to create better working conditions, Pang soldiers savagely beat them down. This brutality was repaid by officials who closed their eyes as the pangs spun their web of corruption.

China's easy defeat during the Sino/Japanese war five years earlier had profoundly effected Ting. Humiliated, the Qing court signed the Treaty of Shimonoseki. The agreement called for Korea's independence and Formosa's ceding to the Japanese. Further concessions allowed Japanese industries in key port cities. Other governments rushed in to grab their share. Foreign influence expanded and Ting's hatred for outsiders turned to obsession. He joined the *I-he-t'suan*, The Society of the Virtuous Harmony Fist. Of the many secret societies dedicated to purging China of foreigners the *I-he-t'suan* was the largest.

In the distance, a blood red cauldron heaved under new explosions. Dragon Mok smiled and let the binoculars rest. "What favors shall I exact from the Bartrums for saving their miserable skins?" he wondered aloud. "Their debt will be immense." Mok turned to Ting. "Your plan went well. So clever to blame the *I-he-t'suan*."

"Their recent attacks against foreign devils make them suspect. Who else would the authorities blame?" Ting stared at the buildings of Shanghai, the great city Westerners had confected for themselves. What he saw was through the eyes of a criminal turned patriot. Lines of coolies trotting up gangplanks discharging China's wealth into ships belonging to foreign devils; skeletal rickshaw runners pulling haughty British and French youths along Western-style boulevards; imperious compradors, reaping huge profits from barbarian exploitation; court-appointed Mandarins, whose greedy fingers touched all. A zealot's fire gathered in Ting's soul, his hate focusing on the Manchus --- the worst enemy of all. Their Empress Dowager Ci Xi --- a Manchurian whore sitting on the celestial throne of heaven, she and her rubbery court eunuchs plotting, scheming and gorging on China's riches. If not for the Manchus, the rape of the Middle Kingdom would not have been possible.

Ting spat into the hot dust. *If the people believe the I-het'suan is responsible for raining fire on foreign devils they will rush to our banner. The Empress Dowager cannot turn her back on the people in favor of foreign interests. Otherwise, she will be tossed from power sooner, rather than later. And with the army at our side we will crush the barbarians into this dust burning under my sandal.*

The sound of men approaching, turned their heads. Alex and Philip Bartrum followed by the hulking Mr. Jones.

"Shanghai is about to be destroyed because you buggered up," Alex said, glaring at Mok. "I could lose everything. There's enough kerosene down there to lay waste to the whole of China."

Mok glared back. "Stand back, barbarian, or I shall slit that wagging tongue."

Alex Bartrum tensed. The giant, Mr. Jones nearby, ready to kill.

Ting moved next to Mok, a throwing knife in his palm.

"Stop it!" Philip Bartrum stepped between them. "Killing each other won't solve our problems. All of us stand to lose everything. The best we can hope for is that a fire break can be established in time."

An explosion, larger than the others, shook the night. All men turned toward. Mok adjusted his binoculars.

"What the bloody hell was that?" Philip asked.

Dragon Mok smiled into his hands cupped around the binoculars. "Gradek International's southern warehouse."

*   *   *

THE fire reached the canal, sending shafts of flame over the water to where Eric's godown once stood. Then the wind shifted and the streets suddenly quieted. All eyes focused on the wall of fire. The fire began retreating on pulsating air. Screams of joy filled the night as the wind reversed itself. Then the people blessed the god or gods of their ancestors that they would live to see another day.

Flames retraced their path, sucking down the heat onto the smoldering cinders. It probably would have burned itself out had it not been for the elevation around the depot where Havershire's once stood. There the earth fell away, following the Huangpu River's easterly flow towards the Yangtze. It was this area that the Huangpu and adjacent land leading to the shantytown had soaked up an ocean of kerosene.

Shanghai's fire marshal leaned on his ax. His hands were burned and cut. Blood ran down his cheek. He glanced at Eric. "Praise God. Looks like the bloody nightmare's over. I hate to think of the consequences if that monster had jumped the canal."

Eric's eyes were fixed on the spot where his warehouse, containing a season's worth of silk, had stood minutes before.

The Fire Marshall followed Eric's gaze. "Sorry about the bad joss, Mr. Gradek. Your godown and silk..... I mean, but the alternative would have --- " An eruption of orange light turned them around. "Bloody Christ." The Fire Marshall grabbed a nearby assistant. "Get the sirens going. Round up whatever men and hoses you can find. Maybe there's time to create a break."

Rushing to face new dangers, the Fire Marshall was barely aware Eric Gradek had disappeared.

* * *

FIRST to be consumed were the sampan homes and fishing boats clustered in the Floating City. Then the flames moved towards the shantytown.

Eric was propped against a tin hut, his head hanging between raised knees, the bag of dynamite beside him. What made him think he could make it to the south shore before the entire shantytown was gone? Already his lungs were bursting. Kerosene fumes fouled the remaining air.

Lifting his head, Eric saw a young girl holding her child. Her hollowed out eyes reflected fire and anguish. He had no words for her. Words from a Westerner wouldn't mean a thing while thousands of Chinese burned alive.

Eric struggled to his feet. The girl was gone, but her image was embedded in his brain. *God, if there is a god, give me strength.* Grabbing the bag of dynamite, he lurched into the night. He was somewhere near the center of the shantytown and running towards the dikes on the lower river.

The fire had sealed the northern and eastern borders. Access to the river was cut as the blaze swept through the Floating City. The only safe route was due west --- an option that was rapidly diminishing. The sick and elderly fell under the human tide. Mothers, too exhausted to stand, passed their shrieking children to strangers --- only to have them discarded in the nearest refuse heap.

Eric had to cut back from one dead end to another. A small voice kept reminding him that he was on a collision course with the fire as it moved from the river into the shantytown. He stopped.   A human wall had congealed in front of him. Ducking into a hovel, he raced out the back door in the direction of the river. But now his energy well was depleted. Was the girl with the screaming child safe?

Don't think, a voice inside said. *Put one foot in front of the other. Forget the horror. Get to the river.*

Reaching inside himself, Eric found a pocket of strength and broke through the line of tin shacks. The dike loomed ahead. Behind the seawall, flames danced on the water as the fishing boats and sampans sank.

The reservoir was full, but there was little time.

Only one charge.

Eric crawled crab-like along the sea wall. The fire was gaining, but he cursed away his fear. More scrambling until finding a crevice. He jammed in the dynamite and lit the fuse.

*   *   *

"WHERE are you, Taipan?" Tong-Po stared at the window, but

his fuzzy image only gave back the question. The dwarf shuddered. Dawn was approaching and Eric had not returned.

Devil-eyed fool's probably lying dead somewhere in the shantytown. Did he really think he could make a difference against that dragon fire? A flea attacking an elephant.

Tong-Po's gaze moved to the quay. The southern docks were smoldering but under control. Men were busy clearing rubble from walkways.

Deh neh loh moh, on all fires. Our hong is devastated. Under-insured --- a season of silk lost --- months of rebuilding.

In the heat minutes melted into hours.

Tong-Po spoke into the darkness. "Gods, if you are listening, I beg you bring this man back."

From the harbor came the somber boom of a cargo ship. The same kind of ship he had smuggled a dying boy off so many years ago.

Two

S hanghai, 1887

NORTHERN STAR WAS TWO HOURS OUT OF SHANGHAI when Tong-Po tossed the last of his books overboard. *My looking glass into the workings of the Western mind,* he thought. *Such a primitive lens, compared to the fine prism of Chinese writing.* More than a hundred kilos of the combined writings of Dickens, Dante, Homer, Aristotle, and the other classics --- about the same weight as one green-eyed barbarian. Returning to his cabin, Tong-Po locked the door and began cutting air holes in the side of his empty footlocker.

Tong-Po found it incredible that the barbarian with flashing eyes had risked his life for him. *Foolish man.* It was something he would never have done for a foreign devil. Memories conjured of the bullying and insults he'd suffered while studying in England. Still, this barbarian was different. Of course, there was the problem of the debt. And such a vast debt. How to repay it? If he managed to smuggle him off the ship, then what? Should he leave him on the docks to die? Or, take him to see Jing-Jiang?

Since childhood, Tong-Po had been with the powerful warlord of Hangzhou. Jing-Jiang had found him starving in a village after a battle, his diminutive figure smaller still. Now, the dwarf was his personal advisor. And what would Jing-Jiang's reaction be if he returned with a barbarian? Tong-Po chuckled. "Interesting, if nothing else."

It had been three years since Jing-Jiang sent him to England.

"I want you to go to learn about foreign devils and their mercantile practices," the old warlord said. "If we are to shed the Manchu yoke then China must join the modern world." Jing-Jiang folded his hands. "I dream of the day when the rivers of China are opened to free trade. Trade managed by Chinese instead of foreigners. I see factories throughout the interior with barges delivering goods to deprived people. A China co-joined of the ancient and the new will rise from the abyss."

"But, there is much trade already with foreign devils."

"Bah, that is not trade." Jing-Jiang's eyes were calm, reading his country's history. "It is organized thievery between barbarians and their Manchu lackeys. The Chinese people are exploited for labor."

Tong-Po finished the air holes and put the knife away. It wasn't long before the knock came. He opened the door and looked up at the ship's Chinese cook.

Fortunately, it was early morning and most of the crew and passengers were asleep. Working quickly, Tong-Po and the cook had Eric inside the footlocker in minimal time. Two hours later, he was stowed on the junk sent by Jing-Jiang.

27

*   *   *

ERIC awoke in a strange room several days later to find Tong-Po sitting across from him, swinging his stumpy legs. The dwarf wore black pantaloons and a red silk Mandarin jacket buttoned at the neck. His queue fell to his waist in a long braid. "Ah. At last you are awake."

A sharp clap of his hands and two girls in blue *cheong-soms* appeared. One carried a black-lacquered tray that held a red porcelain teapot with matching cups. The other carried a tray set with bowls of rice and fresh fruits.

"They have been tending your wound for the past three days," Tong-Po said. "Fortunately your fever has broken, but you have lost much blood."

Eric stared at the sweat stained nightgown, aware of his rancid nakedness beneath. The girls sat with heads bowed, their faces betray no emotion.

Tong-Po's eyes held a hint of amusement. "I'm quite sure this sudden change is disorienting."

Eric tried to rise, but was stopped by a sharp pain. He kept his eyes on the dwarf. "You were in the hold."

"Do not move suddenly," Tong-Po said. "Your wound has not yet had time to mend." He inclined his head toward the two girls. "You are a guest in the house of Jing-Jiang."

The girls lifted Eric's nightgown. "What in God's name are you doing?" He tried to cover himself, but pain threw him back.

Tong-Po smiled to himself. *Foolish barbarian.* "Let them look at you," he said. "They are skilled in the art of healing. And just who do you think has been changing your dressing these past days --- Alex Bartrum?"

The silk sutures held and Tong-Po dismissed the girls. Eric started to speak, but the dwarf touched a finger to his lips. "Eat first. You need nourishment." Lifting the teapot, the dwarf poured two cups. "Tea and food before conversation, *heya*? It will help clarify matters."

Tong-Po tried to show Eric how to use chopsticks. The slim pieces of ivory, inlaid with jade and onyx, were cool against his fingers. Yet, despite their beauty, Eric somehow felt offended trying to eat with heathen utensils. Under Tong-Po's eyes, he made several attempts to pick up his food. Frustrated by his failure, he set them aside and ate with his hands.

The two girls arrived with fresh tea and hot towels. They cleared the table and Eric looked at Tong-Po. "You saved my life. And I'm grateful." His words trailed. Conversation was difficult.

They watched each other.

Tong-Po put his teacup down. "Fate has brought us together. For what purpose I cannot say. But we must talk."

"Where am I?"

"Hangzhou! A city not far from Shanghai. It is the silk capital of China. As I said, you are a guest in the house of Jing-Jiang." Tong-Po then told Eric the details of how he had smuggled him off *Northern Star*.

Eric's mind conjured images of Alex Bartrum and his knife-wielding bodyguard. Anger roiled. "I need to get to Shanghai as soon as possible."

Tong-Po looked away from the fire in Eric's eyes. "Perhaps it would be better to proceed with caution. You have a powerful enemy in Shanghai."

"Thanks for the advice." Eric's chin jutted. "But, I'll figure a way to handle Bartrum and that sodding Jones."

Tong-Po smiled to himself, at the defiant boy in the night-shirt. Yet, in some ways he was like a man. "How old are you?"

"Seventeen."

Is it to be my karma to be joined with this boy-man? Tong-Po sighed. "You have much to learn if you are to survive in China. If you go to Shanghai now Alex Bartrum could have you killed as easily as stepping on an ant."

"I'm going to cut Bartrum's heart out. Then I'll take care of Jones."

"The deer does not attack the Tiger." Tong-Po stared at Eric. "For now, it would be best to stay under the protection of Jing-Jiang."

Eric looked at the dwarf. At that moment, he had no way of knowing that the next eight years of his life would be carefully crafted by Jing-Jiang, with Tong-Po weaving in and out of their lives on his stumpy legs. The first two would be spent learning Chinese and the complexities of the silk industry.

On their second anniversary together Jing-Jang, with the faithful dwarf beside him, would tell Eric how he'd be spending the next six.

*   *   *

Eric and Tong-Po were seated opposite Jing-Jiang at a black-lacquered table in the courtyard at the Inn of Three Blossoms. A hostess was pouring tea. Dinner at the Inn always marked a special occasion. Red lanterns lighted the narrow stone walks of the teahouse, located in one of the famed Hangzhou gardens. In the back, singsong girls, dressed in bright *cheong-soms*, slit high on the sides, were making final preparations for an evening of entertaining.

Jing-Jiang accepted a cup and raised it to his lips. There was a timelessness about his face, round and flat with a wispy white beard and mustache. His skin was smooth, as if preserved in an ancient gallery of time.

"The Dragon Well teas of Hangzhou have no peers," Jing-Jiang said. "A quite famous writer, whose name escapes me, once likened its liquor to the *dew of heaven.*"

Eric nodded. The warlord had come to evoke a sense of both mystery and majesty. In a real sense, Jing-Jiang was the father he never had. Yet, these emotions had been slow developing. At the beginning, Eric was treated like any common worker. His rage had been great, but he owed Jing-Jiang and Tong-Po his life. They had asked him to stay and he'd accepted. With that thought, he vowed to put himself through his period of servitude without complaint.

Curiously, the normally clannish coolies accepted him as one of their own. Evenings found him at their fires, eating rice with his fingers from clay bowls. Afterwards, he gambled his few coppers at the *mah jong* tables, laughing and cursing with them, his language increasingly fluent. Time passed and they became a part of him.

Later, when Jing-Jiang moved him to the temple where the monks could refine his Chinese, Eric spent hours contemplating the enigma of the coolies. Their humped backs, bobbing heads, and toothless smiles floated in his dreams. Sometimes Tong-Po was with them, his face an enigma. *Northern Star* would heel against the sea, tumbling the coolies, then he would wake up.

The hostess arrived with assorted steamed dumplings and fresh tea. Eric waited respectfully for Jing-Jiang to make the first selection. The old general chose a steamed prawn wrapped in cabbage and sticky rice dough, then watched the ease with which Eric lifted one of the smaller more delicate varieties with his chopsticks. He remembered observing Eric's first attempts with Tong-Po.

The dwarf's gaze had met Jing-Jiang's in quiet humor. "The clumsiness of his hands belies his true nature," Tong-Po whispered. "Inside, he possesses a rare confidence, without the bravado so commonly found in the *fan-gwoiloh*. He will be a leader of men."

Yes, Jing-Jiang thought. There was a great spirit within Eric. All it needed was judicious nurturing and he would rise high. Jing-Jang looked across the table. "I have made a decision about your future."

Eric set his chopsticks down.

Jing-Jiang's gaze seemed to encompass everything around him. "My friendship is given freely, but I have two conditions for my future assistance." He folded his hands. "The first is that you travel the Yangtze. Tong-Po will accompany you, acting as guide. It is important that you learn the ways of our land --- absorb her secrets, her language. The Middle Kingdom is comprised of many peoples. Know them and you will understand the true nature of China."

Eric was stunned. He looked at Tong-Po, but the dwarf's face was unreadable. The Yangtze slashed through China from the sea to the Himalayan mountains. This was not part of his plans. There was a score to be settled with Alex Bartrum. "That, that will take a long time."

"Time has a much different meaning here than in the West," Jing-Jiang said. "To compete in life you must be strong of spirit, but to win you must be smart. Survival is accorded those who adapt to their environment." Jing-Jiang formed a claw and held it in front of Eric's face. "Like a coiled leopard you wait for your revenge against Alex Bartrum. In this undertaking you have my support." The claw retracted. "But it is important to remember Bartrum is a tiger who rules an unfamiliar jungle. If you are ill prepared, death will be your reward."

Eric studied his teacup. "You mentioned two conditions."

"Ah. So I did." Jing-Jiang stared across the table. What he saw was not a foreign devil, but a young man ready to make his mark in the world. *He does not yet understand how we Chinese exact revenge. So easy to kill Alex Bartrum for his crimes, but first, my son, you shall have the pleasure of diminishing him before all of Shanghai.   Afterwards, you may kill him at your leisure.* Jing-Jiang smiled. "After completing your travels, my second condition is for you to attend the English University in Singapore."

Eric was about to protest, but Jing-Jiang lifted a finger. "It is imperative you receive a formal education. When you make your appearance in Shanghai, it will be as a taipan, not a common seaman. No one, not even Alex Bartrum will be able to recognize you."

*   *   *

AFTER dinner, Tong-Po excused himself while Eric and Jing-Jiang strolled through the garden. The old general's words were soft against the scent of flowers. "I have killed countless numbers of my own people. And I've battled warlords and landowners, whose names I barely remember. Late in life, I discovered the fallacy of my ways." Jing-Jiang sighed. "I purged the land of one tyrant after another. My accomplishment has been nothing more than paving the way for yet another."

They approached a bridge. Colorful carp swam in the pond.

Jing-Jiang tossed a few bread crumbs. "See how they respond. When there is something to eat there will always be something to eat it." The old general chuckled. "In some ways we are all held hostage to an endless stream of predators." He looked at Eric. "That's what happened to China. A land of many with power in the hands of a few. The tyrants. Our people must be exposed to the outside world. To avoid outside predators, we must have trade controlled by Chinese."

Eric thought for a moment. "England could not survive without trade to keep her factories going. There's not that many natural resources, and without trade there'd be no jobs. The big difference is England's fast-paced, while here steadiness is valued over speed. China is so steady that progress has suffocated. Cocoons are shipped along the Grand Canal the same way as in Marco Polo's day. The Chinese content themselves to slog along like the rest of the world doesn't exist. But time hasn't stood still. And that's why foreigners control trade."

"Most observant." Jing-Jiang frowned, watching the languid carp in the pond. "Despite her great deeds and contributions across thousands of years, China is a land that is always just beginning. We have been set upon by Mongrels, Russians, Japanese, and Western powers. Still, the onslaught continues." The old general's voice dropped to a grim whisper. "*Fangwoiloh* are relentless in their quest for wealth. Nothing it appears can stop them. The English and other seaborne barbarians come like waves upon our shores. Now the China Sea is a British port --- Hong Kong their prize for the Opium War." It was quiet in the garden. Soft breezes rustled the leaves. A bird sang as Jing-Jiang studied Eric's eyes. "China has reached a point where tradition and progress confront each other."

Eric felt Jing-Jiang's power. Their relationship was about to reach a new level. "Yet once you were the most advanced civilization on earth. What happened to change all of that?"

"We became intoxicated with our own senses, our own achievements. As you say, China was considered the center of the universe. Anything from the outside was worthless. Suddenly, prosperity peaked and a period of thoughtless consumption was ushered in. A rot of the spirit inexorably followed." Jing-Jiang smiled sadly. "Since the Mongol invasion we have contented ourselves to languish in a state of decline. China will be destroyed if we fail to adapt to our new environment." A few more bread crumbs dropped to the carp. "Commerce will open our eyes. It is my dream to have free trade along the rivers of China. They are our access to the people from the outside world. The rivers will carry our rebirth. Our people, even the great masses, will recover their identity through commerce. But until that time memories of barbarian imperialism will keep the door closed." Jing-Jiang stared at Eric. "Nothing under heaven is easy my son, but perhaps a boy from the sea, and I, can make my dream reality."

Three

ERIC'S HEAD WAS RINGING AS HE PULLED himself out of the debris. The last thing he remembered was the dynamite's deafening blast. Standing, on shaky legs, he looked around. Darkness in the eastern sky was being displaced by a crimson sun. *Unconscious --- at least an hour.* Water flowed in rivulets through a gaping hole in the dike. Beyond, where the shantytown once stood, shadows moved through morning fog.

The sun continued to rise, burning away the mist. Eric looked at the charred corpses dotting the landscape. "My God." He climbed down the dike, not wanting to believe his eyes. A woman was staring vacantly into space, her naked child's liquid bowel running down her arm. Hollow-eyed people trudged by, their clothes black with blood and ash. Rats squealed as they scavenged the dead. The world stank of death and kerosene.

Eric began to walk. Several steps later, he stumbled over a

---

metal sheet that once served as a roof for one of the hovels. Printed across the face was the symbol for Trident Industries.

*   *   *

TING se-Bing spotted Eric at the foot of the dike and began to follow. He was not following the barbarian as a lieutenant in Dragon Mok's Red Pang, but as a patriot of the I-he-t'suan.

Why would a fan-gwoiloh risk his life in such a manner?

The fact that Eric had saved tens of thousands of Chinese lives by blowing a hole in the wall astonished him. Why? But the longer Ting thought the more his xenophobic nature asserted itself.

Deh neh loh moh on all foreign devils. What does it matter why a foreign devil does anything? Are not all barbarians brains filled with dung?

Lost in thought, Ting nearly bumped into Eric, who had stopped to rest against a gutted hovel. Twisting to one side, Ting slipped on the mud-slick ground and fell --- on a corpse. Horrified, he rolled away. A living hand was offered. Ting looked up and froze. Eric Gradek. He was staring into the face of a demon. Motes of red, purple, and orange burned in the barbarian's eyes.

Eric helped Ting up, started to say something, but changed his mind and walked away.

Ting stared at Eric's back. Despising himself for accepting the help of a foreign devil, he touched the hilt of his knife. Should he kill the barbarian now? *No! This barbarian will be a hero to the people. It should not be the Society of the Virtuous Harmony Fist who claims his life.*

Ting was shaken. For the brotherhood to throw the foreigners out of China it needed support from the masses. And where would that support come from when the authorities let word out that the Society of the Virtuous Harmony Fist ordered the fire? Thousands of Chinese burned alive. Anyone associated with the *I-he-t'suan* would be perceived as lower than the low. *How to explain the gods blew the breath of hell the wrong direction?* Then a smile creased his lips. There was more than a single river leading to the people's confluence of understanding, wasn't there? Turning, he cast a final look at the barbarian with the opal eyes.

*   *   *

ERIC'S shredded clothes stuck to him as he ghost-walked into the office.

"Taipan." Tong-Po rushed to his side. "Put your hand on my shoulder."

With surprising strength, the forty-two inch dwarf led him to a nearby chair. Tong-Po's eyes took in the cuts and bruises. There was nothing that wouldn't heal with rest and medication. "Your joss is good, Taipan."

Pauline Han, the office manager, appeared in the door. "Tong-Po, is the Taipan...?"

"No, Pauline. He needs sleep and nourishment."

"I'll have food prepared immediately." Pauline turned to the young woman peeking around the door. "Su-Mei, prepare a bath for the Taipan and lay out fresh clothes. Be quick or you will find yourself gawking at the ceiling from a mattress in the Red Lantern brothel."

The girl fled to Eric's chamber.

When Pauline left, Tong-Po said, "By the celestial guardians,

Taipan, you look like a mangy dog and smell worse than a buffalo fart. First some brandy, then a hot bath." He went to the bar. "Afterwards you get plenty of sleep, *heya?*"

"Was the fire started by the Society of the Virtuous Harmony Fist?"

"Eh?"

"The *I-he-t'suan.* Do you think they are responsible?"

The suddenness of the question surprised Tong-Po. He stood still, his chest pushed out.

Eric waited.

Tong-Po poured two brandies from a crystal decanter and handed Eric a glass. "It seems logical, Taipan. The *I-he-t'suan* is reported to be well organized, with backing from powerful allies."

"They're not so secret now. The bloody bastards just roasted tens of thousands of their own people."

Tong-Po swung his legs. "I heard."

"A dozen or so red banners are in front of the Commerce Club. The Society of the Virtuous Harmony Fist is giving foreigners an ultimatum. *Big noses with white faces out of China or die.*" Eric swallowed his drink and reached for the decanter.

Tong-Po's sources had already sent word about the threat. "This could be a difficult political situation, Taipan. Obviously, the *I-he-t'suan* did not plan for so many Chinese to die. Had it not been for a shift in the wind all of Shanghai would have been destroyed."

"Two other things." Eric set his glass on the table. "Part of the message read: *Behind every tree a soldier waits.* Also, at the bottom of each banner there was an ideogram of a serpent coiled around a closed fist."

Tong-Po sipped his brandy. "The words are taken from an

ancient Chinese saying, *Ts'ao Mu Chieh Ping* ---behind every tree and thicket a soldier. The Society of the Virtuous Harmony Fist would like foreigners to believe there is one soldier lying in wait for every one of them. However" --- he raised a finger --- "there is a second meaning only Chinese will understand. *Ts'as Mu Chieh Ping* also means that fear is being spread based on unreality. My guess is the Society of the Virtuous Harmony Fist is obliquely asking for the people to rebel. The fire will serve as their rallying point. If the people rise, the Empress will be forced to support the secret societies." Tong-Po's words were bitter. "Ironic, since the societies are dedicated to destroying the Qing Dynasty."

Eric thought about possible ramifications. "The Qings had been teetering since China's defeat by Japan. If the Empress supported a purge against foreigners it would be the same as a declaration of war. The entire country could erupt."

"The banners make it clear the *I-he-t'suan* is blaming the fire on foreign devils, even though it was their own debacle." Tong-Po looked at Eric. "Concerning the ideogram --- *t'suan* means fist --- the serpent represents death."

"Deadly fist?" Eric leaned back.

"More precisely, an unarmed warrior willing to fight using only his fist."

"Why unarmed?"

Tong-Po shrugged. "Only the Manchus and foreign occupation forces have weapons."

Eric let Tong-Po's reference to occupation forces pass. Instead, he said, "What you're suggesting is we're fighting an army of boxers."

*   *   *

ALEX Bartrum surveyed the carnage along the docks from his third story office window on the Bund. His lips were compressed into a thin line as he watched groups of men carrying torches pick through the debris for bodies. Retaining his swarthy good looks over the years, Alex was still a powerful man. The only difference, he was a little softer and heavier than his days aboard the *Northern Star*.

Despite almost losing the city, things were turning out nicely. Bartrum & Sons now controlled kerosene supplies in Shanghai. Folding his hands behind his back, he contented himself that his money problems would soon be resolved. He turned to his elder brother, Philip, who was at the desk making calculations. Abacus beads clicked in the silence. "Hard to imagine what would have happened if the wind hadn't changed direction."

Philip did not look up. He was of fairer complexion and several inches shorter than Alex. The majority of his time was spent in London handling the financial interests of Bartrum & Sons and acting as Trident Industry's Senior Director of Asian Operations. His duel position was not a conflict since Bartrum & Sons acted as Trident's exclusive Far East distributor.

"A good thing it did, or our depot would've gone up with the others," Philip said. "We'd be bloody well bankrupt." The abacus clicked. "There would've been no way to make our option payment to Trident." Philip felt a chill. "Christ, I never imagined such a hellstorm. If it hadn't been for Eric Gradek we wouldn't be having this conversation right now."

"A pox on Eric Gradek," Alex said. "That sod lost more than a godown. I heard there was a season's worth of silk in his warehouse." He looked at his brother. "The only thing to be grateful for is that the wind changed direction. Now our option payment will be made, and we control the kerosene market. Our joss was good."

"It could've gone the other way." Philip mopped his brow, hating the kerosene stink, hating Dragon Mok and his Red Pang --- hating Shanghai. "Joss or no joss, I'm glad this is over. The next boat to London won't be leaving soon enough to suit me." His hand rested on the abacus. "We'll need to increase kerosene prices fifteen percent for the next three months before letting the market settle back to current levels."

Alex nodded. He was aware of his brother's dislike of the Orient. Alex, however, preferred Asia and the free-for-all world of trade whereas Philip thrived in the financial centers of Europe. "Will that give us sufficient capital to cover trading losses for the first half of the year?"

"Yes, with a bit to spare." Philip clicked an abacus bead with his thumb. "What will the other hongs say about our raising prices?"

"What can they say?" Alex smiled. "We're the only source for kerosene. Besides, they're in debt on the tanker fleet and we hold the paper. Does a bit to spare mean we'll have enough operating capital until year's end?"

Philip glanced at his notes. "If there are no unexpected losses we should turn a profit. On the other hand, any more fiascoes like the sugar contracts would be disastrous."

Alex winced. The first half of the year had been dismal. He had speculated on Philippine sugar futures in anticipation of a bumper crop. Two devastating typhoons had destroyed the harvest. There had been major losses with rubber and cotton as well. The only bright spot was opium. It was the only commodity that consistently turned a profit, and good income had been derived from the company's dealings with Dragon Mok.

But problems loomed. A combined effort between foreign and Chinese authorities was underway to crack down on illegal trafficking. The thought was unnerving. Then there was the problem of what to do about Mok. The pang leader was getting harder to control. And now Alex owed him for arranging the fire.

Walking to the bar, Alex poured a brandy. "We're on a razor's edge. Perhaps it was a mistake to invest our reserves in Trident shares."

"We knew the risks when we signed the agreement," Philip said. "What I hadn't counted on was the difficulty dealing with Sutton and Rosenberg. If we fail to meet our payments we'll be in the bloody street."

"They owe us a few considerations," Alex said irritably. "Without us, not a drop of kerosene would reach Asia. The syndicate controls the tankers, and we control the syndicate."

Philip's laugh was caustic. "Sutton and Rosenberg could buy a hundred fleets. Our problem is making the option payments next year. Once our stock reaches parity with theirs we'll be sitting nicely. The entire Asian concession will be ours. Until then we have to do whatever's necessary to keep our position."

Yes, dear brother, we'll do whatever's necessary, Alex thought. The oil concession brings unlimited power. I'll be king of China while you sip brandy and smoke cigars in London. But first, Bartrum & Sons' debt must be retired.

Returning to the window, Alex focused on the spot where Gradek International's godown stood the night before. He wondered if Eric was inside one of the remaining buildings. Smoke rose from dying embers, slowly fading into gray sky.

Word had reached Alex that Eric had saved thousands of Chinese from the fire. There would be honors bestowed on him from the British and Chinese.

Eric Gradek. Bastard.

Three times Eric had made a laughing stock out of him. Anger pricked Alex's skin like a rash. Eric Gradek would be destroyed. What Alex needed was the method. Distant smoke curled from glowing embers.

Of course.

The answer had been right in front of his nose.

Alex smiled and turned to Philip.

* * *

THE next day Eric stood on the canal easement looking at the spot where his godown had stood the night before. Charred boards, metal table tops, pieces of silk, and half the roof lay in the shallows. A paste of gray soot floated on the water. Eric knelt and dug some loose dirt up with his knife and smelled it. Smoke swirled around him from smoldering ashes as he inhaled the scents of gunpowder and kerosene.

Eric stood up, dusted his hands off, and walked to the water's edge. Gulls wheeled overhead as he stared into the distance. The sun was perched along the edge of the horizon, painting the harbor gold.

Four

GARRETT BOTHA COULD NOT SLEEP, SO HE contented himself by watching shadows of palm fronds play across the ceiling. He could hear them rustling beyond the window, a cooling presence. Inside, a mosquito buzzed around the bed's gossamer net.

Next to him, Jacqueline stirred. As Garrett's eyes traced the outline of his wife he could hear the soft rhythm of her breathing. *How lucky I am to have this woman.* Garrett was tempted to wrap himself around her, but now wasn't the time. Palm fronds whispered, inviting him back to the ceiling shadows.

It had taken Garrett half his life to reach this room at the Raffles Hotel in Singapore. The journey began fifteen years ago when his father, Janvillem van de Botha, decided to send him to the United States. The Industrial Revolution was underway and Holland's Ambassador at Large wanted the finest education for his son. He chose the Massachusetts Institute of

---

Technology. But first, Garrett had to complete primary school-ing, so he went to live with his father's brother on a Pennsylvania farm, near the small town of Titusville.

"MIT is the best place for you to learn how to make things happen," his father had said. "A quality that seems to be disap-pearing in Europe. Yankees are making a business out of becoming the biggest and the best, while our staid countrymen content themselves with stroking their beards."

Two years later, during Garrett's final year of school, a geo-logical team from New York arrived at his uncle's farm. A month later the team came back with the news. "Mr. Botha, we've made a remarkable discovery on your property," one of them had said. Garrett mused over that. Remarkable, indeed. Titusville would never be a sleepy little farming community again.

"Oil." Garrett uttered the word reverently. An ugly, dirty combustible liquid that was revolutionizing the world. And he was part of the revolution. He remembered dinner following graduation from MIT and the tall, silent man with piercing pale-blue eyes next to his father. *Percival D. Sutton.* Over prime rib the Robber Baron asked him to work for Classic Oil.

"Thus far our primary focus has been on refining and distri-bution," Sutton had said. "However, we are considering estab-lishing our own production and exploration division. Naturally, we are looking for the best to head up the project. Your pro-fessors tell me that you're the finest geologist MIT has ever pro-duced."

What a joke, Garrett thought of those times. School never prepared him for the lessons of *real life* Sutton would teach him over the next half dozen years. Garrett settled his head deeper into the pillows. Truth be known, he'd enjoyed the experience.

He learned everything about the inner workings of the oil business. Best of all, he'd gained knowledge. And that was the most valuable asset of all, wasn't it?

Garrett became an integral part of Sutton's expansion plans. He was made point man in Classic Oil's war against Star Petroleum, another large oil company owned by Europe's powerful banking family, the Rosenbergs. The war lasted several years with neither side gaining advantage. Then there was a brief period when European demand exceeded supply and prices rose. Sutton was ready for such eventuality. Classic Oil had been holding huge inventories purchased during soft market conditions and had flooded Europe with cheap kerosene.

The market collapsed.

The Rosenbergs fought back. Using their massive financial resources, they further cut prices. In the end neither side could claim victory. A draw. Millions squandered on a hopeless war. Set backs for Sutton and the Rosenbergs, each who had been posturing to monopolize the oil industry. *Where do we go from here?* The question in boardrooms of New York and London.

Garrett learned the answer two years later in Classic Oil's corporate dining room. Percival D. Sutton had been standing by the bar, brandy decanter in hand. His normally dispassionate face held a strange smile. "I don't believe any introductions are necessary." Inclining his head, Sutton said, "You remember Baron Rosenberg."

Garrett stared at the Baron. "How could I forget?"

The Baron stood, handshakes were exchanged. "We meet under more congenial circumstances this time, eh, Mr. Botha?" Baron Rosenberg's family had financed governments, wars, and most of Europe's new railroad system. They owned a refinery at Fiume, on the Adriatic, and monopolized Russia's oil reserves. "Mr. Sutton speaks highly of you." The Baron's eyes crinkled with amusement. "He says you are the finest oilman in the business."

"Oil is a developing science," Garrett replied, "and finding it is an art. One tries to stay on top."

Lunch was pleasant, with conversation resonating between cheerful and serious. Afterwards, Havanas were lighted and brandy was poured.

"No need to keep you guessing any longer, Garrett," Sutton said. The strange smile returned. "Baron Rosenberg was correct about my assessment of your abilities. Precisely why you are one of the first to know about what has developed between us." Sutton looked at the Baron. "A rash of smaller companies have marginally come into their own while the two of us have been at each others' throats. These gadflies and our foolish feud have destabilized world prices."

The Baron grunted. "Impossible to maintain profitable operations under such conditions."

"Quite so," Sutton agreed. He lifted his brandy glass and sipped. "The Baron and I have held a series of meetings. I believe them to be historic in nature. They will have a profound effect on global development during the twentieth century." Pale-blue eyes rested on Garrett. "The Baron and I have concluded an agreement to merge Classic Oil and Star Petroleum under a holding company, Trident Industries. A grand alliance, if you will."

"Once a board has been configured, Trident Industries will begin a worldwide strategy aimed at stabilizing the market. *Our Plan,* a euphemism for Mr. Sutton's and my shared vision, is the tool by which we will manage oil prices as the new century dawns." Cigar smoke swirled around the Baron's words.

"The world is becoming dependent on oil, which means supply and demand must be managed with care. We plan to assimilate smaller competitors into Trident Industries to maintain price stability."

"A trading firm with considerable influence in Asia will be participating with us," Sutton said. "Their involvement insures a totally integrated world wide distribution program. Classic Oil will concentrate in the Americas, Star Petroleum in Europe and Africa, while our Asian partner manages operations east of the Suez. Crude oil, refined kerosene, and other derivatives will be shipped from terminals most accessible to markets."

Sutton refilled glasses. "For example, Classic Oil has maintained a virtual monopoly in Asia by shipping bulk kerosene around the Horn of Africa. This inefficient method will be ended now that the Baron has arranged for our tankers to pass through the Suez Canal. Russian oil piped from Baku to the port of Bantum will service that market. American oil will replace Russian oil as Europe's primary supply."

"Russia is closer, but rail shipment through the mountainous terrain is dangerous and expensive," the Baron said. "It's easy to see that with shipping and distribution minimized, profits will rise along with general market consumption."

Sutton's brandy glass rose. "Garrett, you can play a vital role in making Trident Industry's vision a reality."

"You're talking about controlling the world's oil supply," Garrett said flatly. "A total monopoly."

"Control is perhaps a bit strong," Sutton replied. "Manage would be a more appropriate word." A thin smile appeared. "*Our Plan* is what's best for the future."

Sutton's and Rosenberg's eyes fell on Garrett.

Classic Oil and Star Petroleum teamed up with another powerful third party? Garrett was stunned. Two years ago Sutton and Rosenberg were in the trenches against each other. Now they were plotting to corner the world's oil market. *Incredible!* Assimilating companies meant running competitors out of business if they refused to sell. Every Joe who dropped a hole in the ground would get squashed.

The silence thickened. Garrett felt their eyes on him. When his voice came it sounded like it was coming from a dream. "What can I do to help?"

The Baron leaned forward. "We have substantial interest in Russia, especially in the Baku region. A vast market awaits in Asia and we need Baku fully operational to meet demand. We want you to develop the fields, lay a pipeline to the port of Bantum and construct distribution centers in key Asian cities." The Baron's eyes sparkled. "The Russian terrain is difficult, but no expense will be spared getting you the finest equipment and personnel for the task."

Garrett's mouth opened.

"I'm aware of the sacrifice," Sutton said. "The project will take years and be difficult for Jacqueline and Marianna. However, sacrifice brings reward. If you are successful, I see no reason why a board seat would not be waiting for you."

A knock interrupted the conversation. Sutton opened the door. "Ahh, glad you could make it. Just in time to meet our new vice president in charge of operations." He led two men into the room. "Garrett, I want you to meet our Asian partners, Alex and Philip Bartrum."

Five

GARRETT'S EYES WERE OPEN WHEN FIRST dawn crept through the jalousie. As Jacqueline slept quietly beside him, he thought about how cleverly he had been cheated out of his shares in Trident Industries. Not that it particularly bothered him. He had plans that would more than even that score.

The *Grand Alliance* wasn't going to be so grand by the time he got finished. If things went according to plan, Philip and Alex would be smashed within the year. Of course, Sutton and Rosenberg were too powerful to be destroyed --- but they could be crippled. *And humiliated.* After all, he knew their secrets.

Garrett had to admit, Sutton and Rosenberg played their parts well. Dangled all the right carrots --- complete freedom in all geological development activities, stock equity, club memberships --- a board seat. *You will become a wealthy man, Garrett. Just make sure we're operational and into the Asian market on schedule.*

Well, he sure as hell had done that, hadn't he? *And, in under three years.* The Baku fields modernized --- the pipeline to Batum completed --- storage centers constructed in every major Asian port. *And how'd they repay me?* Garrett took a breath. *Don't get angry,* he reminded himself. *What they did was business as usual. I was up against the best and got clobbered.*

Garrett smiled.

Truth be known, he bore Sutton and Rosenberg no malice. Rather, in some perverse way, he admired their audacity. But not enough to allow them to monopolize the world market. And he had the power to stop them. Information about dummy corporations, systematic price fixing, political payoffs and the rest of the dirt that could sink or cripple the *Grand Alliance* was filed nicely away. Garrett sighed pleasantly. Not that he didn't have plans to make the information public. Well, not until it suited him. And what suited him at the moment was settling his score with Alex Bartrum.

It had been four years since their last conversation. Garrett would play the game with the others, but what he had planned for Alex Bartrum was personal. After all this time, he still could not shake the image of Bartrum's sneering face.

Shanghai, 1897

"YOU'RE out, Botha. Finished." Bartrum glared. "I had to sign a contract with Eric Gradek to produce oil containers because of your stupidity." A copy of the agreement landed on Garrett's desk. "Look at that --- twenty-five percent more than what he was charging Classic Oil. For five years we're locked in with that sodding bastard. It will cost a fortune."

Garrett stood, palms on his desk. "Out --- after I've made us the most cost-efficient producer in the world? Building a god-damned kerosene drum factory wasn"t part of my responsibili-ties, Alex. We've got one of the finest oil producing operations in the world because of me. How was I supposed to know every Classic Oil drum in Asia had been bought up? The Far East is your backyard, chum. Or, did you conveniently forget that little point? If anyone's stupid here --- it's you."

Bartrum's face went dead. "I'll let that remark pass, Botha. But only this one time." He removed a document and slid it across the desk. "Your severance papers. You're of no further use to me or anyone else connected with Trident Industries. Now get out."

Garrett picked up the paper. "What makes you think I'll let you get away with this?"

Bartrum laughed. "I already have, chum." Bartrum opened the door to the receptionist area where his bodyguard was standing. "Mr. Jones, make sure our ex-associate is packed and gone before noon."

*   *   *

"DADDY"

Garrett turned and found himself gazing into the dark eyes of his eight year old daughter, Marianna. His heart swelled, and he smiled that special smile reserved for father and daughter. "Morning sweetheart," he whispered.

"Can I sleep with you and mommy?"

He gathered her in his arms. "You betcha. But we've got to be very quiet not to wake her."

"I love you, daddy."

"I love you, princess."

*   *   *

BANKER Franz Mikolits enjoyed Singapore more than any city on earth. It was a society predisposed to opium and alcohol --- a place where any pleasure could be had for a price. To this end, he placed the proper amount into a pair of matching cloth handbags. He could hear the squeals of delight from the two girls taking advantage of the hotel's modern shower facilities.

Franz walked to the window, drew open the drapes and looked out. He wondered what his staid contemporaries would think if they knew about his night of pleasure. Mikolits smiled. If all went well with Garrett Botha, he would have the concierge make similar arrangements for this evening.

The banker turned his thoughts to his business with Garrett. There would be limitless power and prestige for his bank, the Banque de Swisse Credit, and Switzerland, if he were successful. *Great danger as well,* he reminded himself. The world was realigning itself. Enemies and allies were going to be made and lost. And for what?

Oil.

Was it a force destined to change the world like Garrett Botha and the American shipbuilder Matthew Clay believed? Ships powered by oil instead of coal? Heating, and all manner of machines, becoming oil dependent? *Incredible!* Yet, Franz Mikolits had become a believer. Countries would wage war to dominate this new energy. Powerful men would cheat, lie, steal --- even kill for it. Classic Oil and Star Petroleum had already fought such a war. Others would follow.

Mikolits folded his hands behind his back. Man's flirtation with peace was coming to an end. Bismark had been forced from power and Kaiser Wilhelm had set Prussia on an independent course in foreign affairs. Expansionism would follow, putting Prussia on a collision course with Britain and France. The Kaiser's forces would be invincible on land, but Britain ruled the seas. Which meant Prussia would be forced to expand its navy. Mikolits shivered. War was becoming a real possibility. Switzerland's neutrality might be compromised, his bank put in jeopardy.

Foolish to think that our mountains will protect us if the Hun is beating on our door.

Ah, but the rewards.

Profits from supplying Prussia with oil and naval technology would be huge. Swiss neutrality --- allegiance to no government over another --- would transform his tiny mountain land into the world's banking center. Thoughts of the future filled his mind. Secrecy was key. Every client assigned a numbered account, accessed by coded wire transfer or the bearer of such a number appearing in person. Swiss banks, with Banque de Swisse Credit taking the lead, would house the clandestine fortunes of government and business. Mikolits smiled. And, of course, the bankers would guard the greatest treasures of all. Their secrets.

The sound of a door opening interrupted his thoughts. The two Malay girls came out of the bathroom speaking in their village dialect about the strange Swiss man's toad-belly skin and unproductive yang. Being an astute banker, Franz Mikolits rewarded them at the door with a nod and generous tip.

A glance at his watch said there was two hours before his meeting with Garrett. He went to the desk and removed a folder from his briefcase. An hour and a half later, he filed it back inside the attaché.

Afterwards, he sat there thinking about Kaiser Wilhelm.

Six

GARRETT FOLLOWED THE BATIK-CLAD HOSTESS to a corner table of the Raffles Hotel outdoor restaurant. A breeze drifted in from the sea. At a nearby palm tree a lone Tokay basked in early sun. Except for the circuitous rolling of its lidded eyes the gecko could have been a piece of bark.

Squinting into the distance, Garrett thought about the change that had come over Jacqueline. Singapore was an exotic island and her spirits had been much brighter this morning. Maybe she was getting used to Asia.

What we need is another child. A brother for Marianne would be nice. Take some time off for ourselves and go away someplace exotic and make a baby. Yes, that would be grand. But first I've got to get Telaga Said fully operational.

Only two other people knew the code name for the oil field Garrett was developing in Sumatra --- his father and Franz Mikolits.

So much oil in one place!

Still, it hadn't been easy. For the past two years Garrett had fought the Sumatran jungles. But he had made it --- despite rain, leeches, bugs, tarantulas, cobras, and whatever else that crawled out of that emerald canopy. Now *Telaga Said* was a reality. Had it been worth it?

Garrett closed his eyes.

God, yes --- a million times yes. Telaga Said. A geologist's dream in northeast Sumatra, and it's mine.

Garrett first learned about the find in Sumatra shortly after leaving Trident Industries. While in Amsterdam visiting his father an old friend, Jans Kessler, looked him up. Kessler had worked as Garrett's foreman in the Baku oilfields before moving to the East Indies and going into the trading business.

Kessler was at a coffee plantation in the jungle when he ran across a mineral wax local natives used as a caulking compound. It was during the monsoon season. Kessler and a local native overseer, a *mandur,* were forced to take refuge in an abandoned shack. Once inside, the *mandur* lit a firebrand torch. A stunned Kessler immediately asked how the fire had been created? The *mandur* showed him a pouch filled with the same muddy mineral wax he had discovered earlier. That was when Kessler decided to get in touch with Garrett.

"It's the goddamnest stuff you've ever seen," Kessler told Garrett. "Bloody goo seals anything. It'll be interesting seeing what you think about it." The two men had just finished dinner and were in Kessler's hotel suite with a bottle of brandy.

Kessler went to the closet and removed several small wooden boxes from his duffel bag. "Looks like mud," Garrett observed. He sniffed, recognizing the substance as a quality grade paraffin.

Garrett replaced the sample and looked at Jans.

"Doesn't smell much like mud, does it?"

"No --- it doesn't," Garrett said. "You knew what you were dealing with from the beginning, so why all the talk about a caulking compound?"

Kessler refilled their glasses. "If word got out that I was here with a bag full of quality paraffin every leech in Amsterdam would be out for blood. This situation is much too grand to screw up by making mistakes. Where I got these samples, paraffin covers the earth like a second skin."

"Good God."

"I left for Amsterdam right afterwards. Problem was I didn't know how to get in touch with you. So I figured your father would be my best way." Kessler picked up the wax sample. "But, of course, here you are."

"Why not Trident Industries?"

Kessler's laugh was harsh. "After what they did to you they'd string me out like fish bait. Besides, I'm out of my depth. It requires a helluva lot more money and expertise than I've got."

Garrett stared across the table. "What about the problems?"

"The jungles are none too friendly and logistics will be a nightmare. Still, it can be done. One big advantage is the site's near the mouth of the Balaban River, which flows directly into the Straits of Mallacca."

"What kind of deal are you looking for, Jans?"

Kessler shrugged. "Make me the same offer you would expect if our chairs were reversed."

Garrett kept his face closed. "Let me sleep on it and we'll work out the details tomorrow."

*   *   *

JANVILLEM van de Botha steepled his fingers and listened to his son describe the meeting with Jans Kessler. When Garrett finished talking he leaned back and closed his eyes. The implications of the Dutch East Indies becoming a major oil producer were enormous. World power would be redefined.

Will I be here to see it...?

Not if you listen to your doctors.

Prussia was expanding. War would inevitably follow. Kaiser Wilhelm would be forced to seize, or gain access by treaty to Russian oil. Either way, Trident Industries would be forced to withdraw from Russia. As a consequence, their Asian operations would suffer.

Such irony, especially after the unforgivable way they treated Garrett. Ah. My dear son, how they wronged you. But because of you, I learned their secrets, which are worth more than all of the gold in Africa. And there are other secrets I know that remain in my province alone. The question is how to best use them to politically maneuver the Netherlands.

The Ambassador masked his excitement. The Dutch were a nation of seafarers, and with oil reserves their influence would be felt around the world. Holland would become a powerful piece in the international chess game.

"Can Kessler be trusted?"

"Yes. He's staking his future on it."

Nodding, the Ambassador took a cigar from the humidor. "We must take this matter into our own hands. Something of such importance cannot be left to politicians. Within hours news of the discovery would reach Trident Industries."

The Ambassador lit his cigar. Years in the diplomatic arena had taught him to appear detached in critical situations. But beneath the cool facade, he could see his fingerprints on the pages of history. Smoke drifted toward the ceiling. "I'm still not certain about this Matthew Clay fellow. Are you certain he's developed an oil engine powerful enough to propel tanker ships?"

"I've been aboard the prototype and seen it work," Garrett said. "It's faster and more cost efficient than anything ever put to sea. Trident's fleet will be antiquated by the internal combustion engine. Of course, there are a few design problems, but Matt will get them worked out. Just a matter of time."

"What about security?" the Ambassador asked.

"Matt has the experimental tanker miles offshore. The location is constantly changing. Engineers and crew are on board for the duration." Garrett held his father's eyes. "I've known Matt since MIT. If we come up with the financing, he'll work with us."

The Ambassador grunted. "Money is a powerful weapon. A commodity that's virtually limitless where the Rosenbergs and Sutton are concerned. What if they go to Clay Shipyards and increase the offer?"

"There's an abiding enmity between Clay Shipyards and Classic Oil that transcends money. When Percy D. pulled Classic Oil's European shipping contract from them and gave it to the tanker fleet financed by the Bartrum syndicate he made a grievous error."

The Ambassador's eyebrows arched.

"The Clay's are old line gentry who look at Sutton and his kind as common upstarts --- criminals operating with money, rather than guns. The only reason Matt took me into his confidence was because of the screwing I got from Bartrum."

A thin smile creased the Ambassador's lips. "The first thing we need to do is get a concession from the Sultan of Langkat."

*   *   *

A SHADOW passed in front of Garrett's eyes breaking his reverie. He looked up at Franz Mikolits.

"Good morning, Garrett." The banker glanced at his watch. "I see you arrived a bit early."

"Franz. Nice to see you. Hope the accommodations are to your liking."

"Ahh, yes. Quite comfortable."

Garrett signaled for a waiter. Inwardly, he wondered what kind of education the Malay girls bestowed on such a cold fish?

Two years ago, the Ambassador introduced Garrett to Mikolits over dinner in Zurich. They had just been granted the oil concession from the Sultan of Langkat.

"From time to time, our government utilizes the services of Herr Mikolits's bank," the Ambassador said. "His institution possesses impeccable credentials and discretion. During these past months Herr Mikolits and I have had a series of discussions regarding our project, *Telaga Said.*"

Garrett was speechless when his father spoke the code word used for the field in Sumatra.

The Ambassador's eyes showed nothing. "Herr Mikolits has informed me that his bank, the Banque de Swisse Credit, is disposed to act as the lead institution for funding our tanker fleet."

Since then Garrett had met twice with the banker. First, in Singapore --- then Boston, where Mikolits took a three hour ride on Matthew Clay's oil powered tanker.

Pastry arrived. "Your father tells me a great deal has taken place since we last met." Mikolits picked up a jellied roll.

"How long has it been? Six months? We have much to talk about."

Garrett nodded. "A lot has happened."

Mikolits took a bite out of his roll. "I take it the final design changes have been completed for the new tankers."

"Yes."

"And --- production schedules?"

"Proceeding according to plan," Garrett replied. "Except --- there've been several changes since we last met."

"Oh?" Mikolits's eyes hardened. Significant changes meant significant outlays of capital.

"Don't worry, Franz. These alterations are ones you'll love to finance." Garrett took a sip of coffee. "The tankers like the one you rode on will reduce shipping cost by twenty percent. All we've done is add a few modifications to make them more cost-efficient."

"My budget has already been established --- based on your own figures." Mikolits patted his leather folder.

"The costs will be a pittance compared to the profits generated." Garrett leaned forward. "I had Matt make modifications so each vessel can be steam-cleaned at the port of discharge. In addition, we installed modern freight handling equipment." Garrett's eyes glittered. "Franz, that means return trips won't be empty and unprofitable. Our tankers will be loaded with other goods. The system is so good that we can even haul foodstuffs without contamination. Shipping profits will be instantly doubled. We'll be positioned to carry crude or refined petroleum products anywhere in the world at a fraction of what it currently costs Trident Industries."

Mikolits was impressed. The additional costs were marginal and, more importantly, because of the new freight capabilities any underwriting problems he might have had with Prussia had just been eradicated. The Banker was warmed. After all, the Kaiser had nowhere else to go for such ships --- except through him.

After making several mental calculations, Mikolits arrived at a figure that would allow him flexibility, while maintaining excellent profit margins. "This is good news," he said cautiously. "Certainly, it will make my job a lot easier. I will include the additional costs and have a draft of the new financing agreement for you in the morning. The basic terms of the lease-back will remain as we originally agreed. Ten year amortization, at a rate of twelve percent per annum."

Garrett's eyes turned hard. "You can do better than that, Franz. Cost overruns to develop *Telaga Said* have been mounting. There've been equipment delays and disease has claimed hundreds of workers. During the rainy season we had to literally swim to a nearby village to bring supplies in."

Mikolits's expression was one of deep concern, but inside was a different matter. The fleet was his gold. If Garrett failed to develop *Telaga Said* on schedule, he could always sell or lease the tankers to Trident Industries or to the Kaiser's government at double the cost. "Had I been apprised of your problems earlier --- perhaps I could have helped. However, it will be extremely difficult to ask our investors to reduce their percentage at this late date." Mikolits folded his hands. "How long before *Telaga Said* will be fully functional?"

"Eight months."

"In that case, there still might be time to speak to them. Especially in light these new technological improvements."

Garrett faced the banker. He would be satisfied with eight percent, but would try for six. "Franz, any risk will be cut in half because of the improvements we've incorporated. Your investors should be happy with five percent."

Mikolits almost choked.

"Call a meeting," Garrett said. "I'll personally explain the benefits of the new tanker design to them."

"Impossible." Mikolits' jaw was set. "You know our policy of confidentiality."

"In that case tell them to make some concessions or we'll take our business elsewhere," Garrett said. "There are other institutions who would be glad to get our business. Oil is the future. If you and your people want to be part of it, a few sacrifices will be required."

The banker was shocked by Garrett's tone. "Come now, Mr. Botha. I doubt you will be taking your business elsewhere. You need speed, coordination, and secrecy. Exactly what I offer. Any attempt to deal with major European or American banks will expose your plans. I'm sure Mr. Sutton and Baron Rosenberg would take extreme measures to shut you down." Mikolits smiled, but like his sexual frolics it was devoid of warmth. "You need the one commodity I provide. Secrecy. Without that, *Telaga Said* will turn from a dream into a nightmare."

Mikolits's words slapped Garrett, but he knew the banker was right. If he dealt with commercial banks, word of his plans would be common knowledge within hours. His enemies would make Asia a sea of free oil in order to stop him.

Garrett's tone turned conciliatory. "We entered into this project together, Franz. I want to keep it that way. And, you're right about secrecy being essential. Still, the fact is that we're overextended. If we're unable to meet our obligations, it would be better for us to take our chances. Look for a more favorable rate elsewhere." He stared at the Banker. "Hell, Franz, I'm depending on you. Talk to your people. Ask for four percent and settle for five."

"Five percent is unrealistic," Mikolits said. "Perhaps, I could persuade them to look at eight."

"If we're to turn a profit we can't go higher than six," Garret replied.

Mikolits remained silent for a moment. "Seven is the best I can do."

Garrett frowned. "Agreed," he said at length. "But --- I want it written into the agreement that we have the right to renegotiate the rate after two years."

The two men shook hands. "When are you going to approach Eric Gradek?"

"As soon as *Telaga Said* is ready for inspection."

"Gradek's participation is essential if you hope to undercut Trident Industries. None of the other trading houses will help you. They are tied to Alex Bartrum." Mikolits regarded Garrett shrewdly. "You've never met Eric Gradek. What makes you so confident he will risk huge capital outlays to finance refining and storage facilities in Asian ports?"

"There's been enmity between Eric Gradek and Alex Bartrum for years, starting when Bartrum lost the Shanghai silk concession to Gradek. It's China's most prestigious concession and Alex lost a lot of face. Then Gradek married Katheryn Worthington, the territorial governor's daughter."

"Ah," Mikolits said. "So, Bartrum had designs on Miss Worthington?"

Garrett nodded. "Then Alex gave Gradek's company an exclusive contract to manufacture oil and kerosene drums for Trident Industries."

"Why would Bartrum do that?" A pastry crumb clung to the banker's astonished face.

"Because Gradek was already set up making the drums for Classic Oil," Garrett said. "Alex had nowhere else to go and was forced to pay outrageous prices for the drums in order to salvage Trident's first large shipment to Asia. Been fuming ever since."

Mikolits massaged his chin. "Is hatred of Bartrum enough motivation for Eric Gradek to risk such capital?"

A cargo steamer's horn sounded in the distance. Garrett stared out at the sea and caught sight of the Union Jack. Another two hours before it docked. Turning back to Mikolits, he said, "I suspect Gradek's animosity for Bartrum runs deeper than anything I'm aware of. Other than that, I'd say the Opal Eye Devil will want to team up with me because it's good business."

"Opal Eye Devil?" Mikolits looked at Garrett. Such descriptions were foreign to his banker's lexicon.

Garrett smiled thinly. "He has unusual eyes. The Chinese are facinated by them."

Seven

ERIC PAUSED AT THE ENTRANCE OF THE common-wealth-shanghai lobby to light a cheroot. It was early and people were already making deposits and withdrawals. He walked to Pierce Stafford's office amidst the careful routines.of clerks stamping and signing documents for one transaction or another. Though Eric's own business had been ravaged, he felt good seeing Shanghai returning to normal in the fire's aftermath.

"Ah. Eric come in," Stafford said. "Tea or coffee?"

"Tea. Thank you."

Handshakes were exchanged and Eric took a seat across from the bank president.

Stafford sent his clerk out for tea and tapped the newspaper on his desk. "Dreadful, these murderous Boxers, what? Nothing is safe. Millions worth of property and inventories destroyed." Stafford shook his head. "The bloody heathens have slaughtered thousands of Westerners and Christian Chinese. Now they've overrun our legation in Peking. Imagine, the Empress Dowager supporting them by declaring war against *foreign elements*."

Eric accepted a cup of tea, refusing cream and sugar. "The Empress temporarily avoided civil war by siding with the Boxers. Just a matter of time before the Qings will be forced from power."

Stafford grunted. "I for one hope the bloody Manchus are forced out sooner than later. The fleet needs to be called in."

Eric smiled. "Slay a tiger and find a dragon at the turn."

"Eh?" Stafford looked up.

"Nothing," Eric said. "I've got a pressing day, Pierce. I need to extend my credit line."

Stafford's gaze focused on the top of his desk. "It's been a rotten year all around, Eric. All the major *hongs* have suffered losses. Yours more than most. The bank is shoring its defenses against future calamities, like the fire."

Eric's stomach tightened. "That's understandable, Pierce. But what's that got to do with my credit line?"

"I apologize for not being able to inform you about his earlier," Stafford said. "Just yesterday, I got word by cable that London decided to sell a large parcel of our loan portfolio. Your notes were part of the package. Rotten joss. Perhaps things would have been different had you not been underinsured." Stafford removed a handkerchief and mopped his brow. "Really wish there was something I could do, Eric. But, under the circumstances my hands are tied. Perhaps, another bank....."

Stunned, Eric set his teacup down. In a month, he was scheduled to take delivery of Jing-Jiang's yearly allotment of silk. "Why now, Pierce? We've discussed what my financial commitments would be since the fire. And now, on the eve of my taking delivery for this season's silk, you chop my credit. How in the bloody hell do you expect me to find that kind of money on such short notice?"

The banker's handkerchief returned to his brow. "If it were my decision your credit would be intact. Frankly, I'm as surprised as you are over London's decision. They've never interfered to such an extent with the running of the bank."

Motes of color swam in Eric's eyes. "What kind of calamity do you think the bank would have suffered had I chosen to save my silk and not blown my godown to bloody hell?" The words hung precariously. "I'd have an account full of money and Shanghai would be a pile of cinders."

Stafford's head dropped a fraction.

"Look at me, Pierce." Eric's voice was soft. "Has someone twisted arms in London to single me out for this special treatment?"

*　　*　　*

ERIC looked out on the harbor, but saw nothing as his rickshaw made its way toward his office.

Now what?

It was inconceivable that the bank would pull his credit, yet the inconceivable had occurred. Complicating matters, Stafford wouldn't or couldn't say if the Bartrums were involved. Eric didn't really blame him for that. Stafford was due to retire in less than a year. Why bugger up his pension?

But now the possibility of bankruptcy had become a crushing reality. It was only a matter of time before word leaked to the business community that his credit line had been cut. No other bank would be interested in pulling him out of the muck.

So, how to maneuver?

Eric considered going to Jing-Jiang, but decided against it. Face was involved and his was already diminished. Other options included using Tong-Po as an intermediary or approaching Katheryn's father, Sir Geoffrey.

That's not the way, old chum, he told himself. You're the taipan, and you made the decision to sacrifice the silk. If you go down, don't do it begging.

The rickshaw runner suddenly stopped. Eric looked up, finding himself at his office. Paying the fare, he walked inside and picked up a copy of the Shanghai Times.

"Good morning, Pauline," he said. "A pot of tea, please. And have Tong-Po stop by my office."

Eric seated himself behind his desk and opened the paper. Headlines about the Boxers taking over the foreign legations in Peking stared back at him. "Traders Demand Sir Geoffrey call in the Fleet......" Eric tossed the paper aside. *Bloody Christ.* He'd forgotten he was scheduled to attend a meeting at the Governor's residence later in the day. And right now the last thing he wanted was to discuss the current crisis in Peking. He had his own problems. And besides Alex Bartrum would be there.

Godrot his soul.

Eric turned in his chair and looked out the window. Gulls circled, waiting for the fishing boats to discharge entrails. *Scavengers picking at the remains.* Nothing his enemies wouldn't do to him, given the opportunity.

Tong-Po knocked and entered, followed by Pauline, who was carrying a black lacquered tray holding a pot of tea and rice cakes.

"You wanted to see me, Taipan?"

Eric moved from his desk to the conference table and waited for Tong-Po to climb into his elevated chair. After serving tea, Pauline left. Eric picked up a rice cake and took a bite without tasting it. "The bank refused to extend our credit line."

Tong-Po's teacup stopped midway to his lips. The two men stared across the table, each holding his own peculiar silence. "They cannot do that," Tong-Po finally said. "The silk..... We have to take delivery. What about another bank?"

"Officially, we're as good as bankrupt," Eric said. "No other bank will touch us. London decided to sell a large block of the bank's risky paper. Our notes were among the lot."

Tong-Po was strickened. "As sure as dogs defecate in the streets, the Bartrums are responsible," he said. "We must go to Jing-Jiang for help. Otherwise the co-hong will take the concession."

"No." Eric's eyes flashed. "I've no doubt the Bartrums are behind this, but I've lost more than enough face to go begging to Jing-Jiang. It was my decision to dynamite the warehouse. Our inventory was under insured and we're paying the price. I'm responsible."

Tong-Po saw the pain and something else etched in Eric's face. "Then we need to raise money. We can sell our personal property---"

"Thanks for the thought, old friend." Eric smiled grimly. "I've considered that, but we haven't got the time. The co-hong expects payment in less than a month. Time has all but run out."

"What then.....?"

"We need a bloody miracle."

Eric turned and gazed out the window. Gulls were still circling. It was time for him to go to Sir Geoffrey's. *Then what?* The bad news was he didn't know.

*   *   *

"GOOD-DAY, Mr. Gradek."

Eric nodded to Sir Geoffrey's secretary, Willoughby, and entered the Governor's office. It was a richly appointed anteroom, dominated by a large Rosewood conference table. The Governor was seated at the head of the table, flanked by General Harold Potter and Admiral Richard Klees.

"Gentlemen."

"Ah. Eric, good of you to come," Sir Geoffrey said. "Brandy? Sherry?"

Eric exchanged handshakes. "Brandy, please."

"Mr. Bartrum will be joining us shortly. We'll wait for him to avoid unnecessary repetition."

Conversation confined itself to general trade topics for the next ten minutes until Alex Bartrum arrived. After exchanging handshakes with the other men, Alex nodded at Eric. "You wanted to see me, Sir Geoffrey."

"Yes, Alex. Please take a seat." Sir Geoffrey glared at his secretary who was busy examining a hang nail. "Quit dithering, Willoughby. See to Mr. Bartrum's brandy."

"Yes sir."

Sir Geoffrey took a pinch of snuff and sneezed. Passages freshened, he shifted his gaze to Eric and Bartrum. "As leaders in the business community, I've asked you to join us to discuss the crisis with our legation in Peking."

"Excuse me, sir," the general said. "Seizing sovereign

British territory is an act of war. This is a military matter. I hardly see the need to consult with local business leaders."

"Quite right," the admiral agreed. "The fleet needs to be called in to blockade the Yangtze. Cut off supplies to those contemptible anarchists."

"And it will be the army's job to drive the bloody Boxers into hell," the general added.

"Gentlemen," Sir Geoffrey said. "There are political and trade consequences to consider."

"Other than freeing our legation, the military should not be used," Eric said. "The Empress has allied herself with the Boxers to avoid being overthrown. The *I-he-t'suan* is but one of thousands of secret societies dedicated to toppling the Qings. If she were to side with foreign powers she would be inviting civil war. A military solution would not be in England's best interest."

"Poppycock," Bartrum said. "The only thing Chinese respect is power. Military power. Doing nothing will make us appear weak. The secret societies will become emboldened and intensify attacks against English property. What we need to do is hang the lot of them."

"That's impossible." Eric's eyes locked with Bartrum's. One day he'd have the satisfaction of telling him who he was before settling scores from the *Northern Star.* "You can't hang every Chinese who wants to overthrow a foreign dynasty. There are millions of members in the secret societies. Plus, if we act alone militarily, we'd be snubbing the French, Germans, Japanese, and Russians."

Bartrum's gaze was taunting. "What do you suggest, Gradek --- sitting down with bloody anarchists and having tea? We need the military to protect our interests. The China Trade will be jeopardized if we let them get away with seizing our legation."

"Don't be ridiculous, Bartrum. I won't waste my time answering." The tension became palpable.

"Of course we need the military," Sir Geoffrey said hurriedly. "Trade is England's life blood and needs to be protected. But, Eric's right about maintaining our relationships with the other foreign powers."

The Admiral and General exchanged a glance. "I respectfully repeat, sir," the General said. "This is a military matter and should be decided between the Admiral and myself. An act of war has been committed against His Majesty's government. Certainly a matter well beyond the province of business people."

"Thank you, gentlemen," Sir Geoffrey said. "I want the army and navy made ready to move quickly. London has cabled authority to use military force to secure our legation. First, however, I must discuss an overall strategy with my European, Russian and Japanese counterparts."

"Compensation for property damage and trade concessions would be in order," Bartrum said.

Eric remained silent. Taking the matter up with the other foreign powers would result in endless bickering. Perhaps Sir Geoffrey could broker a political settlement in the meantime.

"I'll take that under consideration, Mr. Bartrum. Now, I think another round of brandy would be in order." Sir Geoffrey motioned to his secretary.

*　　*　　*

ERIC was still at his desk when the clock told him it was two in the morning. The cup of tea in his hand was tepid. He watched dim lights blink from cargo ships in the harbor. A familiar sight, but now the lights mocked him. Since leaving the bank, Eric had examined and re-examined ways to extricate his company from impending bankruptcy. He had discarded them all. Except for one. The only avenue that remained open to him was going to Jing-Jiang. *Beg for help.* But that really wasn't an option, was it?

Weary from it all, Eric decided to go home and slipped on his jacket. So many people depending on him. Did he dare go to Jing-Jiang?

"You stay plenty late tonight, Taipan," said a voice from behind.

"Real bugger today," Eric replied.

Watchman Choy, the man-servant who had come with him from Hangzhou to Shanghai so many years ago, walked into the office. Choy watched over the premises and maintained quarters in the basement.

Shadowed by Choy, Eric went downstairs and glanced around the offices. *A bugger today. But tomorrow will be better.*

Choy held the door as Eric stepped outside. He stood a moment looking at the harbor, the salt breeze fresh on his face. He began walking. Water lapped against the seawall. Dawn would announce a new day in four hours.

Fifty yards later, Eric heard a crate shatter. There were sounds of men struggling. "Hold the sodding bastard, he's squirming like --- "

"Pop the bleeder on the nog!"

"Bugger off. I want this godcursed heathen to see the smile on me face afore I relieve him of his bloody innards. Hand me the rope."

Eric raced down the dock, hurtling over several drunks. A muffled cry from under the pier. Peering over the side, he saw four men on a loading platform. Three were white --- the fourth was a tall Chinese, gagged and tied.

Steel glinted in the moonlight. The knife tip was placed next to the Chinese man's throat. "Feel that, heathen? I'm gonna use it to cut your yellow hide."

"Gouge the sod and get it over with," one of the other men said.

"Yeah, let's get the bloody hell outta here," said another.

"In a minute," the man with the knife said. Blood darkened at the point of the knife tip. "I want to hear this bugger beg for mercy."

Eric landed on the platform and was on the man with the knife. Wrapping an arm around the man's neck, he jerked back on the knife, inverting the angle and slamming it inward. The body disappeared into the dark maw of the harbor. Eric's eyes blazed with opalescent fire. The smaller of the two men reacted first. Holding a belaying pin, he launched himself. Eric ducked. The weapon crashed against a mooring post. Eric's fist sank into the exposed ribcage. Bones cracked. The man crumpled.

The third man, knife in hand, was closing. Eric spun, partially losing his balance. The blade flashed. Fire burned across Eric's arm. The knife arced again, but Eric was prepared. Sidestepping, he grabbed the extended arm, slammed the man's head into the seawall and raked his face down the barnacles, taking out an eye. A shriek of pain.

Eric pulled the man over and hilted the knife into his gut. Silence.

Eric cut the Chinese man's bonds and rolled him on his back. Blood gurgled from a gash in the abdomen. "You need a doctor." Eric cut the shirt into strips for a bandage. "I'm going to need your help to get back to my office."

The Chinese man's eyes glazed with pain. "Nevermind. Help me up the ladder and I will manage."

"You'll manage about ten paces before you bloody well bleed to death." Eric lifted him to his feet.

*　*　*

NIGHT was dissolving when they stumbled inside Eric's office. He put the wounded man in a chair, relocked the door and lit an oil lamp.

Watchman Choy stepped out of the semi-darkness, a fighting hatchet in his hand. "Taipan. I thought you were a bandit." The servant's eyes widened seeing the blood and grime covering Eric's clothes. *"Oh ko!* Your arm, Taipan --- how you wounded so?"

"No need to worry," Eric said wearily. "It's a flesh wound."

"Ayeeee, Taipan --- you look plenty terrible." Choy's eyes went to the Chinese man slumped in the chair. "He look worse."

"He's lost a lot of blood."

"Eeeee, so big for a civilized person, *heya?* His ancestors are no doubt fornicating mongrels from the north."

"Get some hot water and towels up to the guest quarters. Then I want you to fetch Tong-Po and a Chinese doctor." After Choy had gone, Eric felt the reaction to the fight. He had killed two men and wounded a third. For a moment he felt sick. The Chinese man watched him, his eyes filmed with pain.

78

---

*   *   *

ERIC had the Chinese man cleaned up and in bed by the time Tong-Po arrived with the doctor. The dwarf looked at the man's face. *Formidable Fung Xio Ling. By all gods, how did the Taipan manage to become involved with this foul dragon?* A first fear settled in. "Come," he said to Eric, "We must talk."

After two cups of tea, Eric recounted the events.

Tong-Po paled. "Two men dead --- a third beaten. Can the third man recognize you?"

"It's possible," Eric replied. "But even if he can, I doubt it will come to anything. He failed and will probably be killed by whoever hired him."

Tong-Po shook his head. "Foolish to have gotten involved."

Eric was too tired to respond.

"Listen to me," Tong-Po said. "The man you saved is Formidable Fung Xio Ling, supreme dragon of the Green Pang. If he lives, you will not have seen the last of him. This could be bad joss."

Eric stared at the dwarf. "Why bad joss?"

Tong-Po shrugged. "Maybe bad. Maybe good. Who can say? But, one thing for certain, your karma is now entwined with his."

Eric's eyebrow arched.

"You saved him from dying and are responsible for changing his joss. According to Chinese tradition you are now the owner of his life for having saved it."

*   *   *

BLOOD gouted from the man's mouth. Vaguely aware that his front teeth had been shattered, he writhed on the dirt floor in

---

Dragon Mok's warehouse.

"Enough," Mok barked.

Alex Bartrum watched impassively as a bucket of cold water was thrown over the man's head.

Mr. Jones set the thirty-six inch broom handle, wrapped in black tape, on the table. Without looking at the man, he removed his knife from the scabbard tied on his forearm. He began stropping the ten inch blade across the sheath he'd made from a razor strap. The back and forth movements possessed a monstrous sensuality.

Dragon Mok glared at the beaten man. "Kill this worthless dog."

Petrified, the man began to babble through broken teeth. "So help me God, I told the truth. It was Eric Gradek hisself."

Mok beckoned to one of his men. "Take this turtle dung outside and feed the crabs."

"Hold on," Bartrum said. His men had botched the assassination attempt and he needed to recover a measure of face. An impression needed to be made on Mok to keep their relationship on an even keel. "Let Mr. Jones handle it."

Jones jerked the man up and pulled him towards the door. The terrified man gave off a sour smell.

Bartrum smiled at Mok. "Death is good for Mr. Jones. Inflicting it makes him feel alive."

A blur of movement as Jones' knife opened the man's throat from carotid artery to jugular vein. The man gaped into the leering face of Mr. Jones. For a split second he had no idea what had been done to him, then he collapsed, hands to his neck and the spraying blood.

Dragon Mok looked on impassively, but felt his scrotum tighten.

Bartrum marveled at the speed with which Jones wielded his knife. An impression had been made. But, the rawness felt about Eric Gradek remained. Even so, he did not believe Eric's interference was anything other than happenstance.

Sodding bastard.

*   *   *

MOK slurped his tea. They were in his office, a single lamp burning. Ting se-Bing, Mok's High Tiger, a brooding presence in the shadows.

"Bad joss, Eric Gradek saving Formidable Fung's miserable life," Mok said. "An alliance will be formed. Fung's debt to the Opal Eye Devil is great."

Bartrum let Mok's reference to Eric as the Opal Eye Devil slide. It had become a moniker of respect the Chinese gave him after the fire. The other taipan had taken to using it as well. "Any alliance will be short lived. I hold Gradek's notes. What's left of his hong will revert to me next month."

Mok's eyes narrowed. "Until then we are confronted by a pair of wounded tigers. A condition when predators are most dangerous."

Bartrum sipped his tea. "After we sell our opium, Formidable Fung and the Green Pang will be finished."

Mok remained silent. The foreign devil was right. Still, things could go wrong. An entire season's supply of opium sailing down the Yangtze posed great dangers. A whisper of such a shipment would attract every pirate on the seas and rivers of China. Fear brushed Mok's backside. If it weren't for the armor and cannon of Bartrum's ships he would never have taken the risk. But the risk worth it. It was his chance to destroy Fung's

Green Pang. His customers would be forced to turn to him for their supply. And without customers Fung's money supply would evaporate. His soldiers would desert like rats fleeing a sinking ship.

Fung will be finished.

Mok stared at Bartrum. "When do you think the shipment will arrive at Chongming Dao?"

"Two weeks, give or take a day."

"What about reserve crews to take your ships to Shanghai after the cargo's been unloaded?" Mok asked. "Too dangerous to leave the original crew alive. So much opium would start tongues wagging."

"Don't worry," Bartrum said. "Men from my Hong Kong office who know nothing about the shipment will be downriver. Just make sure the opium is bloody well protected until it can be dispersed."

Mok smiled.

Bartrum smiled back, pleased he had doubled the size of his mercenary force arriving from Hong Kong.

Mok scratched his armpit. One day he would have to kill this pea-brained barbarian. He opened a drawer and pulled out a bottle of brandy. "What will happen now that the Boxers have attacked the foreign legations in Peking? The Empress has declared war against foreign devils."

Bartrum studied him. Mok's tone was casual --- too casual. *Little shit's digging for information.* "Within days they will be crushed." Bartrum watched Mok's face crack then smooth into an oriental calm. "An international fleet is preparing to sail to Peking and lay waste to the city if the legations are not surrendered immediately. The Empress will pay for her support of the Boxers. Her declaration of war against Western powers could well bring down the Qings. Either way, it's time for the Chinese and their bloody Manchu overlords to learn that we are here for good. As for the godrotten Boxers --- they will be publicly hanged."

Bartrum's revelations were not surprising. Still, Mok secretly vowed to castrate him publicly. *May you drown in your own feces for your impertinence, you son of a lice-infected whore.* Mok poured brandy into three cups. Ting se-Bing stepped forward. Bartrum accepted one. Raising his cup, Mox said, "To our success at Chongming Dao."

"And a black pox on all Boxers," Bartrum added.

The two men downed their drinks.

Neither could see the hatred burning in Ting se-Bing's eyes, nor did they notice that his cup never touched his lips.

Eight

KATHERYN STUDIED ERIC'S PROFILE AS HE stood on their second story balcony. Night was falling and distant noises from the city drifted through the open window.

Watching him reminded Katheryn how much she wanted to be included in his secret thoughts. She sensed his despair and ached for him. Losing the warehouse and a season's worth of silk was terrible, but surely not the end of everything, was it? Certainly, the Commonwealth-Shanghai Bank would help them sort things out. *Mr. Stafford is such a dear.* Still, since the fire, things had not been right. Eric never spoke of trouble, but Katheryn knew it was there. She saw it in his eyes.

Ah, those eyes, so green --- green like the leaves of a tree.

Katheryn wrapped her arms around her chest. Eric's eyes could by turn contain laughter, or reach into her soul, or reveal how much he loved her when she was in his embrace. But then there was that other light which spoke to violence and primal anger. Katheryn had seen the fire in Eric's eyes, but she knew it would never focus on her. Some cruel experience had forged and honed that fire, but it was not for her. Thank God, it was not for her.

Eric was both hero and enigma to Katheryn. In her mind, he was a man of great talents, great thoughts and great wrongs. When he came home with his arm cut she had been frantic. He said it was an accident, but she knew better. *How ignorant I am about his business.* Complicating matters, she realized it had been a deliberate effort on her part to be that way. She'd never had the courage to face the darker side of his nature. Nor did she have the courage to ask about the woman in his past, Hsi Shih. Twice, when he was asleep, she heard him whisper her name. Was he in love with her? Or worse, did he still...?

Katheryn's amah, Ah-Sook, told her the name Hsi Shih meant *beauty of beauties.*

"Original Hsi Shih *weerry* famous courtesan in ancient China. On outside she great lady --- trained in fine womanly arts of singing, dancing, playing music, composing poetry, writing, and conversing. But --- during pillow time great lady replaced by shameless whore. Oh yes," Ah-Sook said, "Hsi Shih very artful --- supreme master at weaving the silken web. Once ensnared in its shimmering strands no man ever escape."

Katheryn touched her cheek. Could it be that she'd not been daring enough with Eric? She sat up. Their intimate times were wonderful, weren't they? He was never demanding. Yet, she'd never acted like a whore in their bed.

You're a married woman. Free to explore your wildest fantasies.

Distant sounds from the city touched her. Familiar sounds,

yet tonight strangely hypnotic. Katheryn leaned back, watching Eric, so quiet yet composed on the balcony. She'd met him at a party hosted by her father, Sir Geoffrey Worthington, the acting territorial governor.

Such a grand occasion.

Lanterns illuminated the tree-lined terraces and manicured lawns of the Ambassador's residence. In the background, darkened sampans and junks glided along the Huangpu like giant bats.

Katheryn was standing between her father and mother, Lady Ann, when Eric came in. Bored, she was listening complacently to the music being played by the military band. She heard her father saying, "Katheryn dear, I want you to meet Mr. Eric Gradek, taipan of Gradek International."

She looked up and into the most incredible green eyes she had ever seen. "My pleasure," she said. Heat filled her, and her voice sounded small and strangely unreal.

"No the pleasure is mine, Kate." Eric took her hand, kissed it lightly. "Perhaps later in the evening you would honor me with a dance?"

"That would be nice," she replied. Eric's touch was electric. She had never been called Kate before.

Minutes crawled into an hour and the line thinned. Katheryn glanced at her father, who was speaking with the Governor of Hong Kong. She slipped away into the crowd looking for Eric. Occasionally, she paused to chat with a guest, hoping to catch a glimpse of him.

"Good evening Katheryn."

"Good evening Mr. Bartrum." She managed a smile.

For months, Bartrum had pursued her --- sending gifts --- hinting at marriage. "You look lovely tonight, Katheryn." The compliment was given in that kind of obvious manner she abhorred. "I have grand plans for the future. Nothing could please me more than to see you become part of those plans."

When she failed to reply, he touched her arm. "I was hoping we might speak privately."

Katheryn's fan fluttered. "Really, Mr. Bartrum, I'm rather busy."

Bartrum's grip tightened. "I don't want to lose you, Katheryn."

Cocking her head, she regarded him curiously. "Mr. Bartrum, I find it difficult to comprehend how you could loose something you never had. Now if you will excuse me."

Something moved in Bartrum's eyes. He was about to say something, but Eric arrived. "Evening, Alex." Eric's gaze never left Katheryn. "I came to collect my dance, Kate." The tone of his voice was soft, but loud enough for Bartrum to hear.

"That would be quite nice, Mr. Gradek."

On the dance floor, Katheryn saw Bartrum's face twist with rage. Eric took her in his arms. His eyes seemed to peer into her soul.

"You are a grand woman, Kate."

"Mr. Bartrum seemes to be quite angry."

"Forget him. Let's enjoy the dance."

*　　*　　*

KATHERYN smiled, looking back on that evening. Eric had blown into her life like the wind. No, she corrected herself, more like a tempest. *Father almost had a seizure when I mentioned our plans to be married.*

"Eric Gradek," Sir Geoffrey had roared. "Absolutely not!

Out of the question."

"But father I love --- "

"Katheryn, we'll have no more talk about it." Sir Geoffrey's face softened. "Dearest, young Gradek's a decent sort, but for you to marry someone with no family background?"

"I love Eric Gradek." Katheryn's eyes steeled. "I'll not allow you or anyone else to stand in the way of my happiness."

"But, he just arrived in Shanghai one day from God knows where. For all we know he's some profiteer with a sordid past." Sir Geoffrey stood from behind his desk. "Perhaps it would be best for you to return to London until you get this foolishness out of your head."

Lady Ann moved to her daughter's side. "Katheryn, dear," she whispered, "give me a few moments alone with your father."

Three months later, Eric and Katheryn were married with Sir Geoffrey's blessing.

Katheryn turned toward the balcony. She could see the orange tip of Eric's cheroot. For a long while, she sat watched her husband. Night had laid down its exquisite mantle. Eric was quite still, a coiled strength in the darkness.

*   *   *

TING se-Bing was in the moss garden at the rear of his house when the message arrived. The terrified courier was detained by guards while Ting meticulously checked the rice paper wrapping, wax seal, and chop. Satisfied there was no tampering, Ting dismissed the courier and set the package on the table.

Servants arrived with brandy and assorted fresh fruits. For some time, Ting brooded and drank, refusing to look at the parcel. The liquor burned his belly, but could not reach the cold pit

inside him. Ever since Alex Bartrum's prediction that an international force would be dispatched to stamp out the Society of
the Virtuous Fist, a creeping dread had gripped Ting.

Setting his glass down, Ting picked up the package. He
stripped the rice paper away and removed a rosewood jewelry
box. Expertly, he traced the small metal padlock for hidden
cuts. Turning the box over, he twisted the hollowed out right
rear leg. The padlock key was inside.

Ting opened the box and stared at the message tube. His fingers trembled over the prospects of what he might find. He
adjusted the wick on the oil lamp, slipped the message out, and
began to read. Each character brought increasingly bad news.
When he reached the final line there was little doubt as to the
state of his brotherhood's cause. "Hope for a better China has
been eclipsed by armies of foreign devils."

Ting stared at the message without seeing. Finally, he closed
his eyes and leaned back. His life had become a hideous joke.
For years, he had sold his soul to Manchu devils and *fan-
gwoiloh* for wealth and power. Then a long dormant inner
voice had whispered to him: *Stand with China.* Ting obeyed
and was quickly infected with the nationalistic fervor sweeping
the country. He met the founder of the Society of the Virtuous
Fist, Wong Sing-wei, and joined the brotherhood. By this time
his inner voice had risen to a tiger's roar.

Finding redemption for his soiled life, Ting committed heart
and soul to the cause. But now the cause had been killed. His
brotherhood smashed, along with the armies of the prune-faced
whore, Empress Dowager. The Society had been duped --- used
by the *fan-gwoiloh* and their Chinese lackeys. *Storm the legations,* they had whispered. *Foreign devils only respect the use
of force. How else can one deal with barbarian dogs?* Ting

buried his head in his hands. *Oh ko.* Like fools they listened to beguiling tongues. Now Ting's brothers had been hanged by foreign devils before jeering mobs.

Rage roiled inside Ting. How smug the international forces must feel entering the celestial city and lifting the siege of their legations. Like whipped dogs the Imperial Court fled to Hsi-an, granting barbarians the unthinkable rights of maintaining troops in Peking and water routes to the sea.

Ting stared at the stars. Night breezes stirred, but gave no answers. *The ways of heaven are treacherous,* he thought. *So fickle are our gods. They give and take* --- protect and destroy. Bartrum had been right when he boasted foreigners would be in China forever. The thought filled Ting with hatred. He despised all things associated with barbarians: their stench and arrogance --- their religion and ridiculous customs. How he longed to kill Bartrum. But that was not possible. At least not now. If a member of the Society of the Virtous Fist was found responsible for the death of a powerful taipan, the foreign devils would have yet another excuse to gain further concessions.

So, what to do?

Ting reread the message. The brotherhood, while not destroyed, would be forced underground. Support from the people had been crushed by the military. Confidence replaced by fear. He read the message again before tossing it into the fire.. Watching it burn, Ting felt the stirrings of an idea. While it was true that all barbarians were enemies, some were better than others. Destroying Alex Bartrum would require that Ting betray Mok.

Was that something he would be willing to do? Ting looked at the stars, but they offered nothing but distant light, long since dead.

*   *   *

FORMIDABLE Fung Xio-Ling opened his eyes. Having survived the night, he would begin the process again. Glancing at the girl curled next to him, he fingered her hair. She cooed, but did not open her eyes. Fung stood, walked across the room, and stood in front of the mirror. The knife wound was healing and beginning to scar. Satisfied, he left the bedroom and prepared for the day.

It had been foolish of him to visit his fourth wife without security. She was obviously a traitor. How else could the three barbarians have known where to intercept him? Fung fastened the last button on his Mandarin jacket. Such stupidity would send him to his ancestors. He moved to the window and stared down on the street. *Sad to exterminate such a fragrant flower.* Of course, he'd had no other option.

Fung watched a beggar woman holding a baby settle on a street corner. Passers-by would hear the child's cries as she artfully used a hidden needle. The sight did not disturb him. Life in Shanghai was hard. Kill or be killed. Feed yourself by whatever means necessary. Or starve. Joss.

Life was fickle, like the gods --- sometimes good, sometimes bad --- but never stagnant. Fung shivered at the thought. Had it not been for the Opal Eye Devil he would be dead. Saved by the same barbarian who risked his life to save the shantytown.

Madness. I would not lift a finger to save the life of one foreign devil. Still --- I owe him my life, and a life is a debt not easily repaid. But to be owed to a fan-gwoiloh?

Fung set the problem aside. Other matters needed his attention. Like what to do about Dragon Mok? He had little doubt that Alex Bartrum, Mok's ally, had been responsible for the attack against him. No question, Shanghai had grown too small for the Green and Red Pangs to coexist.

Shrill cries from the baby. Fung watched as an English woman deposited a coin in the beggar woman's cup. Mok and Bartrum had cornered the season's supply of opium. Fung's growers had betrayed him --- for money. Now his Green Pang faced destruction.

Fung stared out at the city. Ten thousand cannon size balls of opium were sailing down the Yangtze on Bartrum's armed lorchas. The cargo was too dangerous to bring into Shanghai. That meant a warehouse on one of the outer islands. But, which one? And what about the Bartrum's crew? Obviously, marked for assassination. The smallest whisper about such a shipment would attract every pirate on the Yangtze.

Fear touched Formidable Fung's back. Even if he learned the location of the warehouse how would he move such a sizable amount of opium? Soldiers he had, but trained crews to man ships....

A soft knock. Fung looked up to see his guards ushering in Ting se-Bing.

Nine

ERIC WALKED INSIDE THE COMMERCE CLUB, nodding to headwaiter Fong. "Anything of interest?" he quietly asked. Eric had gotten Fong, a third cousin of Tong-Po's, the prestigious job specifically to keep him abreast of club chatter.

"Plenty talk about Boxer rebellion, Taipan. Traders happy Society of Virtuous Harmony Fist smashed and that Empress Dowager's decree of war nothing more than dog howling at moon."

Eric's face hardened. "Fools. The real trouble is only just beginning. A godrotten civil war is staring us in the face."

"Fourth cousin Mung, who works as server at French Club, say that important general say big trouble between foreign governments could develop over where soldiers stationed in Celestial City and along waterways." Fong glanced conspiratorially at Eric. "Who guard what important, *heya?*"

"Be sure cousin Mung keeps his ears free of wax."

Fong helped Eric remove his coat. He was proud to occasionally pass information to the Opal Eye Devil.

Taipan weery smart for fan-gwoiloh. So sad he will forever remain an uncivilized barbarian. Bless all gods that I am civilized and from the Middle Kingdom and therefore superior. How could even the great Opal Eye Devil, who all Chinese revere for saving thousands of lives during great fire, comprehend that the Society of the Virtuous Fist served a valuable purpose by bringing the withered Dowager hag and her court eunuchs a step closer to oblivion? Yes, the vile Manchus and their fornicating Qing Dynasty will soon fall. Eeeee, and after the northern invaders are smashed the dragon of China will rise and cast the fan-gwoiloh and their foul manners and foul religion to the four winds.

Fong smiled, his gold tooth on display. "You prefer table in lounge or dining room.....?"

"Ahh, Eric," said Ian Havershire. "What a pleasant surprise. Haven't seen you in an age." Beside the Welshman was Andrew Pendleton. Havershire, in his early forties, had migrated to Shanghai twenty years earlier and built one of the preeminent trading hongs in China. A beefy man, he was several inches shorter than Eric with flaming red hair and a handlebar mustache. Pendleton, also in his forties, was a slight Englishman with refined features. Fifteen years ago, he inherited a small trading firm from his father. He took the one room operation and built Pendleton & Sons into a giant, equal in stature to that of Havershire's. Both men were predators.

"We've a table reserved, Eric," Pendleton said. "Care to join us for drinks?"

Eric nodded.

Conversation heated as the topic turned to politics and the Boxer Rebellion. "Still can't believe that bloody Empress openly supported those murdering heathens and declared war," Havershire said. "Incompetent bitch."

Other traders wandered over. Soon the merchants grew angry, calling for the government to declare war against Peking and bring the Qing Dynasty down.

"We should seize Shanghai as British territory then pressure Sir Geoffrey to send the fleet to Peking," Pendelton said "We've been coddling a bunch of heathens while our business goes down the pisser."

"Politicians only know how to wag their tongues," an angry voice broke in. "Sodding bastards should keep their noses out of military matters."

Pendelton's gaze found Eric. "No offense intended, Sir Geoffrey being your father-in-law. It's just there's only room for so much talk. Now action is required. I've lost hundreds of thousands because of those heathen renegades."

"We've all been hurt, Andrew," Eric said. "But seizing Shanghai would only strengthen the Qing's. The army would mobilize and seal off the Yangtze. Shanghai, at least temporarily, would be isolated from the interior. Trade would be cut off."

"Our fleet would take care of that!" Havershire said.

"Perhaps," Eric replied. "But consider the possibilities. Taking Shanghai would result in war between China and Great Britain. Japan, Russia, Germany, and France --- all envious of our position in Asia, would support China. A more prudent course would be to diplomatically destroy the Qing Court. If we succeeded, Great Britain would be in the strongest position to deal with any subsequent government."

Conversation ceased as Alex Bartrum stepped in front of Eric. "Just like you, Gradek. Taking the soft approach in dealing with these heathens and their godrotten face. What the Chinese respect is power, military power. Smashing them in Canton was the only reason we got treaty concessions in the first place. The presence of our fleet insures control of the inland waters and China."

Eric stared at Bartrum. "We gain nothing but our own demise if a hundred million armed Chinese line up against us, supported by France, Germany, Japan, and Russia."

"Poppycock. Our fleet can finish the Qing Dynasty once and for all. Great Britain will dictate, not negotiate terms with any subsequent government." Bartrum crossed his arms and looked down on Eric. "But none of that will matter as far as you're concerned."

Eric fought the urge to call Bartrum out for satisfaction.

"Enjoy lunch," Bartrum said. "It'll be one of the last you'll be having here."

"Really?"

The silence thickened. "Really." Bartrum removed a document from his coat and tossed it in front of Eric. "Bartrum & Sons holds your notes --- all of which are due and payable in thirty days. In a month Gradek International will be finished." Bartrum turned a palm up. "Unless you can find a way to make payment in full."

Eric lit a cheroot, ignoring the document. "I'll be here in thirty days to collect my paper." He exhaled a stream of smoke. "Pity that you rather than the bank profits from this transaction."

Bartrum's smile was ugly. "Hollow rhetoric won't save you, Gradek. It's common knowledge you lost an entire season's worth of silk. You need money for this year's allotment and there's not a bank in Asia that'll extend you a shilling's worth of credit."

Eric stood. Anger darkened his emerald eyes. The other traders sat transfixed. "Hear me well, Bartrum. My business isn't common knowledge --- least of all to you." Eric removed a document from his coat and placed it on the table. "Speaking of debts, here's a copy of your last invoice for oil containers." A half-smile pulled at the corners of his mouth. "It's thirty days past due. If anyone's having trouble meeting obligations, it's you."

Bartrum glared.

Eric made his good-byes and left the club humming.

*   *   *

SOUNDS of the harbor greeted Eric on the street. A tanker owned by the syndicate headed by Bartrum & Sons languished along the horizon awaiting clearance to discharge kerosene. Eric stood looking at the ship, Bartrum's words resonating in his mind. *Hollow rhetoric won't save you now.*

Bloody bastard's right. I won the battle in the club, but how to win the war? Thirty days and his notes were due. Gradek International, forced into bankruptcy. Had he built a house that could be so easily swept away?

Eric began walking. In front of the Commonwealth-Shanghai Bank he stopped and stared at the white marble columns supporting the arched facade. *A black pox on you, he thought. No, not a black pox. You need this bank, or another one like it to finance your dreams. Once you figure a way out of your current mess --- figure a way to get the bank. You can use it to destroy Bartrum. All you need is the capital.*

Eric walked on until reaching the Street of Nine Dragons. There he turned toward Nanjing Road and left the calm of the business district. Nanjing Road was old and narrow, residents packed six to a room in tiny flats. Crowds jostled, the din of the city was strident. Smells of spice, incense, charring meats, fish, and boiling soups vied with more rancid odors of urine and decomposing vegetables. Shops, stalls, and foodstands covered by red and gold-trimmed awnings lined the street.

Mah jong tiles clacked. Bands of children, some clothed --- some not, rushed about wildly swinging toy sticks at invisible demons. Carts filled with squealing hogs clattered over cobblestones. Men and women carried loads across their shoulders in twine baskets, supported on bamboo poles.

Eric felt a thousand eyes on him as he sank deeper into the heart of the city. Off to his left was the animal market, where badger, fox, cat, dog, and even owl were sold alive and fresh for human consumption. He stopped to watch the panoply of life that made up Shanghai. The city had an energy of its own --- pushing outwards, ever changing. Yet, in the process of changing, remaining the same. Eric recognized this to be the essence of China itself. It was this essence that made her eternal, and it thrilled him to know he was a part of it. Often times, he felt like his entire life had been spent here. His childhood in England was nothing more than hazy recollections, ending on the *Northern Star* with a knife in his belly, only to be reborn under Tong-Po's ministrations, and Jing-Jiang's mentoring. It had become easy for him to imagine that he had been born an adult into this strange land.

Eric spied a restaurant across the street. Near the front door was a beggar, his bowl on top of a wooden box. The man's head slouched between his knees. Eric knew that this man was under the control of the infamous Beggar King, Kwok-yu. Thousands more lined the streets of Shanghai, all paying a percentage of their meager contributions into Kwok-yu's treasury. Failure to do so resulted in pain and revocation of the right to solicit on the streets. The Beggar King held dominion over a grisly cast of characters ranging from old men and women who garnered their meager coins, or *cumsha,* by threatening tourists and pedestrians with contact from their rotting limbs, to starving children who offered themselves unnaturally for the price of a bowl of rice. These outcasts of humanity were Kwok-yu's family --- his eyes and ears of the city. And, for a fee, any service could be obtained through the Beggar King's maze of sorrow.

Eric watched the beggar swat at a fly. *Why does God, if there is a god, allow such misery for some, while others never know a day of deprivation?* He stepped into the street and deposited a few coins into the beggar's bowl on his way into the restaurant.

The outer wall of the establishment was composed of metal-rimmed glass containers housing a vast assortment of fish. Above, hanging from a trelliswork, were glazed duck, sausage, and pig intestines. An old man was busy cleaving melons, carefully saving the seeds on a burlap bag. Other workers were occupied scaling fish destined for flaming woks or steaming bamboo baskets.

Eric passed inside the restaurant, but did not notice the smile on the beggar's dark lips. People were looking for the Opal Eye Devil. Powerful people. Perhaps Kwok-yu would reward him.

The proprietor was exhorting the waiters to serve with haste to make room for new customers with new money. His mouth dropped when he saw Eric step inside. *The great Opal Eye*

Devil in my restaurant --- waiting for a table? Eeeee, what great face I will gain for serving the illustrious taipan with glittering eyes. He grabbed a waiter. "Clear our best table."

"But a party of five has just placed an order --- "

"Is dung clogging your ears?" The proprietor glared. "I said clear the table. Be quick or I'll have you eviscerating chickens."

The proprietor walked over to Eric. "Great honor to have you visit my humble restaurant. I have plenty good number one table available. Would you like?"

Eric nodded.

The proprietor's toothy smile broadened.

Waiting to be served, Eric remembered Jing-Jiang telling him that war mirrored life. Both were breeding grounds for fear. *I've laughed at danger a thousand times before and always won.* But this time the sand in the hourglass was running out. He had no choice but to go to Jing-Jiang. *With my hand out.* The admission shamed him.

"Excuse, Taipan."

Eric looked up to see the proprietor and two waiters around his table.

"Hope it okay, but we prepare special dinner for you. You like plenty good," he beamed.

"Your efforts will be my good fortune," Eric replied.

As predicted, the fare proved excellent. Especially the special stem of wild rice soup, jiaobai, prepared by the proprietor's wife. Eric belched to show his appreciation. He tried to pay but the proprietor pushed his money away.

"No take money, Taipan," he said softly. "You good joss for my family. Never do you pay one copper in my restaurant. You save many of my relatives from dragon fire. Today all would be visiting ancestors if not for you."

*   *   *

A BLOCK from the restaurant Eric was stopped by five Chinese men. The leader was tall with yellowed teeth and garliced breath. "Please come," he said. "*Weeery* important my master speak with you."

Eric's eyes moved from one man to the next. All appeared lethal. He lit a cheroot, taking his time, asserting control. "Go with you where? And who is your master?"

The leader's eyes darted up and down the street. "We go see my master, Formidable Fung. He say plenty big important he speak with you, *chop, chop* ."

Eric masked his surprise. The incident on the quay had occurred over a month ago. He blew on the tip of his cheroot. Fung had something more in mind than a cup of *cha. But what?*

The leader fidgeted nervously, waiting.

Eric made his decision. There was only one way to find out what the Dragonhead of the Green Pang wanted, wasn't there?

*   *   *

FUNG dismissed his guards when Eric arrived. He was dressed in black silk pants and a quilted red Mandarin jacket with a pair of white and gold egrets embroidered across the breast. The Dragonhead was tall for a Chinese with a wide mouth and strong chin. But the most striking feature about him were his eyes. They held no light.

"So sorry for the inconvenience," Fung said. "But, due to our peculiar circumstances, I was unable to approach you on the street." The flat ebony eyes watched Eric. "Can I offer you some tea or brandy?"

"Tea," Eric replied.

The office in one of Fung's warehouses was meticulously clean and decorated with fine Chinese appointments. In the corner was a red lacquered screen with a black and gold dragon coiled around a tiger. Fung followed Eric's gaze. "For Chinese the dragon represents renewal and strength."

"And the tiger?" Eric asked, knowing the answer.

Fung inclined his head. "Ah, the tiger --- well that's another story." A small smile touched the corners of his mouth. "Please, take a seat."

Eric watched Fung. There was more to this man than his brutal reputation. "How's the wound?"

"Tender and itching," Fung said. He poured tea and waited for Eric to take the first sip.

Eric slurped at the steaming brew. "The flavor is quite unique."

Fung refilled his cup. "Black Dragon. My own special blend."

The two men drank in silence.

"I owe you my life, Eric Gradek," Fung said after a time. "You know our ways. You know that such a debt cannot ever be fully repaid. Today, however, I will make a start."

Eric stared back, saying nothing.

Fung set his cup aside. "Both of us are victims of betrayal that has placed our houses in danger. The Commonwealth-Shanghai Bank was manipulated into revoking your credit line which allowed Bartrum & Sons to gain control of your commercial paper. They are now squeezing you for funds you do not have."

Eric was shocked. The confrontation with Bartrum earlier at the Commerce Club was the first public airing about his financial difficulties. Two hours later, Formidable Fung was describing the noose Bartrum had around his neck. "You are well informed."

Fung stared into Eric's eyes. *Mu Kuang Ju Chu, flaming torches like the dark demons below. Eeeee. What a prized ally the Opal Eye Devil will make, if he can be persuaded. How far will he go to destroy Bartrum? Will he kill like that night on the quay?* Fung leaned back into his chair. "How I learned about your dilemma with Alex Bartrum will no doubt be of interest," he said. "But first, I will tell you about the trap Dragon Mok and Alex Bartrum have snared me in. It will clarify matters."

"I'll take that brandy now," Eric said. Then, after lighting a cheroot, he listened to Fung tell him about an opium shipment that would be unloaded on the island of Chongming Dao in seventeen days.

Ten

E RIC SPENT THE NEXT MORNING THINKING about his arrangement with Formidable Fung. The thought of stealing a fortune in opium was unreal. Blood would be spilled. But that would be between Fung and Mok's men. *At least,* he thought, lighting a cheroot, his own hands would be clean.

Or, would they?

Then there was the possibility of a double-cross. Eric stared out the window, weighing risk against gain. Fung's weakness was not having trained seamen to sail a sizable fleet like Bartrum's. If Fung attempted to off-load the cargo and transport it by junk back to Shanghai, he would be opening himself to piracy.

I'm Fung's insurance policy, by providing the seamen.

No double-cross there.

Eric watched the smoke from his cheroot curl toward the

ceiling. For his efforts, he would receive fifty percent of the profit. More than enough to buy his notes from Bartrum and pay Jing-Jiang for the season's silk production. He smiled. Best of all, he would be doing it with Bartrum's money.

If there are no mistakes.

There was a soft knock on the door.

Pauline Han looked in. "Taipan, a Mr. Garrett Botha is here. He says it's urgent. I told him you've a busy schedule, but he's persistent."

Garrett was standing by an open window in the reception area when Eric walked up. He was wearing a worn Outback hat, khaki shorts, and hiking boots. The Sumatran sun had turned his skin cinnamon and his blond hair platinum.

"How might I be of service, Mr. Botha?"

"Ah, Mr. Gradek. Good of you to see me on such short notice." They shook hands, taking to each other instantly.

"Miss Han informs me you have something urgent to discuss."

The blue eyes hardened. "Indeed I do, Mr. Gradek. I've traveled from some nasty jungles in Sumatra to see you. Is there somewhere we could speak?"

Eric looked at Pauline. "Have some *cha* sent to my office, then see we're not disturbed."

*   *   *

GARRETT sipped his tea. "Hope you don't mind my calling you Eric, but formality will become a bit cumbersome after you've heard what I have to say."

The two men's eyes met, measuring each other.

"I've taken a gamble coming here." Garrett turned a palm

up. "A risk based on the assumption you want to destroy Alex Bartrum as much as I do."

Eric stared back, saying nothing.

"Alex and Philip Bartrum's connection with Trident Industries goes beyond being lead distributor in Asia. They are major shareholders, along with Percival D. Sutton and Baron Albert Rosenberg. Because of that relationship I have a way to legally smash Bartrum & Sons." Garrett set his cup down. "Well, there you have it. The question is, would you help me do it?"

Eric's liking for the man overrode his inclination to remove Garrett from the premises. This sunburnt man from the Sumatran jungle was deliberately baiting him. *Why?* There were stronger trading houses who had scores to settle with Bartrum, but taking Bartrum & Sons down would require power. A great deal of it.

Could this man have such power? Fung and opium, now this. Careful now.

"My company manufactures kerosene containers for Trident Industries," Eric said.

Garrett's eyes crinkled, a first humor. *How different and alive from Fung's,* Eric thought.

"I'm not only aware of the contract with Bartrum, but I'm responsible for your getting it in the first place," Garrett said. "You see, at that time, I was a business associate of his."

Eric's eyebrows raised. "It was a bitter pill for Bartrum, coming to me for help."

"More like taking strychnine. You charged him twenty-five percent more than your contract terms with Classic Oil. Besides, he already hated you for taking his silk business." Garrett smiled. "I can only imagine how he felt when you married Katheryn Worthington."

"You seem to know a lot about me, Mr. Botha. I'm not sure I like it."

But Garrett was already laughing. "Those kerosene receptacles will go down as the greatest balls-up in history. Who would ever have dreamed every Classic Oil container in Asia had been bought up and remanufactured into everything from tin roofs to hibachis?"

Despite himself, Eric smiled. This Garrett had an infectious way about him. "There's an unwritten law in China. *Don't waste anything.* Everything has value and can therefore be turned into profit."

"Look, I'm a geologist by trade," Garrett said, getting serious. "When you got the Classic Oil contract, I was working for Sutton. I later moved to Trident and developed their Baku fields. Afterwards, I set up their Asian facilities. I assumed customers would use the same Classic containers you were manufacturing to receive shipments." Garrett sipped his tea. "Our tankers had passed the Suez Canal with no way to offload. If not for you, the Bartrums would be flat on their rumps and the mighty Trident Industries humbled. Such irony." Garrett eyes smiled with insight. "All for a goddamned tin barrel."

For the next two hours, over cigars, Eric listened to Garrett detail events leading to the *Grand Alliance* between Classic Oil and Star Petroleum.

"The oil wars between Percy D. and the Baron demonstrated that no one group is strong enough to control the world's oil supply." Garrett's expression sobered. "But, a powerful triumvirate is a different proposition. Sutton and Rosenberg already own every pipeline of importance. Trident was established to act as the legal umbrella."

Eric whistled softly.

"Sounds incredible, but it's true," Garrett said. "A transaction the size of Trident was very complicated and top secret. In order to keep government eyebrows from lifting, Sutton and Rosenberg made it appear Trident was a joint venture providing efficient transportation for the industry as a whole. I give them credit for a brilliantly executed ploy."

Something ate at Eric. Since the fire, kerosene prices had risen. Profits of the major hongs were pinched. If Bartrum's ownership in Trident Industries gave him such arbitrary pricing power then the China trade would be his to control. "How does Bartrum figure into the scheme?"

"Baron Rosenberg brought the brothers in. Politically it wouldn't do for a powerful Jewish family to have exclusive privileges through the canal. Bartrum & Sons was the perfect fit. Powerful, British, Protestant --- an internationally recognized trading firm with roots in Asia. All the necessary ingredients." Garrett looked at Eric. "Except one."

Eric leaned forward. "Which was?"

"Money. For several seasons their trading company had taken a battering. They were cash poor for a transaction of that size. That's where Philip Bartrum came in." Garrett set his teacup on the desk. "The Bartrums agreed to make a substantial cash contribution and provide a modern tanker fleet. In return, they would receive limited equity and stock options for an equal future position. So, Philip mortgaged Bartrum & Sons to come up with the down payment. The problem was there was no money left to finance the fleet."

Eric's eyes widened. "That's why Alex Bartrum formed the syndicate."

"It wasn't difficult getting the taipan to come up with the money," Garrett went on. "Bartrum offered them a share of the profit from tanker operations and guaranteed allocations at stable prices. Anyone who wouldn't go along forfeited kerosene shipments." Garrett smiled ruefully. "Of course, everything he promised was bullshit. Now the poor sods are up to their arses in debt. There were no shipping profits and prices have been set according to his whim."

Eric was appalled. "Bloody fools, why don't they band together and abrogate the agreement?"

"Too late," Garrett replied. "Bartrum & Sons control the collateral and distribution. Philip ran the inflated financing package through their London bank." Garrett's lips compressed. "All without a penny of their own capital. Pretty slick, eh?"

"Good God."

"The bright side is Bartrum & Sons is still teetering," Garrett said. "Doing business with Percival D. Sutton and Baron Albert Rosenberg was unlike anything the brothers were used to. Cash expenditures were tremendous and now they're caught in a financial box. It they fail to meet option deadlines, accumulated equity is forfeited."

Eric took a breath. It made sense. Bartrum's storage facility was the only one undamaged by the fire. Any reservations he'd harbored about stealing the opium vanished.

Garrett caught Eric's expression. "Bartrum & Sons are still the most powerful economic force in Asia. They are engaged in a strategy that will make Alex a monarch in Asia." Garrett studied the tip of his cigar. "If they're successful."

"How are you are privy to Bartrum's plans?" Eric asked.

"As I mentioned, I worked with him," Garrett replied simply. "He knows that whoever controls the oil markets in the next decade will control the world."

Eric finished his tea. "The United States and England are free societies. Trident can't hold back the tide. What's to prevent other companies from working together and getting involved in the oil game?"

Garrett's eyes hardened. "Sutton and Rosenberg have the will and the resources. Promising patents are purchased --- new companies assimilated. If the owner doesn't accept their offer to buy, then they run him out of business by cutting prices. If that fails, other tactics are employed."

"So how do you plan to bring Bartrum & Sons down? They're part of Trident."

"I hate Alex Bartrum deep in here." Garrett jabbed a thumb at his chest. "He screwed me out of millions after I'd built the most efficient oil distribution network in the world. Putting that aside, I know how he thinks and he cannot be allowed to control Asian oil. Sutton and Rosenberg, on the other hand, are untouchable. The best I can hope for is to sting their pride."

Eric saw the anger in Garrett's face, and it mirrored his own as bitter memories welled up. He saw himself holding Tong-Po as Mr. Jones charged with a knife. He felt the pain of cold steel entering his side and saw shadows of Alex Bartrum and Mr. Jones over him.

Do you want me to finish him now Mr. Bartrum?

God's blood no. Nothing so easy for this stinking sod. Throw the bloody bastard into the hole and let him bleed to death.

Seventeen years old.

"My motives for seeking you out as a partner are not altruistic," Garrett said. "You are as essential to the success of my plan as I am."

Eric stood and poured two brandies. "I'm interested, but I'm making no commitments. All I'm promising is my attention."

"Fair enough." Garrett accepted a glass. Relaxing, he lit a fresh cigar. "Sutton and Rosenberg knew that efficiently servicing the Asian market was essential for their plan to succeed. First, three things had to happen. They needed to develop their Russian holdings at Baku and build a pipeline to Bantum. This, of course, was done by yours truly. They needed access to the market. That required Baron Rosenberg to secure right of passage for Trident's tankers through the Suez Canal. And, they needed Bartrum & Sons to distribute refined oil and kerosene in Asia."

Garrett removed a map from his valise and spread it on the desk. He touched a circled area in Russia along the Caspian Sea. His fingernail was hard and dark "This is Baku, located here on the Apsheron Peninsula," he explained. "The dotted line is the pipeline that runs from Baku to Bantum, a major port city on the Black Sea." The dark fingernail moved on. "At Bantum the oil is loaded on tankers and shipped around the tip of Turkey to the Mediterranean. Then it passes through the Suez Canal, into the Red Sea, and onward to Asia. What you see is the fastest, most efficient, way to move kerosene to the Orient. Until now. Bartrum & Sons' Achilles heel is in their own back yard and they haven't a clue. South of Singapore is the big island of the Dutch East Indies, Sumatra." Garrett touched the map. "Jans Kessler, an old chum I worked with in Baku, brought me some paraffin samples he found on a Sumatran coffee plantation. They contained a high concentration of kerosene. I left for the Indies on the next boat and did a series of geological studies." Garrett looked at Eric. "What I found was a sea of oil --- the largest field I've ever seen."

Eric hid his surprise. "What's your connection with the field?"

"My father is the Netherlands Ambassador at Large. He pulled some strings and got me the concession from the Sultan of Langkat. Nothing incorrect because of my expertise." Garrett returned to the map. "The field sits at the mouth of the Balaban River. It's a damn good waterway that flows directly into the Straits of Mallacca. That's where the refinery's located. I've already got the field outfitted, but there's work left on the pipeline and refinery that should be completed within the year." Garrett grinned at Eric. "About the same time your contract with Trident expires."

Eric stood and stretched. "You're plan is to squeeze Bartrum out with lower prices from reduced shipping costs. Sounds nice, but what makes you think Trident will take it lying down? They'll flood Asia with cheap kerosene."

"If they drop prices we'll undercut them by ten percent. That is unless they're willing to give it away. And even Percy D. and the Baron can't do that indefinitely." Garrett's excitement couldn't be contained. "You see, we have the backing of the Danish Government! After my father apprised Queen Wilhelmina of Trident's plans she gave him magisterial powers to develop Holland's oil resources. She wants to expand The Netherlands' political presence in Asia. Being a major oil supplier will allow her to do that. But her overriding concern is domestic interest. War is becoming a real possibility. The Americans have destroyed the Spanish Navy and taken possession of the Philippines, Cuba, Guam, and Puerto Rico; the Boars and the Brits are fighting in South Africa; European powers are saber rattling; Russia and Japan are at odds; China on the brink of civil war. Whoever's got the oil will play the pivotal role!"

Eric hoped his own excitement was well hidden. "Outside of my personal animosity for Bartrum why come to me with this proposition? You've got the oil --- the political support --- everything tied up in a neat little package. What do you want with me?"

Garrett counted off his jungle hardened hand. "Three things: Money, expertise, and your commitment to see this through. I need distribution and you're the only major taipan not wedded to Bartrum financially. The larger houses like Havershire's or Pendleton & Sons wouldn't throw in with me, even if they wanted to. They've got too much capital tied up with the tanker syndicate. My plan depends on speed and secrecy. If I approached one of the larger hongs I'd have Bartrum and every other syndicate member out for my balls. Thirdly, there's a lot of uncertainty in China and you know more about the Chinese than anybody."

"You still haven't explained why you consider me vital to this operation."

"I've got the oil concession, and financial backing of the Royal Dutch Government and you've got offices and manufac-turing facilities for containers in every major Asian port city. You produce Trident's receptacles and have the list of every kerosene user in Asia. That's the key to capturing the market. Overnight, before anyone knows what's happened, we'll be in and Trident will be out." Garrett snapped his fingers. "For those things, and the money you'll need to buy land for storage and distribution depots, you get half interest in distribution profits. Coming in with me won't come cheap, but it'll be worth it."

Eric stared out the window. *A half share in distribution prof-*

its. And I believe him. Such vast potential. Large enough to help China's development. Open up the kind of trade Jing-Jiang has dreamed about. Millions of people having access to lighting oil for the first time. I could light up the world. Not bad for a seventeen year old with a knife stuck in his gut. Eric refocused his attention on Garrett. "One detail we haven't discussed are tankers."

Garrett nodded. "Our tankers are the most cost-efficient way of transporting oil. Twice the size and twice as fast. We'll have eight outfitted by year's end and another four three months later. And, you know what...? You won't find a particle of coal dust on board. They're powered by oil."

"What!"

Garrett nodded. "Soon every major naval and commercial fleet in the world will be powered by oil. A schoolmate of mine at MIT, Matthew Clay, developed the technology. His family's big in shipping. They handled Classic Oil's European shipments until Percy D. severed the contract. Cost Matt's family millions." Garrett bit the bottom of his lip. "That was a serious mistake by Sutton. Instead of Trident having the most modern tanker fleet in the world --- we do. Joss, eh?"

Eric lit a cheroot. "Joss."

"Here's something you'll appreciate," Garrett said. "I had Matt outfit our ships with modern steam cleaning and freight handling equipment. We'll be able to clean the holds in port and return with a full load of whatever we contract to ship. The equipment works so well that we can transport food without contamination."

"Sweet Jesus," Eric said. "With tankers like those we could bloody well rule the world. But where's the money coming from?"

Garrett checked his watch. "Three o'clock. Why don't we have a bite of lunch and I'll tell you all about Mr. Franz Mikolits --- a mysterious little banker from Switzerland."

*   *   *

ERIC and Garrett worked into the evening on land and storage requirements for Asian ports. Cost estimates had been high, but that was acceptable. Potiential profits more than justified the outlay. And, Eric was confident Jing-Jiang would provide the financing. It would pave the way for making his dream reality.

"I'll need three weeks before I can give you a firm commitment," Eric told Garrett. "The only condition is that I'm satisfied with everything you've presented."

"We'll make arrangements for you to visit the site in Sumatra," Garrett said. "After that, I'd like you to meet Matthew Clay. I'll also arrange for my father and Franz Mikolits to be on hand." He passed Eric a sheet of paper. "These are the notes outlining our partnership arrangement. If everything's in order I'll make a duplicate for us to initial.'

Eric studied the sheet, finding nothing amiss.

"What made you go after the Classic Oil contract in the first place?" Garrett asked, writing the copy. "Lighting oil receptacles and silk are worlds apart."

"I needed to expand my office network into other Asian cities. The contract came along and I took it. None of the other taipan wanted it." Eric smiled. "If things work out between us, it might be the best deal I ever made."

Initialing the papers, Garrett handed them to Eric. "Let's hope they work out."

"Where's the best spot to cable you with my response?"

Garrett wrote down a name and cable number. "I'll be here for the next four weeks. I'll assume we don't have a deal if I haven't heard from you by the end of that time. But if everything's in order let me know by a cable. We'll need a code. No need risking any wrong parties being made aware of our association, eh?" Garrett's face hardened. "At least not now. Once I receive your cable, I'll respond with a like message to confirm receipt. Within thirty days after that I'll meet you back in Shanghai."

Nodding, Eric said, "Obviously you've got something in mind for the code?"

"Yes. I've got a good feeling about this so we'll use the name for our field in Sumatra. Only two other people, my father and Franz Mikolits, know it." Garrett scribbled a name on a sheet of paper. "Send these two words and we're partners."

Eric stared at the paper. *Telega Said.* The words jumped off the page. "By the way, what's the Teahouse of the Golden Carp?"

"A quiet little inn outside Kyoto. Beautiful gardens, great baths. Jacqueline and I are going to watch the cherry blossoms fall."

"Your wife?"

"Yes."

"A holiday?"

"Of sorts. We're going there to make a baby."

Eric laughed. "One of life's more pleasant tasks."

Silence gathered.

"What is it?" Garrett asked.

"You know a lot about me. Some of it is common knowledge."

Garrett nodded. "That's right."

"What else do you know? Understand, I take no offense if you've had me investigated, given the nature of this business venture."

"You recently killed two men, injured a third."

"Go on."

"That's all," Garrett said. "But it's an important measure of the man."

"And you?"

Garrett looked at Eric without fear. "Let's just say I'm a jungle man with jungle ways."

Eric nodded. "Perhaps that speaks well for a partnership."

Eleven

I T WAS PAST DINNER TIME WHEN ERIC ARRIVED home. euphoria held him now that he'd committed in principal to a partnership with Garrett. If there was a way to put the pieces together he would find it. An inner voice whispered, probably the same one that had spoken to Caesar and Napoleon. *This is your moment, seize it.*

Eric stopped at the front door, thinking about Garrett. *Odd we hit it off so well.* Except for Tong-Po and Jing-Jiang, who were more like family, he'd never had a friend. Garrett was everything he wasn't. Born into a rich family, the right schools, the right connections, doting parents.

As a kid on the English docks, Eric had to fight his way to school.

Dad was a godcursed alcoholic who beat me and mum senseless every chance he got. The hard London life reasserted itself, and the memory stabbed his gut. *Beat us until I turned sixteen.*

Eric remembered blood filling his eyes when he returned home that rain-soaked evening. His father, standing over his mother, her face badly bruised. "You'll not be giving me no more sass, you old bag." He raised his hand to strike.

"If you hit her dad, it'll be the last time."

His father reeled, laughing in drunken rage. The resounding smack rang in Eric's ears. His mother screamed. Eric went for his father. After a pitched battle, the man who sired him lay sprawled on the floor. The event proved too much for his mother. She died the following year. After arranging a proper burial, Eric sailed for China. As for his invalid father, he left without a backwards glance.

Rotten sod never gave mum anything but a parcel of hell.

"Taipan?"

"Eh?"

Katheryn's cherished amah, Ah-Sook, was standing in the open door. "Come in," she ordered imperiously. "What you doing standing in dark? *Oh ko,*" the old woman clucked. "Look at you. Lean as a willow. Have you had dinner? Mistress give orders to properly feed you, and have nice bath waiting."

Eric grinned. "Just a snack. I had a late lunch."

After a light dinner, Eric went to the bath house. He'd had it designed after similar bath houses found in Hangzhou. The famous *fung-shui* man he'd contracted had also found the best location for attracting good spirits. A spot in the back yard's maple grove was selected. Eric smiled. *Imagine. A British taipan consulting a heathen soothsayer about where to build a bath house.*

Eric crossed the courtyard to the sounds of frogs and cicada.

Lanterns highlighted the path with its multi-colored mosses. Red candles burned inside, casting shadows on the lacquered bamboo walls. Steam rose from the wooden tub.

A servant served tea and helped him out of his clothes. Afterwards, Eric sat on a stool and was scrubbed with pumice. He sank into the bath, letting the heat take him, and thought about his meeting with Tong-Po. The dwarf's face had congested with excitement, first on how he planned to help Formidable Fung steal the opium, then about Garrett's proposition.

"Easy to understand why Fung needs your help to seize the opium," Tong-Po had said. "If he tries to recruit trained seamen he risks word getting back to Mok. But remember, Taipan, you are about to put your head inside the dragon's jaws. What happens after Fung's taken possession of the prize? Your value withers like the lining of an old whore."

"Fung's not beyond treachery, but he owes me his life," Eric replied. "Plus, he'll need my services in the future if he wants to bring the poppy in by river."

Tong-Po stared at Eric. "You've struck a long-term arrangement with Fung? Have you entered into an *Old Friend* relationship?"

"If there'd been another way I'd have taken it," Eric said. "It was the only way to get enough advance money out of this mess. Besides, the arrangement is for transportation, not distribution. I hate the godcursed poppy, but it was here long before I arrived. Christ, it's a bloody stinking way of life."

You are wise in many things Taipan, Tong-Po had thought. *Entering into Old Friend relationship with Formidable Fung was clever. But sometimes your logic is unfathomable. This guilt you feel is astonishing. Of course, the opium trade was here before you arrived and it will remain long after you leave, or are thrown out.* The dwarf looked at Eric with renewed excitement. "*Ayeeee,* great benefits could be reaped from *Old Friend* relationship with Formidable Fung, especially if Dragon Mok's Red Pang is smashed. As sure as gods fornicate, civil war is coming to China. We could use a strong arm like Fung to help protect our interest. Besides, as you so wisely pointed out, success in this venture will allow us to approach Jing-Jiang about the Garrett Botha matter."

Eric opened his eyes and found Katheryn standing at the end of the tub. She was wearing a red silk robe tied at the waist, her hair falling about her shoulders in golden ringlets. Her eyes were luminous. She untied the sash, letting the robe part and drop to the floor. Eric's eyes explored the landscape of her body. The faint scent of her perfume came to him. His wife had never been so beautiful to him as she was now.

Katheryn watched his eyes. She realized her life had been lived inside some sort of puritanical Victorian dream. *Ahh, but it's so nice to be awake.* She moved forward and slipped into the tub, resting her head at the opposite end. Her toes brushed his thigh --- then their legs were intertwined. Perfume filled his nostrils.

Eric watched his wife's hair fan around her.

*   *   *

THEY retired to their bedroom and made love with their hands and mouths and bodies until early morning. Sated they joined as *yin* and *yang* and loved each other with their minds.

Afterwards they cleansed each other with hot towels, drawing themselves back into the present.

Eric patted her back dry. "This is so unlike you, Kate."

"Not unlike me at all," she said. "You've never seen the real me. Probably because I've kept her hidden away, even from myself. Since childhood, I've been treated like a doll that would break in the real world. When we married, I bloomed."

"And bloom you did," Eric said, setting aside the towel.

"You liked the way I slipped off my robe?"

Eric took Katheryn's hand and squeezed. "Very much. You're a beautiful woman, Kate."

Katheryn inclined her head. "I doubt the idea ever occurred to you to invite me to share your bath. Can't blame you really. I was appalled like everyone else when you had the bath house built." She laughed softly. "I can still see that funny little *fung shui* man mapping out dragon veins in our back yard."

Eric smiled. "But now you drop your robe and let your hair fan free in the water."

"I was reared to the sound of stodgy Victorian voices and the evils of being naked."

Eric kissed her cheeks. "I like you naked."

Katheryn looked deeply into his eyes. "I'm your wife and want to share your life. I want us to esperience each other's hurts and triumphs. The bad as well as the good." Her gaze sharpened. "I know we have a parcel of trouble since that wretched Alex Bartrum got our notes. I'd like to be included in such --- "

"So the whole bloody world knows." Eric shook his head.

"Shanghai's really a very small place, my love. The way you took Alex Bartrum's face at the Commerce Club is quite the talk. Of course, no one speaks openly to me about our problems, but everyone knows."

"I'd hoped to spare you."

"That's the point darling. Don't. I can take care of myself. Imagine how it makes me feel to learn about these things from other men's wives. Today at Lillian Havershire's, I could feel the other women salivating behind my back about our imminent demise." Katheryn chuckled. "Actually, this afternoon gave me some insight about who our friends are."

"And who might they be?"

Again, the soft chuckle. "Sorry darling --- we don't have any. So I played the blissful little wife and innocuously dropped a tantalizing bit of information into the old biddies' laps. By now it will be the gossip of Shanghai."

Eric's eyebrows lifted. "What?"

"Everyone was talking about the terrible trading year facing us because of poor crop reports and the damage caused by those awful *Boxers*. Lillian asked how it would affect us. I smiled innocently and said we were concerned about the frightful state of affairs. Then I told her we were looking forward to a banner year now that you'd arranged new financing to cover our expanding silk markets in the United States." She crinkled her nose distastefully. "You should have seen the expressions on their faces."

Eric heaved up onto one elbow. "You what? My God, Kate, I'm up to my neck in debt. It will take a bloody miracle to pay off Bartrum, much less Jing-Jiang."

"Calm yourself, dear. If it's a bloody miracle we need, it's a bloody miracle we'll get. If I know anything about you at all, you've got something working. Meanwhile think of all the fuss stirred around town. Everyone will be wondering what the Opal Eye Devil is up to. Bartrum will be thrown off balance. A lot can happen in seventeen days. *Chieh Tsu Hsien Teng, heya?*" Knowing her inflection was perfect, Katheryn beamed inwardly at her use of the Chinese proverb meaning the nimble of foot get there first.

Brilliant, Eric thought. If he was successful in stealing Bartrum's opium, groundwork was laid explaining where he got the money to buy our paper back. The only one who would know the truth was Bartrum. He smiled to himself and took Katheryn's hand. Loving her greatly, he began talking to her like a wife and friend. Speaking about his past was difficult, but once the words began to flow, all the serious emotions he'd buried since his youth were freed. He withheld nothing, except his plans to steal Bartrum's opium and his pledge to Jing-Jiang to use his resources to open China to the world of trade.

Katheryn was horrified to learn he'd been stabbed by Mr. Jones and left to die in the ship's hole. "What about the law? Why didn't you contact the police and have him taken before a magistrate?"

Eric searched her eyes. "Listen and remember. The law is nothing more than a feeble human attempt at decency. Bartrum's above whatever bloody law there is in Shanghai."

Katheryn shuddered at the force of his words, while other parts of her mind damned Bartrum and blessed Tong-Po for saving the man she loved. Lastly, she cursed Eric for exacting revenge against Bartrum by marrying her. Biting back the urge to verbally assault him, she remembered Ah-Sook telling her, *The secrets of a man's heart are learned by opening the ears rather than the mouth.*

Katheryn opened her ears and listened.

"There's a vastness about China beyond our comprehension," Eric said. "Out there" --- a sweep of his arm --- "is a land of more than two hundred million people. Half the world's population lying in wait. There're ethnic divisions and thousands of village dialects, but they're all first and foremost Chinese. The timelessness of the land bonds them together." Eric's eyes took on a strange glow. "They're locked in a primitive time vacuum without an inkling of what modern civilization means. But one day that will change." Eric stared at Katheryn. "Think of the consequences when those lost millions are reached. A market will be created that'll shake the bloody world."

Katheryn held the shiver inside. She had always known China was a vast country, but nothing like what was now being described. It had never occurred to her that the peasants would remain anything but peasants. She remembered going with her parents to Peking on an official visit to the Dowager Court. Part of the protocol was a side trip to Shanhaiguan. She had been awestruck to see the Great Wall rising like a great serpent out of the ocean surf. It somehow seemed alive, able to shake off the clinging gray waters as it twisted across a narrow plain to the *First Gate of Heaven* where she was standing. From there it uncoiled, writhing through the peaks of the Yan Shan range.

Wind whipped her hair as she stared. "Why on earth was it ever built in the first place?" she asked.

"Stone Serpent represents the threshold of civilization," the guide said. "Everything depends on which side one dwells. Inside Gate of Heaven we are in the Middle Kingdom where all things are Chinese and therefore civilized." Katheryn caught the hate behind the guide's eyes. "Out there are the barbarian outlands. Chinese people make supreme sacrifice and build Great Wall to keep our lands free from their foul ways."

They really despise us, she thought. Even the lowest coolie thinks we are barbarians and inferior. Yet, Eric seems as much at home with them as with his own kind. I wonder if he's Christian? He never goes to church even though I've nagged.

She considered it for a moment and found herself unconcerned.
It doesn't matter. Our life together will be grand, regardless.

"I'll be leaving for Hangzhou tomorrow with Tong-Po."

Katheryn looked up. "How long will you be away?"

"Not more than a week. Adair will look after things until I get back."

"Is she there?"

"Who?"

Sitting very still, Katheryn stared at him.

"No," he said softly. "Hsi Shih happened a long time ago in another lifetime. You and I are happening in this lifetime."

"You loved her very much, didn't you?"

"There was a time when I heard her whispers the same way leaves rustle in the wind."

"How did you get over her?"

"The days rolled into each other and the pain became less." He moved closer to her.

Katheryn hugged him, squeezing back tears. "I can imagine how you felt. The pain, I mean. Surely, I would die from grief if I were to lose you."

*   *   *

KATHERYN awoke several hours later. Eric was gone. He would be well on his way towards Hangzhou. Sighing, she stretched and reached for his pillow. She pressed it to her breasts. Their lovemaking had always been pleasurable, but last night? Had it not been for the dull pain between her legs she would have thought it was a wild dream.

I should be ashamed. A true English lady would never have acted the way I did, would she? But then again, I'm not a true English lady. At least, not anymore.

Twelve

ERIC LEANED AGAINST THE *LORCHA'S* guardrail watching the panoply of life along the Grand Canal. They were in mid-channel with thousands of other junks and sampans near the suburbs of Hangzhou. Many of the craft carried quilted sails made from myriad scraps of discarded fabric. They curved in the light breeze, sending the vessels forward. Eric smiled. Another reminder of the Chinese propensity not to waste anything.

Tong-Po stood on tip toe and pointed a finger at the planes of mud and rice. "Look there." Men were following their buffalo as they plowed the earth, while women in conical hats plodded barefoot through the paddies harvesting the crop. "A pastoral scene as old as time," he said. "The only thing that changes are the people who replace themselves as the wheel of life turns."

"I suppose," Eric said. He was reminded of the day he had set off on his two year journey into China. At the dock Jing-

Jiang had told him: "My son, you will learn many lessons, pleasant and unpleasant, but the important thing is you will learn."

Jing-Jang's words held true. During his travels, Eric began to absorb the essence of China. Tong-Po had told him while he was bleeding to death in the hole of *Northern Star* that he would not die. Indeed he had not. Instead, he had been transformed.

The evening breeze freshened. Ahead, Eric saw Precious Stone Hill. At the summit was Bao Shu Pagoda, where the monks had refined his street Chinese and made him fluent. West of the pagoda, midway down the small mountain, was Jing-Jang's fortress home. Beyond, rimmed on three sides by mountains which were perpetually shrouded by clouds, was the ethereal West Lake.

Eric heard the temple bell calling the monks to evening prayers. It rolled across the waters, timeless, spiritual. In his mind, he could hear their incantations. It was a sound that pleased him greatly, a soothing rythym for the soul. "The bell is the voice of Buddha," Hsi Shih told him years ago. "Each bell has its own spirit. Copper plates from the donors and paper prayers from the people are added to the molten metal to become the soul of the bell."

Hsi Shih.

She was Jing-Jiang's niece, who at the age of five had been promised to a high official in the Dowager Court.

What's her life like now?

On the eve of his departure to Shanghai, Eric said to Jing-Jiang, "I'm not going to let her go. I want to take her with me."

"That is not possible," Jing-Jiang said. "Her fate has been sealed. Hsi Shih will go to the Empress's court as her contract reads. You must never attempt to find her."

The pain in Eric's eyes softened the old man's heart.

"She cannot be seen with you, my son. Do you want her to be reviled as the lowest form of whore? A *fan-gwoiloh's* whore?" Jing-Jang touched Eric's shoulder. "Today's sorrow is the price for yesterday's happiness."

The lorcha entered the part of the canal that paralleled the market district. Ten barges were roped together. Stevedores unloaded silkworm cocoons for delivery to silk factories a few blocks away. Eric recognized the family members. For generations they had lived and died aboard these barges, seldom setting foot on dry land. A half-dozen or so young boys were on deck wearing leashes to keep them from falling overboard. There were a few girls, but they were unfettered.

Eric saw the patriarch, Riverman Po, stitching up a ripped bag than had spilled out cocoons. Jing-Jiang had commissioned him to captain the junk that had taken Eric on his two year odyssey up the Yangtze into the heart of China.

Now if I can get the old pirate to ferry me and my crew to Chongming Dao.

Riverman Po gathered the spilled cocoons and stuffed them into the repaired bag. Looking up, he caught sight of Eric's lorcha. "*Hola,* Taipan. You come for *cha* tonight, *heya?*"

Eric waved. "Tonight, no can. Tomorrow, morning can, heya?"

"Tomorrow. I wait for you."

Ahead, Eric saw the torches lighting the pier. Bannermen, carrying Jing-Jiang's insignia, flanked a pair of red and gold sedan chairs that would transport him and Tong-Po.

*   *   *

JING-JIANG'S wisp of beard was snow-white and he seemed older to Eric. Still, his eyes remained both youthful and wise. He wore a silk gown of emerald green with a tiger of gold and black embroidered on the back. Laying his chopsticks on a silver filigreed holder, he belched and nodded to his chef.

Tong-Po patted his stomach and belched his appreciation. "Chef Cheong, I have missed your peerless culinary offerings."

Using the arms of his chair, Jing-Jiang stood and turned to his majordomo. "We will take *cha* and brandy in my study. After that we are to be left undisturbed."

Eric followed Tong-Po and Jing-Jiang to the study and was saddened to see the old general's back a little more bowed. But, the aura of power that always surrounded him was undiminished. A servant led them inside and closed the door. It was a spartan room with a stone fireplace and shelved walls to hold his collection of books.

"Since you left for Shanghai my books and memoirs companion me these days," Jing-Jiang said. A small reminder that Tong-Po had thrown his Western books over *Northern Star's* railing. Under the circumstances, an understandable act but, nonetheless, shortsighted. Tong-Po's face reddened, but he said nothing. Jing-Jiang touched a stack of papers on his desk. "Perhaps my penmanship will contain something of value." He chuckled. "After all, I have the luxury of looking back from the high hill of my old age."

A knock at the door announced the arrival of the majordomo.

After tea was served, Jing-Jiang looked at Eric. "We have much to discuss. You mentioned problems with Alex Bartrum."

"Bartrum & Sons hold our commercial paper," Eric said. "If payment is not made within the month Gradek International's assets will revert to them."

"What is the amount due?"

When Eric told him, Jing-Jiang closed his eyes. "*Ayeeee,* such an amount. There has been no default on our obligations. Are not all of our financial dealings confidential and confined to the Commonwealth-Shanghai Bank?"

"After the fire, future prospects weren't good. Our ability to repay outstanding loans had been diminished. Knowing this, Philip Bartrum arranged for the London headquarters of Commonwealth-Shanghai Bank to sell them our notes at a discount. What Philip did was legal. It's common practice for banks to sell questionable loans to other financial institutions. Besides, Bartrum's allies, the Rosenbergs, are large purchasers of this kind of commercial paper."

"All gods piss on barbarian banks." Jing-Jiang's eyes narrowed. "How long have you been aware of this problem?"

"Thirteen days."

Jing-Jiang cast Eric a stern look. *My son, I will not tell you how proud I am you did not ask for my help directly. Now you have learned about power. So tangible when one possesses it, so ephemeral when one does not. You have sunk to the depths. Are you prepared to rise to the heights?* "It is time you learn that face is one thing --- survival another," he said. "No man is truly alone. Emperors and kings need vassals, armies, and allies to survive. By failing to come to me you jeopardized the hong we have so carefully constructed." Jing-Jiang's words hung in still air. "When does this money need to be paid?"

Eric sensed Jing-Jiang was already aware of the problems with Bartrum. The Old General's response to the amount of money owed was too casual. *Tong-Po must have told him after the incident at the club. If so, it's a bloody blessing. Face has been saved on both sides.* Eric looked into Jing-Jiang's eyes.

"In seventeen days."

Jing-Jiang toyed with the end of his beard. He was mildly irritated by the amount he had to pay. Still, a small price for the face Eric had gained in the barbarian and Chinese communities. By sacrificing the silk, Eric saved Shanghai from annihilation. And, by saving the people in the shantytown, he'd earned the respect of the Chinese people. *A fair exchange.* "Fortunately there is still time to deal with Bartrum," Jing-Jiang said. "Funds to buy back our notes will be transferred to your account. This year's silk consignment will be delivered to your godown as originally scheduled." The Old General leaned back. "Now tell me about Formidable Fung and this man Garrett Botha."

For the next several hours, Eric recounted the details about his meetings with Fung and Garrett.

Jing-Jiang listened silently, inserting a question here and there. When Eric finished, the old man stared into the fireplace. *Oil.* Eric would be able to take it out of the hands of foreign devils and have it distributed to the interior by Chinese merchantmen. But, there were questions. Could this magical substance bring about modernization? Could his dream pass from fantasy into reality? Jing-Jiang tapped a forefinger against his lips and thought it through. Satisfied, he turned his attention to Formidable Fung. Eighteen thousand five-kilo balls of opium were going to be discharged at Chongming Dao. Such an amount had not been seen since the opium wars. And three million barbarian golden guineas was their share. *Ahh, such irony. I can hear the gods laughing at their divine jest. Imagine paying Bartrum back with his own money.* Finding no obvious flaw to Eric's plan, Jing-Jiang looked up. "We have reached the final confrontation in our battle against Alex Bartrum. One side or the other will be destroyed. Fortunately, we appear to have the element of surprise."

Tong-Po chuckled, glad to find a voice after the two men had talked so intensely. "Finality is sometimes sublime --- sometimes dire. Either way it gets the energy flowing, *heya?*"

Jing-Jiang stared at Eric. "Never have I wished for life as much as I do now. We are on the threshold of achieving great things. My fear is I will not be here to see them come to pass." His eyes glittered. "You must see them for me, my son. Then my legacy will have fulfillment."

Thirteen

ERIC ARRIVED EARLY AT RIVERMAN-PO'S BARGE. After tea and rice cakes, he asked about ferrying him and his men to Chongming Dao.

"You want me to transport one hundred seamen down the Yangtze in middle of night? *Eeeee,* and in total secrecy. Am I magic?" Eric could hear abacus beads clicking. "There will be great danger, *heya?*"

"There will be danger."

Riverman-Po watched a beetle roll a piece of dung across the deck. "This matter important for survival of your hong?"

"Yes."

"Do you go against son of sow-belly whore, Bartrum?"

Eric nodded.

Riverman-Po's head moved a hairsbreadth. "How much danger involved, Taipan?"

Eric shrugged. "That is a matter for the gods to decide,

heya?"

A smile split the old man's face. "Look there."

Eric saw a cormorant lifting out of the water, a fish in its beak.

"The fisher bird feels secure with his catch. Such arrogance will be his undoing," Riverman-Po said. "Nothing is what it seems. Yet, everything is exactly as is. An unseen enemy lurks."

Eric looked up. A black speck hovered.

"Now we see if it is the fisher-bird's joss to feast."

The two men watched the dark form plummet towards earth, shaping into a sea eagle. Talons bared, the predator bore down. The cormorant screeched as the eagle tore into its back and wrested the fish away.

"Joss. There is no controlling it." Riverman-Po scratched his groin. "I will transport you and your men to Chongming Dao, Taipan."

Eric nodded. His eyes turned to the eagle. All he saw was a black speck.

*   *   *

"DOES that fornicating piece of dog shit think he's dealing with the Golden Emperor?" Tong-Po looked up, his face purpled at learning how much it was going to cost for Riverman Po to ferry Eric and his men to Chongming Dao.

Eric stopped at the door. "Money well spent, my friend. Riverman-Po has a closed mouth and knows the Yangtze better than anyone."

Grunting, Tong-Po picked up a rice cake and stared out the window. Beyond the wharves junks and sampans filled the sea lanes, winding sluggishly in and out of the larger ocean-going cargo ships. Overhead, gulls circled in an incredibly blue sky.

Ah, Taipan, you alone look on me as a man and not a jest of the gods. And for that spark of dignity, my opal eyed friend, I would follow you to the bowels of hell. Eeeee, if only I were Tong-Po the tall --- Tong-Po the strong, and not Tong-Po the dwarf. Then I could accompany you to Chongming Dao.

*   *   *

DRAGON Mok smiled thinly. Two boys were about to steal their breakfast from a street vendor. The larger youth, approaching the fruit stand from the left, knocked over several baskets of fruit. While the enraged vendor went to reclaim his merchandise, the second youth darted in and made off with their morning meal.

"Is all in readiness for tonight?" Mok continued to watch the cursing fruit vendor.

"Sentries line the river in sampans downstream from Chongming Dao," Ting replied, glancing at Bartrum.

"Good. What about your Hong Kong crew?"

"After your men dispatch the original crews, Mr. Jones will bring them in by junk to sail my lorchas back to Shanghai."

Mok frowned.

"Don't worry," Bartrum said. "Pour yourself a drink. If we stick to the plan nothing will go wrong and we'll both wind up getting what we want."

Ting watched them drink.

*   *   *

THE president of the Commonwealth-Shanghai Bank, Pierce Stafford, delicately set Eric's statement aside. "I thought Bartrum had you," he said. "Glad to see you saved yourself. Of course, there've been rumors that you have a new financing source. Some American institution, I understand?"

Eric lit a cheroot. "In three days my notes come due. Between now and then, I wouldn't want to hear any gossip about my financial resurrection."

"You can rest assured that I --- that the bank, will be discreet."

"Glad to know I can count on you, Pierce." Eric exhaled a stream of smoke. "I'm leaving for Hangzhou to check on this season's silk production. If I haven't returned in two days, Adair MacAlister will issue Bartrum the sight draft in exchange for the notes." Eric removed a document from his coat pocket. "This is his power of attorney."

*   *   *

KATHERYN was waiting for Eric in the dining room when he arrived home. He ordered Ah-Sook away and gathered her in his arms. "Ahh, Kate, you are a wise woman. You should have seen Stafford's expression when Jing-Jiang's funds were transferred into our account. He thinks I've got the backing of a large American bank. All of Shanghai is buzzing over the little rumor you dropped at Lillian Havershire's."

"Darling, why have you increased security around the house?"

Eric released her. "Since I'll be out of town for the next several days I thought it necessary."

Katheryn's eyes flashed. "Eric, don't toy with me. You've

gone out of town before without turning our house into a citadel. Even the servants are chattering over the extra men."

"Nothing to worry about, love. Just a precaution in case Bartrum overreacts about me climbing out of his trap."

"You think he would send someone here to make trouble?"

Eric poured a brandy. "Anything's possible where that sod's concerned."

"This feud you've got won't be put to rest until one of you is dead, will it?"

"For Christ's sake, Kate. The rotter came within a hairsbreadth of bankrupting us. Besides Bartrum's bad for China."

"Bad for China? What about bad for us? You think I'm looking forward to someone telling me they've fished your body out of the harbor? Have you considered the consequences?"

"I've considered the consequences," Eric said. "Garrett Botha has provided the opportunity and I'm going to seize it. Once I've run Bartrum out of Asia then I can create something worthwhile for China."

"And the consequences be damned if you fail?"

"By God, I'll not fail."

Eric fixed her with a penetrating gaze. Katheryn had seen that kind of look before, hunting with her father. She remembered the hooded bird riding on his gauntleted arm and her excitement when the first covey of grouse was flushed. Her father removed the falcon's hood. It was then she glimpsed the dark marble eyes of the predator as they fixed on the grouse.

"I'll not fail," Eric said again.

Katheryn was chilled. Her husband's eyes were the same as the falcon's, except they were emerald green and full of fire.

Fourteen

ERIC STEPPED OUT OF RIVERMAN-PO'S CABIN and breathed deeply. The fresh air and sense of impending danger broomed away his fatigue. He gripped the handles of the fighting knives in his waistband. The Huangpu River was flecked with gold as darkness approached. Hundreds of junks and sampans threaded their way through the dappled light.

Leaning against the guardrail, Eric was careful to keep his shoulders stooped. His face was blackened and and shrouded by a conical hat. He wore loose-fitting black pantaloons and shirt. Braziers glowed on the decks as men huddled around them to cook evening meals. Aside for the creaking ropes and an occasional curse the river remained quiet.

"*Eeeee,* Taipan, you look like a first class coolie." Riverman Po stepped up and sniffed the wind. "Tonight promises to be a fine night, Taipan." A toothless smile split his leathery face. "A

---

fine night for killing, *heya?*"

"With joss that won't be necessary."

"In the end everything will be decided by joss. We have many armed men aboard. If your enemy at Chongming Dao is as well prepared....." The Riverman shrugged.

Eric did not reply. Instead, his eyes scanned the deck. The hand-picked seamen from his lorcha crews were eating rice and charcoaled meats from round bowls. It was essential the opium be stowed in the holds before they boarded Bartrum's lorchas. If the crew discovered its existence he could be faced with a mutinous mob.

Captains you can count on, but not the men. Greed turns men's loyalty.

The wind freshened as night closed around them, leaving the heavens bright with stars. Eric watched Riverman-Po's second son, who was carefully maneuvering the barge convoy down the river.

Eric lit a cheroot and wondered if they were sailing into hell.

*   *   *

THEY entered the mouth of the Yangtze at ten o'clock. The river was more than a half mile wide and traffic had thinned. Riverman-Po ordered his son to take them closer to shore. "Plenty pirate in this part of river. Plenty," he explained to Eric. "Close to shore we open to attack one side only."

Eric stared at the expanse of the river. The barge cut a small swathe of ripples across the black and silver moonlit surface. Ting had told them where Mok's sentries would be posted. Had Fung been successful in killing them? Dark shadows of junks and sampans glided by in wraithlike silence. Did any of them house the enemy? A thousand unseen eyes seemed to be boring into him. Sweat stuck his shirt. He left Riverman Po by the rail and went for a final meeting with his captains.

*   *   *

THE man was running towards the river bank. His lungs were straining, but the river offered hope of freedom. At water's edge the man jerked to a stop, his eyes rolling back. A final convulsion and he fell.

Formidable Fung walked up and pulled the fighting hatchet out of the Red Pang soldier's head. At the same moment, a Cantonese seamen Bartrum had brought in from Hong Kong crawled out from beneath a canvas covering in a small boat and began sculling downstream. Fung wiped the hatchet blade on the back of the dead man's shirt, then kicked the body into the river. For a moment he stared at the corpse. The turtles would soon find him.

It was just after midnight. There had been a short vicious battle, but the element of surprise had been his. He'd held his men back when the opium-laden vessels arrived. As Ting predicted, the captains and crew were marched inside the warehouse and shot. During the excitement, Fung and his men attacked. Now the opium was his. His.....

If the Opal Eye Devil and his men are waiting downstream.

The bodies of Dragon Mok's men were everywhere. Along the dock Bartrum's lorchas were lined up neatly.

Fung sheathed his hatchet, walked to the pier and dispatched a sampan to signal Eric. Then he ordered a pit dug for a mass grave. This gesture was not out of any reverence for the dead. It was merely a method of concealing evidence of a massacre from Chinese authorities.

* * *

TENSION thickened on Riverman-Po's barge. Seconds dragged into minutes and Eric felt the men's unease as they lingered downstream. On the far side of the river, he saw a small boat sculling. Who would be on the river this late? A vagrant fisherman? Or, did it house a spy for Mok and Bartrum? His eyes followed the craft until it was swallowed by darkness.

Christ. What's taking so bloody long?

Then Eric caught a lantern blinking. It flashed four times. Thirty seconds later the signal was repeated. He turned to Riverman Po. "Time to go."

* * *

THE small boat sculled alongside a sailing junk a hundred yards astern from Riverman Po's convoy. Seventy-five Cantonese crowded the junk's deck. Bartrum's backup crew were dressed in black and heavily armed.

"Well?" Mr. Jones said to the Cantonese.

"*Weeery* much trouble," he replied, panting. "All deaded." He lifted his head and ran his forefinger across his throat.

"Watdaya mean all deaded?" Mr. Jones grabbed the man's tunic. "Who's dead?"

The Cantonese felt the barbarian's spittle. "Hong Kong sailors and Red Pang soldiers deaded. All deaded," he wailed. "We attacked. Attacked by Green Pang."

Mr. Jones lifted the man up. "Green Pang? You sodding bastard. Why'd you not warn me sooner?"

"Too many people. *Weeery* much fighting. I hide under boat canvas until safe to warn you."

"Hid under the boat canvass, did you?" Mr. Jones's knife slid into his hand. He gutted the Cantonese cutting left, then right, then up to the sternum.

Seconds later, when the man was tossed into the waiting river, he had no idea that he was dead.

*   *   *

A HALF hour later the first grappling hook fell on Riverman Po's aft barge. More grappling hooks were thrown. Seconds later, Mr. Jones and Bartrum's mercenary force were on board.

It had not taken long for Mr. Jones's speedier junk to catch Riverman Po's convoy. Earlier he had seen the anchored barges, but had paid them little attention. Only a few men leaning over the guardrail. But things had changed. Jones estimated a force of at least a hundred men now occupied the deck of the lead barge.

The barge heeled to port after the first grapple had been secured. "We're being boarded," Riverman Po said. "Alert all hands."

Eric yelled out the alarm. Pulling a knife from his belt, he saw shadows within shadows scurrying across the decks. Moments later, Eric and his men were fighting for their lives.

Eric ducked a Cantonese who rushed him with a short sword. The man was fast, but Eric was faster. He sprang out of a crouched position and hafted his knife under the man's lower rib. The Cantonese screamed then fell to the deck.

A gunshot rang and one of the mercenaries dropped. Eric saw Mr. Jones slashing through a group of his men. "God's blood! Now's as good a time as any." He leaped over a body and fought his way toward Mr. Jones. Another shot and another mercenary fell. Suddenly, two Cantonese were blocking him. Eric grabbed the shorter one by the throat and slammed his head into the deck. The other mercenary rushed in with a Chinese fighting knife. Had it not been for the sturdy bamboo weave of Eric's conical hat he would have been blinded. The blade caught the rim of the hat deflecting it away from his right eye. Eric tore the shredded hat off and hurled it at his attacker. The mercenary hesitated, stunned to find he was fighting a Westerner. The pause was long enough for Eric's knife to do its work.

Eric's men beat back the first wave of mercenaries but more were coming. Mr. Jones cut a man down, maimed another --- then caught sight of Eric rushing in his direction. Mr. Jones couldn't see Eric's face in the dim light, but knew he wasn't Chinese. So, Fung had gotten a bloody European to pilot the lorchas. Mr. Jones stepped out to meet Eric's challenge.

The second wave of mercenaries were repulsed. A volley of gunshots sounded, dropping a half-dozen Cantonese. Another volley. A bullet slammed into Mr. Jones's left shoulder, spinning him around. Dropping to his knees, he scurried behind some crates.

Mr. Jones saw his forces in disarray. There was no way to fight repeating rifles. He shouted something in Cantonese and his men began retreating. Looking around, he saw the damned European closing. He lifted a packing crate with his good arm and threw. Eric was caught on his thigh and knocked to the deck. Palming his knife, Mr. Jones lunged forward. Eric jumped to his feet. More shots --- more men fell. A bullet creased Jones's cheek, twisting his head. Mr. Jones retreated over stacked bodies. Casting a final look in Eric's direction, he shook his fist --- then raced back toward his junk and disappeared.

* * *

GREEN Pang soldiers surrounded Eric and his men when they stamped ashore. Others were filling the pit with bodies. Occasionally, a shriek or moan could be heard from one of the wounded before being tossed into the grave. The stench of death was everywhere.

Eric was nauseated.

Formidable Fung left the warehouse and joined Eric on the dock. Ting se-Bing was by his side. "We heard gunshots."

"Cantonese mercenaries," Eric said. "Bartrum's bullyboy, Mr. Jones, was the leader." He turned to Ting. "You never mentioned a small army hidden downstream."

Ting cowered beneath the fiery eyes. "I did not know."

"We'll discuss it later," Eric said. "Is the cargo safely stowed?"

"In wooden crates," Fung replied. "We can leave now."

"Good. Get your men together."

Eric signaled to his captains to board their ships.

* * *

MR. JONES watched from across the river. Bartrum and Mok would deal with Fung and Ting. Of that, he was certain. But he wanted the godrotten Westerner who had challenged him. He smiled grimly. Something was familiar about him, but with the coolies garb and blackened face he couldn't be sure. He watched three men jump aboard the lead lorcha. Well, he would find out who it was soon enough.

Mr. Jones turned and ordered the junk back to Shanghai.

* * *

TWO hours later, Eric saw the outline of Chushan Island, where the opium would be discharged. Lightning flashed along the horizon, silhouetting a line of dark cumulus.

Formidable Fung studied Eric. His foot was propped on the mid-rail, a cheroot in his mouth --- brown hair blowing in the breeze. *A man who's friendship is not given easily,* he thought. Yet he risked his life for mine. *Are we destined to become friends, Opal Eye Devil?* Distant thunder broke into his thoughts. "Will there be storm?"

Eric turned. "We should get a bit of rain." There was growing unease about his relationship with Fung. He needed a powerful Chinese ally now that the other taipan would be allied with Bartrum against him. But, what about Fung himself? There were qualities about him that Eric both admired and detested. A trusted ally on one hand --- a cold-blooded killer on the other. Then again, had he not just described himself?

Fung stared at the river.

The light rain began to fall. There had been too much death tonight. Eric had lost a dozen men, with twenty others wounded. Riverman Po's third son, for one. At least they were safely aboard the barges back to Hangzhou.

Christ, what a bloody muck. If only I'd known....

If only you'd known what? the familiar inner voice replied. *You wouldn't have called the raid off. You'd have sacrificed anyone or anything for that opium and perdition on those who stood in your way. More cold blooded than Fung.....*

Eric closed his eyes.

"How much longer until we reach Chusan?" Fung asked.

"Twenty minutes or so."

"Do you think Jones recognized you?"

"My face was blackened." Eric flicked the cheroot into the river. "I'll find out soon enough after I get back to Shanghai."

"Jones is dangerous. Bartrum and Mok will cordon off the city looking for you if they suspect involvement on your part. I would feel better if several of my fighters accompany you back."

"No need. Tong-Po will be waiting with reinforcements."

"As you wish," Fung said. Then he turned and faced Eric. "Be careful, Taipan. We have dynasties to build."

Fifteen

ERIC GRADEK'S CALM SURPRISED MANY WHEN HE *stepped out on the balcony of the Commerce Club. He had been back from Chongming Dao for two days and rumors were rampant. A fortune in opium had been stolen from Dragon Mok and Alex Bartrum by Formidable Fung and an unknown barbarian. Formidable Fung had gained immense face in the Chinese community while Dragon Mok's was reduced to the level of running dog. The question now --- Who was the unknown barbarian?*

Many, like Headwaiter Fong were betting on Eric. After all, it was common knowledge that great hatred existed between the Opal Eye Devil and Odious Mountain of Dung. Everyone knew that Bartrum was holding the Opal Eye Devil's commercial paper. It would be perfect irony for Eric to extricate himself from imminent bankruptcy with Bartrum's opium money.

Could the Opal Eye Devil redeem his notes on this the final day before Bartrum foreclosed? Betting was furious. The only consensus was that it would be a day of reckoning and --- a day of death.

*   *   *

ERIC gripped the handrail. He had sent the cable to Garrett containing the words, *Telega Said.* Eric's green eyes scanned the crowds gathering along the Bund. People were coming into the business district from all parts of the city. Festive crowds converged around a wooden platform that had been erected at harbor's edge where Han-Zu would make his entrance. Firecrackers exploded --- lion dancers snaked through the melee to the sounds of cymbals and bells. The entire atmosphere was charged with primal excitement and a cocophony of sounds.

Declining offers of conversation, Eric sipped hot tea alone. His suit jacket and cravat hung over a nearby chair. His white shirt was unbuttoned at the neck and his black leather boots polished to a high gloss. Behind him the room buzzed with conversation.

"Look at him, as calm as you please. Nary a bead of sweat on his brow,"Andrew Pendleton said. "His whole bloody world about to collapse and he looks like he hasn't a care. Flaming bastard must have ice for blood."

Havershire twirled his mustach. He looked at Eric, wondering if he had helped Fung steal ten thousand opium balls from Bartrum and Mok. Such a quantity in a single shipment was unbelievable. The Welshman lifted his tankard of ale and drained it. If the rumor was true, Bartrum & Sons would be grievously crippled. That would make Havershire's future brighter.

Brighter, if it weren't for your godcursed involvement with the tanker syndicate. Should never have tied myself to one supplier. Stupid, stupid.

A fresh tankard of ale arrived. Havershire took a drink. "Rumor is Gradek has a new source of financing in the United States."

Pendleton smiled. "My good fellow, that's precisely what it is, rumor. I'd wager Bartrum has his balls in a rock crusher this time."

Havershire wiped his forehead. "A hundred pounds sterling says you're wrong."

"Done, by God." By the time Pendleton extended his hand Havershire was making his way toward Eric.

"Much too hot for an execution, eh, Eric?"

Eric nodded, his eyes fixed on the crowds below.

Havershire took a drink and began considering his options. If the rumor was true, Gradek's power would grow. Should he extend an olive branch or wait and see? "You'd bloody well think Han-Zu would end this charade. This makes the third sacrificial offering within the past two weeks."

Another nod.

A roar from the crowd sounded as a drumbeat announced Han-Zu's arrival. The crowd parted to allow the procession through. First in line were Manchu bannermen, followed by flag-bearers hoisting banners and emblems representing the Qing Dynasty and Empress Dowager. Next, came Han-Zu's red and gold curtained sedan chair, surrounded by bannermen. Behind the viceroy, stripped to the waist, was the executioner -- a giant with a scimitar sword holstered in his sash. His head was shaved, except for his braided queue, which hung to his hips. Frog-marching in the rear were a half-dozen prisoners, each manacled and chained to a common yoke. The crowd cursed them, then, with equal passion, yelled greetings and well-wishes for the doomed men's spirits on their journey to the after-life.

The prisoners stumbled along, laughing and joking with the crowds lining the gauntlet. Occasionally, one would shout a curse or blessing to an acquaintance as he plodded toward the raised platform.

Havershire finished his tankard and belched. "Poor devils. Their minds are besotted on opium."

"Mine would be too if I were marching up to the block," Eric said.

Havershire followed Eric's gaze. Bartrum and Mr. Jones were pushing through the crowd towards the club. Eric's face appeared untroubled, but his eyes held fire. *God's blood,* Havershire thought, *I wouldn't want this devil against me.*

The drumbeat ceased. Han-Zu climbed from his sedan chair in full ceremonial dress. He carried a slender ivory baton, tipped at both ends with balls of Burmese Jade. On the back of his jacket was a tiger with smoldering sapphire-blue eyes. The tiger, poised to strike, symbolized the power of the Qing Dynasty.

A bannerman sounded a gong and everyone kowtowed three times. Han-Zu unrolled a paper scroll and began reading in a sing-song voice.

"Wonder what the sod's saying?" Havershire said.

Eric shrugged and opened his ears.

"By authority invested in me by the Empress Dowager Ci-Xi, guardian of the Celestial Throne of Heaven, I hereby sentence these unworthy dogs to death for criminal acts against the laws

*of civilized society." Han-Zu glared imperiously at the prison-
ers. "Let this sentence be a warning to those who plot crimes,
now or in the future, against property of foreign devils who
reside within selected areas of the Middle Kingdom, at the
pleasure of the court, for the general purpose of trade."*

Eric smiled at the reference about foreign devils being guests
in China at the pleasure of the court.

*"Any and all persons suspected of complicity in such acts
will be put to immediate death after suffering the humiliation of
being chained and dragged through the streets like the lowest
form of human carrion."*

Another gong. The Viceroy rolled the scroll and handed it to
the commanding officer, who issued an order. The prisoners
were taken to the top of the platform and forced to kneel in a
row with their heads extended. In the background, arms
crossed over his naked chest, stood the executioner. Playing to
his audience and taking time for tension to reach a new level,
the executioner positioned himself beside the first prisoner. He
drew his sword and raised it. A collective gasp from the crowd,
then breathless silence.

Glinting in the sun, the blade twisted downward. A sharp
crack, followed by a fountain of blood arcing from the severed
neck, then the rolling, mouth gaping, head. The crowd roared
approval of the executioner's skill at removing the head with a
single pass.

Eric turned and pushed his way through other traders rushing outside for a better view. Another crack --- another round
of applause. Walking into the empty bar, Eric spotted Bartrum
talking with Pierce Stafford. Mr. Jones leaned against the wall,
his arm in a sling. Had the banker tipped Bartrum that he had
the funds to purchase his notes? *No matter.* Either way,

Stafford would have to bear witness he had the money prior to the opium hijacking. Of course, that would be the public version. He would make sure Bartrum knew the truth.

Eric ordered a brandy. He looked at the balcony as the crowd roared. Havershire and the other traders were laughing and drinking, drawing pleasure from the beheadings.

Adair MacAlister stepped inside the club as the executioner's blade made its final arc. The traders grumbled and shuffled into the main room. Stafford and Bartrum, followed by Mr. Jones, walked up to Eric.

Nodding at Stafford, Eric set the glass on the bar.

The banker adjusted his wire-rimmed glasses. "Good afternoon, Eric. Bloody heathens will never learn how to administer proper English law." Extending his hand, Stafford wondered how Eric remained so cool in the sultry heat. "Frightful, all these executions, what?"

"Appears to be no end in sight to Han-Zu's bloodletting," Eric replied.

"I'm glad to be a banker and not a bloody politician." Stafford's nervousness increased as Eric's gaze found Bartrum. "Can't wait until I'm retired and in England away from all of this ungodly nonsense."

Bartrum's eyes were bloodshot. Eric Gradek wasn't on the brink of financial ruin, he was. The urge to kill gripped him, but with supreme effort he resisted reaching for the pistol inside his belt. He needed Eric to purchase his notes --- even if it was with his money. It was his only hope of survival. With joss, Philip would be able to leverage the funds and pull them out of the muck. Two more option payments to Trident Industries, then he'd settle with Mr. Eric godrot Gradek.

Eric nodded at Bartrum. "Care for a brandy?"

Bartrum opened his mouth to speak but no sound came out. Traders surrounded them. The silence deepened.

Eric lit a cheroot, exhaled a long stream of smoke. "Brandy all around," he said to the bartender. A chorus of cheers followed as traders pressed against the bar.

Ignoring the stench of body sweat and liquored breath, Eric turned to Stafford. "Pierce, you'll be getting back to England at a rather good time. Since the Boxers were defeated, Shanghai has become a bloody haven for pirates and thieves. Nothing is safe anymore."

"Enough talk." Bartrum removed a folder from his pocket. "Have you got the draft to cover your notes?"

Eric tapped an ash from his cigar. "I told you before I'd be here with the draft." He nodded to MacAlister, who handed him an envelope. Eric stared at Bartrum. "Like I said, my only regret is that you, rather than the bank, profits from this transaction." He tossed the envelope on the bar.

A tick pulsed in the muscle group next to Bartrum's lips. "Where did you get your funding, Gradek? Did you borrow it from your heathen brethren? Or steal it? No right thinking bank would touch you."

The silence thickened. "Whether I borrowed or stole it is of no concern to you, Bartrum." A smile played at the corner of Eric's mouth. "You ought to be glad to get your money. Times are hard, eh?"

Bartrum's neck purpled. He picked up the envelope containing the sight draft.

Eric raised his brandy glass. "You've breached our contract, Bartrum. Bartrum & Sons is sixty days in arrears for lighting oil receptacles. There'll be no future deliveries until your account is settled. Subsequent shipments will be negotiated on a cash only basis."

An uneasy murmur spread through the traders. No receptacles meant no lighting oil deliveries --- which meant no sales. The resulting loss of revenue coupled with the maintenance costs of the tanker fleet spelled ruination for many.

Bartrum felt hammered. He had planned to pick up Eric's receptacle manufacturing operation when he foreclosed. Now that had changed. *Beaten and humiliated by Gradek, again.* Bartrum's hand moved toward the pistol beneath his jacket. Mr. Jones moved to his side.

Eric stood stone still, the derringer inside his belt hot against his skin. He wanted Bartrum to see the vast pleasure he'd derive from killing him. The circle of men surrounding the three men backed away. Fear clutched at their stomachs as they silently cursed or blessed the Opal Eye Devil and his incredible nerve.

The fire in Eric's eyes stayed Bartrum's hand. Stepping back, Bartrum said, "Now's not the time for a fight. You and I will settle our differences soon enough." Bartrum looked at the other traders. "Don't worry about oil deliveries. Gradek will have my bank draft by this afternoon. I'm delinquent because I thought I'd be repossessing his bloody hong today. Four months are left on this godcursed receptacle contract then I'll be providing the containers myself." He cast a final look in Eric's direction and left. Mr. Jones studied Eric carefully before following.

Eric relaxed much in the same way as a cat after a danger had passed. He did not fully unwind until he saw Bartrum and Jones leave through the front door. *Wondering what I look like with my face blackened, Mr. Jones?*

There was a sigh of relief as Bartrum's explanation allayed

the trader's fears. After all, wasn't Bartrum & Sons inviolate?
The Opal Eye Devil had made Alex look like a fool. His joss
had been incredibly good. Tomorrow, well that could be another story.

*   *   *

*OUTSIDE, word had spread that the Opal Eye Devil had again
thwarted Odious Mountain of Dung. For the Chinese the news
was cause for great celebration. Firecrackers popped and the
air filled with sounds of drums and cymbals.*

*Obviously, Eric was the mysterious barbarian who had
aided Formidable Fung at Chongming Dao. How else could
the Opal Eye Devil pull his company back from bankruptcy?*

*Money exchanged hands amidst smiles and curses and Eric's
face grew immensely as the people of Shanghai honored him.
And the people honored Tong-Po, as well. Not that Tong-Po
needed additional face. Was he not second only to the venera-
ble Jing-Jiang in importance, and related to the dwarf god,
P'an-ku, who was hatched from the egg of chaos? And weren't
dwarfs favored by the gods and advisors to the Mings, the true
rulers of China, before the fornicating Manchus seized power?
Yes, Tong-Po was a clever advisor and a most valuable ally to
the Opal Eye Devil. So the people honored him for his cleverness. Surely, a barbarian, even one with the stature of the great
Opal Eye Devil, would not possess the foresight to appropriate
such a vast quantity of opium without the shrewd guidance of a
civilized person like Tong-Po.*

*Vendors arrived, their carts laden with roasting meats and
prawns. Sampans jostled the harbor, carrying steamed crabs,
lobsters, and other fish. And the people, fired by the drama of*

death, celebrated Eric's victory and blessed their joss that they were alive to do so. Today they would feast and make love, and perhaps --- with joss --- become rich tomorrow, like the Opal Eye Devil had become today.

Book II

Sixteen

EVERYTHING WAS PERFECT. ON HER FINAL TEST run, the tanker's oil-fired boilers performed faultlessly, powering the engines to speeds beyond original specifications. Eric and Garrett stood dockside admiring the colossal ship, the first of twelve extra large tankers manufactured by Clay Shipyards for their new company, Crown Petroleum.

The previous day and night had been spent on board with Matthew Clay reviewing the innovative systems. Then, in early morning, Clay navigated the world's first commercial vessel fueled by oil into Boston Harbor for the world to see. Within an hour a huge crowd had gathered, including the mayor and city council.

Matt climbed the podium and begin fielding questions. Unlike his Victorian father, he was a modern man. His engineering genius was responsible for the development of the propulsion system now powering Eric and Garrett's tanker.

"She's faster, more efficient and requires less manpower than anything to date," he responded to the first reporter's question.

"What about Trident Industries? Or do you have another buyer for your tankers?" another reporter asked.

"For now we anticipate acting as a contract carrier for those companies wishing to get their products to market on a more cost-efficient basis."

"Our boy handles the press rather well," Garrett noted.

Eric lit a cheroot. "Maybe Sutton and Rosenberg will be kept off guard long enough for us to make initial deliveries."

"Mr. Clay. Are you going to license the technology?"

"We haven't made that decision as of yet."

"What about the effect of an oil fired boiler on coal?"

"Quite possibly, within a few years, coal will become a secondary source of fuel."

"Well, at least for now, we're non-entities," Eric said.

Garrett focused on the slate-gray tanker. "Ahh, such a beautiful sight. The most modern tanker fleet in the world and it's ours."

"Ours along with Mikolits and his bank," Eric said drily. "It's still hard to believe we can transport food products without contamination. Installing those steam-cleaning systems was pure genius."

"I agree with your assessment." Garrett smiled, and stared at the great ship. "By the way, have you given any thought to what we should christen our little beauty?"

"*Sultan of Langkat* seems appropriate under the circumstances, eh?"

"*Sultan of Langkat* it is," Garrett said. "Our chubby little benefactor should be royally pleased."

Eric looked at the tanker. *There's vast power here,* he

thought. *Enough to put Jing-Jiang's dream of resurrecting China on the path to reality. Oil is going to change the world and I'm going to play a major role in that change.*

Footsteps interrupted his thoughts. Garrett's father, Matthew Clay Sr. and Franz Mikolits were approaching.

"Impressive, is she not?" Mikolits said.

"There's nothing on the seas like her,"Matthew Clay Sr. said, a tall aristocratic man with wavy, snow-white hair. "What you're looking at gentlemen is the making of history. Oil is no longer merely a source of illumination, but, rather, a source of power. *King Coal* has been dethroned. From this day forth the world as we know it will not be the same."

Ambassador Botha removed a linen handkerchief and coughed up bloody phlegm. He knew his time was limited as the insidious disease inside his lungs continued to spread.

The senior Clay removed a cigar from his breast pocket, applied fire and inhaled. Looking at the Ambassador, he said, "Sutton and his kind are in for a time of it once our tankers begin to dominate the seas. It will become increasingly diffi- cult for Trident to maintain control over oil supplies when other producers have ready access to port markets. Our tankers will allow them entry. Already there are rumblings in Washington about building a canal through Panama. Can you imagine the ramifications? Shipping will be open between east and west like never before."

Ambassador Botha nodded. "The canal will open major U.S. ports from the east coast to the west coast. America will be like a juggernaut unleashed on the rest of the world. Great Britian's days as the preeminent trading nation are about to become another chapter in history. The question that concerns me is where will that turn of events leave the Netherlands?"

Eric was stunned. England dethroned as the world's preeminent power? *It'll never happen. Not in a thousand years. The Royal Navy controls the seas and whoever controls the seas controls the wealth of the world.* He was about to say something, but was interrupted by Franz Mikolits.

"The Banque de Swisse Credit has long been interested in the China trade, Mr. Gradek." The banker's eyes were fixed on the tanker. "It is a fertile area that has languished too long. I've been giving serious consideration to establishing a branch in Shanghai. Perhaps our new association will serve as the catalyst for the bank to become more actively involved in the Orient, yes?"

"Perhaps, Herr Mikolits,"Eric replied. "However, I feel compelled to offer a word of caution about venturing so far afield. Banking practices in Shanghai compared to those on the Continent are worlds apart. Fortunes in Asia rise and fall based on intangibles like weather, blight, pestilence, and disease --- all of which affect some remote farmer's ability to produce. Then, of course, you have the question of supply and demand, political stability, economic conditions, and the like. Factors that are bloody impossible to forecast with any accuracy." Eric flicked his cheroot into the harbor. "Hardly fundamental principles for a conservative European financial institution to base a long-term strategy on."

Mikolits nodded, then permitted himself a thin smile. "Touché, Mr. Gradek, but the kind of banking I would be offering are services based on confidentiality. Silence is a commodity that can be appreciated anywhere in the world, yes? And we Swiss are very good at it."

Eric stared at the banker. It occurred to him how powerful Mikolits must be. Hidden beneath an astringent outer facade was a clever and dangerous man; a guardian of secrets. Men and governments could rise and fall according to his whim. All that would be required was a word or whisper in the right ear. There would be uses for a man like Mikolits in the future. A great deal could be learned. *But deal with him carefully,* he reminded himself. It was then that the idea of purchasing controlling interest in the Commonwealth-Shanghai Bank planted itself in Eric's mind. *Why not?* Turning to the harbor, Eric said, "You're right Herr Mikolits, a person's privacy is a valuable commodity. Perhaps, we'll have an opportunity to expand on this conversation before I depart?"

*   *   *

ERIC picked up his key and went directly to his suite. Under the door he found a cable from Katheryn which he immediately decoded.

Dearest:

Much has happened these past five months. The one constant is that Tong-Po has served you well. He is truly an amazing individual. In every major port from Japan to Australia he's secured prime wharfage. Construction on storage facilities and office space is progressing nicely and should be completed by the time you return. Don't ask me how he managed such a feat. He seems to be everywhere at once.

I'm proud to report that all is well at Gradek International in spite of your absence. The season's silk shipments have been made and our storerooms are bare. Addie MacAlister has been stalwart in his management of the company. I believe he is a man to be trusted. Based on this year's figures and barring any international catastrophes, such as war in Europe, Addie believes we can easily double exports for next season.

Father is hosting a reception for the business community this month. The British Trade Ambassador, Gerald Farnsworth, who is currently touring the Orient, will be on hand. I understand he will officially award this year's dredging contract on behalf of the Harbormaster's office.

Since you and Garrett departed, the Pang War has left thousands dead. Formidable Fung is recognized as High Dragon, but there are pockets of resistance still under Dragon Mok's control. Scores of bodies are taken from the harbor daily. One was identified as Ting se-Bing. I understand his corpse was terribly mutilated. Robberies and piracies are frequent. Hundreds of men have been publicly executed or whipped, and the slaughter continues. Father ordered a sunset curfew for Chinese in the British quadrant. But, despite efforts to control the situation, British and Chinese authorities seem quite ineffectual.

All of Shanghai is speculating about your relationship with Garrett now that Jacqueline and Marianne have moved into their new home. It's a marvelous place, one I'm quite sure will be to Garrett's liking. Again, thanks to Tong-Po, there were no construction delays. Jacqueline nearly had a seizure when Lo-Fong, the fung shui man, altered the window and door placement on the guest wing. It was all quite comical. She's really a grand sport, and in the end deferred to his better judgment.

Garrett need not worry as the pregnancy seems to agree with Jacqueline. And, as for Marianne, she is such a dear child. I sometimes catch myself feeling like she's my own. Speaking of which, I think it would be nice if we had a little Marianne of our own. With that to ponder I'll close for now and send you many good thoughts.

Hurry home dearest. I miss you terribly.
All my love,
Kate.

Eric stared at the paper for a long time. Kate had become so much more than a wife; his best friend and right hand. The one person he could completely trust. Jing-Jiang, Tong-Po and Garrett were dear friends, but they had separate agendas. *Home.* Eric rolled the word around in his mouth. Another week in Boston before returning to Sumatra for a stopover --- then home to Kate.

Striking a match he lit the paper and watched it burn in the ashtray. "A little Marianne, eh?" he chuckled. "Howabout a little Eric, instead?"

*   *   *

PERCIVAL D. Sutton sailed for London on the first available ship after the *Sultan of Langat* appeared in Boston Harbor. Now, ten days later, he was staring out at Hyde Park from Baron Rosenberg's third floor office. The sky was turning dark with rain, but Sutton did not focus on the approaching turbulence. Instead, he was sifting through events of the past week and a half. The nightmare began when he received word about Clay Shipyard's new oil-powered tanker. He had been beaten by a phony patrician like Matthew Clay. A bitter pill since Trident had invested millions trying to develop a marine boiler system of its own. Control jets combining oil fuel and air had been the insurmountable problem, now that Clay held the patents, the problem was ingeniously solved.

Two errors were responsible for the current dilemma. Taking the European shipping contract away from Clay

Shipyards, and going along with Alex Bartrum's sacking of Garrett Botha. Stupid on both counts.

"This situation in Sumatra is untenable," Sutton said. "If we allow them to deliver a single barrel of oil *Our Plan* will unravel. Despite our amalgamation, we will no longer be able to control production. More oil in the marketplace will lead to price instability. We'll be back to the days when you and I were at each other's throats."

Baron Rosenberg grunted. "I agree. This development puts a new slant on things, what? It will cost dearly, but it appears we'll be forced to flood the region with cheap kerosene."

"Cutting prices is exactly what they expect us to do," Sutton replied. He turned from the window. "A more decisive course of action is called for. The field in Sumatra along with the present operators must be rendered inoperable."

The Baron's face whitened. "Sabotage is one thing, Percy. Murder is quite another."

"Do we have a choice?" Sutton's tone was glacial. "This is war. Botha and Gradek are poised to wreak havoc on everything we've built. If we cut prices, they will cut deeper. They have the financial wherewithal to do it."

"What makes you so sure?" the Baron asked.

"I know Janvillem van de Botha," Sutton replied. "He'd never allow Garrett to go against us without the backing of Queen Wilhelmina. Plus, they've probably got some sort of arrangement with Franz Mikolits. Cut prices and we'll have a war on our hands. A war that will cost us the Asian market. It takes us weeks to make delivery in Asia from Batum. Their tankers can cross the Strait of Malacca in a matter of hours."

Baron Rosenberg massaged his chin. "How would we go after the field? It's out in the middle of a godforsaken jungle halfway around the world. Also, have you considered the stink Ambassador Botha would raise if anything happened to his son? An international coalition, headed by Queen Wilhelmina, would line up against us."

Sutton seated himself across from the Baron. "It is absolutely essential we remain beyond reproach. But the fact remains that the situation requires immediate, decisive action."

The Baron reached for the decanter and poured two brandies. His hand shook slightly. "I don't know, Percy. We're treading on shakey ground. A hint that we were involved in foul play and every government west of Suez would be out for our privates. It might be wiser to try and reach some sort of accommodation."

Sutton set his glass down. "Why should they negotiate with us? If war breaks out in Europe our Russian holdings will be at risk from Prussian attack, which will make the Dutch East Indies strategically important. Janvillem knows this and will use it for all it's worth."

The two men stared at each other.

"They've got better tankers and financial backing from the Dutch Government," the Baron noted.

"Plus, Gradek's contacts give them instant distribution."

"I see your point," the Baron said. "Russia is our Achilles Heel if war comes. Still, how do we go after them in the jungle without linkage to ourselves?"

Sutton's face hardened. "Several things need to be considered. First, an abiding hatred exists between Alex Bartrum and Eric Gradek. Their feud started when Gradek took the Shanghai silk concession away from Bartrum & Sons. Matters got worse after Gradek married Katheryn Worthington and gutted Alex on the price to produce our containers."

The Baron nodded. "And, since Alex sacked Garrett, there's no love lost in that quarter, either."

"Without us the Bartrums are finished," Sutton said. "Everyone's aware Gradek pirated their opium. They've become laughingstocks."

The Baron swirled his brandy. "I think I see where you're headed, Percy."

"It's quite simple. We call Philip in for a chat and lay out the problem. Our position will be it's a complication for Bartrum & Sons to solve. After all, Asia is their backyard." Sutton smiled thinly. "I understand the Orient is rife with all manner of soldiers of fortune, thieves, pirates and cutthroats. Bartrum & Sons have offices throughout the region. Certainly, they, especially Alex, would have access to someone capable of rendering the kind of service we're looking for."

"What if Philip refuses to go along?"

"He'll go along," Sutton said. "We offer financial relief in return for handling the Sumatran crisis. Philip really has no choice in the matter. If he refuses, we stop the money and Bartrum & Sons is relegated to the slag heap."

Baron Rosenberg nodded. "Very tidy."

Sutton smiled. "It gets better."

The Baron's eyes crinkled as he poured two more brandies, his hand quite steady. "Tell me about it."

Seventeen

"AH, MR. STANLEY. DELIGHTED YOU COULD come." Katheryn stood and shook hands with the senior partner of Melbourne-based Brentwood, Stanley Heavy Equipment. "I trust your voyage was a pleasant one."

"Pleasant indeed.. Thank you." Morgan Stanley gave a short bow. He was a tall sun-baked man with a hawklike nose. "Our results have been most encouraging."

Katheryn smiled. "Wonderful." She rang for tea, then seated herself at the conference table, motioning for the Australian to take the chair opposite her. "I'm anxious to hear about them."

Stanley's eyes crinkled as he removed a folder from his valise and laid it on the table. "Since we entered into negotiations four months ago, Perth's harbor depth has been increased by almost fifty percent. Of course, we didn't have the silt problem you have here."

Katheryn watched at Stanley closely. "And what kind of

results can we anticipate in Shanghai?"

A soft knock interrupted them as Pauline Han entered and served tea.

When they were alone Stanley slid the folder forward. "Here are the time and cost estimates. I've also included a draft of our agreement. Naturally, the key points remain the same. Any changes or addenda that need to be worked out can be handled by your office."

Katheryn picked up the folder and began to read. Cost estimates were in order. The down payment was substantial, but worth it. Especially since Stanley had agreed to provide specialized personnel until their own crews were trained to operate the equipment. More importantly, a deep water channel and increased harbor depth could be maintained for the large tankers to offload.

"Impressive, Mr. Stanley." Katheryn closed the file.

"Impressive enough to wrest the contract away from Bartrum & Sons?"

"Getting the contract will be difficult. Bartrum & Sons has had it for the last twenty years."

"Right. And they're still using the same outdated equipment they started with." Stanley leaned forward. "Depth requirements have changed. Modern dredging equipment must be used for Shanghai to remain a credible harbor."

Katheryn refilled their cups. "Let's see if we can persuade our Harbormaster, Richard Franklin, to recognize that fact tomorrow."

Stanley laughed bitterly. "He's been Bartrum & Sons' puppet for years. I don't see any way he can be persuaded."

Katheryn sipped her tea. "There's always a way, Mr. Stanley. It's a matter of finding it."

"How long before Franklin will give us an answer?"

"Gerald Farnsworth, the British Trade Ambassador, is presently in Shanghai for talks. He will award the contract at a reception my father is holding a month from now." A hint of a smile passed over Katheryn's lips as she looked at Stanley. "I trust you'll be attending as my guest."

Stanley raised his cup. "It will be an honor, and I thank you."

*   *   *

PHILIP Bartrum placed his umbrella into the stand and walked into Baron Rosenberg's office. Percival D. Sutton was seated across from the banker, separated by a Louis XIV table topped with a brandy decanter and ashtray.

Baron Rosenberg was in the beginning stages of lighting a cigar. "Philip, good of you to drop by."

Neither Sutton nor the Baron stood.

Through a cloud of smoke, the Baron motioned for Philip to be seated on the divan. "Some disturbing news has come to our attention," he said without preamble. "We've learned that Clay Shipyards has been secretly building a fleet of very large tankers. They're bigger, faster, and more efficient than anything afloat. Want to know why?"

Philip looked at the Baron. "From the sound of it, I'm quite certain you'll be telling me."

"Because there're powered by oil."

"Oil?"

"Our engineers were sorely lagging on that technology," Sutton said.

Philip was stunned. "If the tankers aren't being built for us, then who's the buyer? We control all serious production."

Baron Rosenberg stared at Philip. "The buyer's in your back yard."

Philip felt a first fear. "I don't understand."

"No, of course you don't." The Baron's bushy eyebrows lifted. "Garrett Botha. Does the name mean anything?"

"The geologist?"

"He's currently in Boston with a group of men inspecting his ships," Sutton said. "One of our people spotted him with Matthew Clay in a hotel lobby. We assigned several investigators and came up with a remarkable scenario." Sutton leaned back. "It seems our former geologist is launching an attack against Trident Industries."

"Three men are accompanying Garrett," the Baron said. "One is his father, Janvillem van de Botha, Holland's Ambassador at Large. Aside from Queen Wilhelmina, Janvillem is the most influential person in the Netherlands. We suspect he's the mastermind behind Garrett's actions." Baron Rosenberg steepled his fingers. "A banker, Franz Mikolits, is also there. He owns the Banque de Swisse Credit --- Switzerland's largest. No doubt, Mikolits is providing financing for the tankers. We ran a routine check on him through our own bank, but the Swiss refused to release information."

Philip held down a laugh. "Garrett Botha attacking Trident Industries? Bloody absurd."

The Baron stood. "Our people backtracked Botha's itinerary before he arrived in Boston. Six weeks ago he was in Sumatra. Any idea what he was up to?"

Philip stared at Rosenberg. "No. Why should I?"

The Baron's eyes were contemptuous. "He was touring his oil field. Complete with refinery and pipeline."

Philip sat unmoving.

"You and Alex have made a real botch of it. How could something of this magnitude take place and you not be aware?"

Philip's gaze turned to the floor. "I have no idea." .

"Botha wasn't alone in Sumatra." Percival D. Sutton's soft voice lifted Philip's head. "He was with his new partner."

"New partner?"

Sutton smiled. "The third man in Boston is Eric Gradek."

The name slammed into Philip. "Gradek! That's not possible."

"It's fact," Baron Rosenberg said. "Mr. Gradek upstaged your brother once again. He stole your opium and redeemed his notes with your money." The Baron chuckled. "Most resourceful sort of chap, I'd say."

"The problem is that your brother's amateurish attempts at cutting it fine have spilled over into the business of Trident Industries," Sutton said.

"Quite right," the Baron agreed. "However, things might not be as bleak as they seem." The old man handed Philip a crystal glass and poured brandy all around. "Obviously, this situation with Botha and Gradek changes things. "We will need to redefine our long-range plans."

"*Our Plan* must not be allowed to fail," Sutton said.

The Baron's eyes hardened. "We are about to enter a mercantile war, Philip. To win requires we play by rules that have nothing to do with the rest of society. Do you understand?"

Philip's palms dampened. "I'm not sure I do."

The Baron cast Philip a withering look. "If Botha and Gradek disappeared, Queen Wilhelmina and the Sultan of Langkat would have no choice but to turn to us. Aside from Garrett Botha, we are the only ones capable of developing Sumatra's oil resources."

The air in the office turned fragile. "You're talking about murder," Philip said.

"An impediment has been placed before us because you and your brother blundered." The Baron leaned forward. "It's up to you to remove it."

Philip felt dizzy. He had no qualms about ruining another man in a business sense --- but murder? Swallowing hard, he said, "That particular kind of vindictiveness is quite beyond my capacity."

"Really?" Sutton's voice was ice. "The fire you and Alex orchestrated last year nearly destroyed Shanghai. Thousands died."

Philip's cheeks colored. "Lies aimed at discrediting us."

"Enough banter." The sharpness of Sutton's voice shook Philip. "Talk has its uses to a point, after that point has been reached action is required." Sutton's pale blue eyes bored in. "The Baron and I have a proposition for you, Philip. I suggest you consider it carefully."

"After what Gradek did to your brother, you are considered high-risk," the Baron said, injecting his voice with regret. He paused to refill Philip's glass with brandy. "Without our financial help you have no hope of survival. Bartrum & Sons is mortgaged to the limit. You've no collateral, no cash. And" --- the Baron raised a finger --- "there's the possibility that criminal charges will be brought against you for fraudulently refinancing the syndicate's tanker fleet. My dear chap, you're boxed in."

Philip felt sick. "You've been bloody well spying on us."

"Come now, Philip. Surely you didn't think Mr. Sutton and I wouldn't be informed about actions you and Alex took regarding the Asian market? Besides you haven't heard our offer."

Sutton rubbed his eyes. "Botha and Gradek must be stopped. The fate of several individuals is of little consequence compared to what we do here."

"We also want the field in Sumatra immobilized," Baron Rosenberg added. "Not destroyed mind you, but shut down. An oil field can die easily." The Baron shrugged. "A vagrant spark, perhaps. Who's to know?"

"We are willing to pay for these services," Sutton said. "We're prepared to underwrite your final option payment and stand behind any liability you've incurred refinancing the tanker fleet."

The Baron smiled. "Bartrum & Sons will be back on a sound financial footing."

The words filtered into Philip's brain in slow motion. Was he facing redemption or damnation? Either way, it didn't matter. All he wanted was out from under the financial burden that was crushing him.

*   *   *

THE male secretary's eyes widened at the sight of Katheryn entering the office carrying a valise.

"Katheryn Gradek and Morgan Stanley to see Mr. Franklin."

The secretary disappeared, returning moments later with the Harbormaster, Richard Franklin.

"Katheryn. So nice to see you. How are Sir Geoffrey and Lady Anne?"

"Well, thank you." Katheryn filed Franklin's failure to inquire about Eric for a later date. "I'd like to present Mr. Morgan Stanley."

"A pleasure, Mr. Stanley."

The two men exchanged handshakes.

"Shall we retire to my office? I understand you have a proposal to discuss." Franklin turned to his secretary. "See that some tea is sent around."

After pleasantries and the first cup of tea, Katheryn removed a folder from her valise and slid it across the desk. "Our proposal is for the dredging contract."

The Harbormaster's eyebrow arched in surprise. "Really? Most unusual to have a bid other than Bartrum & Sons."

Katheryn smiled. "The harbor requires modern facilities if Shanghai is to remain competitive."

Franklin put on his reading glasses and began scanning the document. "Convincing," he said at length. "But, too expensive. The reason Bartrum & Sons have held the contract for so long is that they've kept costs under control. I'm afraid your pricing doesn't merit serious consideration."

Katheryn stared at the Harbormaster. "It depends on what's being considered, doesn't it?" She removed another folder and handed it to Franklin. "Last year's bid by Bartrum & Sons does not take into account creating a deep water channel or deepening existing harbor facilities."

"You don't have a natural harbor," Stanley added. "Shanghai will be relegated to a backwater port without deep water to handle the increased tonnage of modern ships."

Franklin's cheeks flushed. "We've done very well to date with our harbor facilities."

Katheryn and Stanley exchanged a look. "Our bid has been duly filed, Mr. Franklin," she said. "We expect to see it considered based on merit, not on an out of date pricing schedule."

The Harbormaster felt the first signs of a headache. "Are you implying impropiety on the part of this office? If so, I ---"

Katheryn closed her valise and stood. "I'm not implying anything, Mr. Franklin. Merely informing you of my expectations."

Franklin was left staring at his empty tea cup.

*   *   *

IAN Havershire drained his brandy glass and scowled across the table. "The way Lillian's carrying on you'd think King George himself was attending Sir Geoffrey's reception. Her bloody gown is costing a fortune."

"Mary is similarly affected." Andrew Pendleton signaled the waiter for refills, then turned his attention back to Havershire. "What concerns me, Ian, is that the King's Trade Ambassador, Gerald Farnsworth, will be here for the next month sticking his nose in our business."

"The China trade's got enough problems without the government mucking things up more than they already are." Havershire curled his mustache. "Curious, Eric Gradek's ducked out of sight these past months. He's up to something, I'd wager?"

Pendleton grunted. "Imagine running off and leaving his wife in charge."

Havershire smiled faintly. "Rumor has it he had a banner year with the silk trade."

"Joss," Pendleton replied. "It still doesn't alter the fact that women and business don't mix."

"Speaking of business," Havershire said, "it's time we got some bloody relief on kerosene prices."

Pendleton nodded in agreement. "Why don't we speak to a few of the syndicate members and pose that question to Alex Bartrum?"

*   *   *

"WELL?" Alex Bartrum continued sifting through a pile of paperwork.

The Harbormaster's palms went damp. "I thought you should know I was visited by Katheryn Gradek earlier about the dredging contract. She filed a bid."

Bartrum looked up. "Do you have a copy?"

Franklin laid a folder on the desk. "It's quite comprehensive, actually. Deep water channel, increased harbor depth --- "

"And look at the associated costs." Bartrum's eyes scanned the documents. "I'd say they were prohibitive, wouldn't you?"

"They are high, Mr. Bartrum," Franklin replied. "But it's work that needs to be done, if Shanghai's harbor is to remain ---"

"I'm aware of the harbor's needs, Franklin. Plenty of time to take care of them next year."

"Questions might be raised if we don't consider her proposal."

Bartrum glared over his desk. "If you value your position as harbormaster see that Gradek International's bid doesn't see the light of day."

Franklin picked up the folder. "If you say so, Mr. Bartrum."

Alex watched the Harbormaster leave. Once alone, he reread Philip's cable then tossed it into the fire. He walked to the bar, poured a brandy and returned to his desk. So his brother was coming to Shanghai with a plan to pull Bartrum & Sons out of the muck. Well, that couldn't happen soon enough, could it? Syndicate members were taking a hard line on kerosene prices, opium income had evaporated since the Chongming Dao debacle, and a less than spectacular trading year loomed ahead.

The one bright spot was that Franklin would quash Katheryn's challenge on the dredging contract.

Yet, despite the rash of bad news, Alex felt a rush of excitement, like in the old *Northern Star* days. Philip wouldn't be making the trip to China without something substantial in the works. He must have come up with a way to make their final option payments to Trident Industries. That would put Bartrum & Sons back on top. It would probably have the smell of death about it. But that was fine with Alex. In fact, he found it an appealing prospect. Staring through his brandy glass at the fire, the amber liquid winked back, golden and lustrous. *Yes,* it would be grand being back on top. The one unanswered question that continued to nag him was why Katheryn was going after the dredging contract with such resolve. Alex took a sip of brandy, feeling the familiar heat work its way down to his belly. *Nevermind,* he told himself. He would find out soon enough what Eric Gradek was up to.

Eighteen

PHILIP BARTRUM STEPPED OUT ONTO THE cruise ship's upper deck. Shanghai was a distant blur. Inwardly, he cursed the fact that he'd had to return to China. The last time, he'd helped Alex instigate a fire that nearly consumed the city. What a bloody muck up that had been. Afterwards, Philip promised himself never to return. But circumstances had changed, hadn't they? This time he was back as a matter of survival.

Five months since the disaster at Chongming Dao and his world was upside down. Philip remembered his father telling him how treacherous it was dealing in China.

"One day an emperor, the next a running dog."

How apropos.

Eric Gradek was positioned to become the preeminent taipan in China, while the once all-powerful Bartrum & Sons lay bleeding. Curiously, Philip did not hate Eric for stealing their opium. He would have done the same had the roles been reversed. Besides, Eric had given him the resources to keep the company afloat by buying his notes back. For the moment, Bartrum & Sons was still in business and in control of the oil supply. They could raise prices and recoup a portion of their losses. That was the good news. The bad news was there had been nothing left to make their option payment to Trident. So, Philip gambled heavily and refinanced the syndicate's oil tankers under the auspices of renovating the fleet.

Then, suddenly, the banks and lending institutions began distancing themselves. Philip felt like an outsider in London's stately boardrooms, places where he'd once been revered. Small demeaning actions were taken against him by the cliquish power brokers. These slights were subtle, which made them all the more insidious. Why he received such shabby treatment had been a mystery. Then he overheard Chongming Dao mentioned at a social gathering. Philip realized his carefully crafted image had been destroyed by an incident on a remote island a world away. Like his brother, he had been reduced to a laughingstock. His humiliation was so great that he considered suicide. And it was for this reason that he despised Eric Gradek.

Touched by a chill, Philip closed his eyes. Fortunately, he'd lacked the courage to take his own life. Now, he was returning to China with a plan that would restore Bartrum & Sons to power.

If there are no mistakes.

Philip opened his eyes and leaned on the rail. The docks of Shanghai were quite visible now.

*   *   *

THE Chinese opera house was crowded, scents of sweat and perfume co-mingling. Jacqueline shifted uncomfortably. She was six months pregnant and dying for a bit of fresh air. The high-pitched gibberish coming from the stage grated on her nerves. Well, at least it was the final act.

Despite colorful costumes, Jacqueline detested the performance. She hadn't a clue what the presentation was about. Plus, her bladder was going to burst. It would be impossible to last until getting home to relieve herself. She shuddered. The thought of squatting over one of those horrid little holes in the floor was appalling.

Earlier, when Katheryn suggested they attend the opera, Jacqueline envisioned a Shanghai version of a New York, London, or Paris production. *But this.....?* It was so alien. She glanced at Katheryn and felt a sudden warmth. It was wonderful having a friend and a real house after years of living in one hotel after the other.

Katheryn is such a dear. I wonder why she and Eric haven't had children? Well, all good things at their proper ----

Applause. Jacqueline looked up and watched the final curtain fall. Rushing through the crowd, she reached the latrine. The dreadful smell made her ill. When she stepped back into the lobby, crowds were milling. She groped her way outside.

Watchman Choy and Katheryn were suddenly by her side.

Katheryn took her arm. "Poor dear, you look frightful. Shall I send Choy for the doctor?"

Jacqueline leaned against the wall. Several deep breaths and her stomach calmed. She squeezed Katheryn's hand. I'll be fine. It's the pregnancy. And the facilities" --- she held her nose --- "are not the most pleasant."

Katheryn chuckled. "I know what you mean. I've been

caught in them a time or two."

A man watched from across the street. As soon as Watchman Choy settled the two women in a rickshaw the darkly-clad figure fell in behind them.

The night air was invigorating as the rickshaw runner loped toward the Bund. The din of the city welled. Brightly colored lanterns came into view, burning above the endless stalls and shops that lined the street. Katheryn looked at Jacqueline. She seemed caught up in the excitement, occasionally pointing out a shop she intended to visit. A rosy glow had returned to her cheeks and she chatted gaily.

Were all American women so uninhibited? Jacqueline was so effervescent --- a refreshing contrast to the stodgy English matrons Katheryn had grown accustomed to. It was grand having a friend to share common interest, now that Eric and Garrett were away so much. And Marianne was such a delightful child. *I couldn't love her more if she were my own.* Katheryn sighed. Then, unexpectedly, she found herself envying the child Jacqueline carried. Removing such a thought from her mind, she said, "How did you find the Chinese opera?"

Jacqueline wrinkled her nose. "It sounded like cats screeching. Certainly, nothing like Paris or New York."

"European opera can be traced to the Chinese from Marco Polo," Katheryn said.

"Perhaps if I understood the nuances, it might become more meaningful." Jacqueline inclined her head. "For example, why do men play the parts of women? Seems terribly patriarchal."

Katheryn settled in her seat. She had posed the same question to Eric on her first visit to the opera. "The Chinese believe that having men assume women's roles creates the perfect reenactment of what a woman should be as seen through a man's eyes. All very practical, really."

"But the female characters are all so subservient and mousy," Jacqueline observed. "Still, they must have their special charms. It's no secret that most well-to-do Westerners keep one as a mistress. Why Asian women hold such fascination for Western men is quite beyond me. My mother, bless her soul, taught me the importance of a wife keeping her husband satisfied. Garrett will always have a warm bed to come home to." Jacqueline's eyes suddenly misted. "If he ever comes home."

Katheryn patted her arm. "Not to worry. They'll be home soon."

Jacqueline smiled wanly. "Sorry to be making such a fuss. I'm afraid pregnancy tends to fill one with self-pity."

"You've held up remarkably well," Katheryn said. "Most women would've fled to the safety of their parent's house. Besides, everything's about to change. You've got a lovely new home and the baby will be here soon."

Jacqueline dabbed her eyes. "You've been such a dear friend. Except for you, I probably would have gone mad." She stared at Katheryn. "I've lived with loneliness and uncertainty all of my married life. Drifting from one oil field to another is not how I want to raise our children. Things have improved since we moved to Shanghai, but I want more. Garrett should've been here to participate in building our new house. Without his presence, it just doesn't feel like a real home." Jacqueline"s face suffused with emotion. "Dear God, Katheryn, call it women's intuition, but I'm terrified he won't be here when the baby comes."

"Don't even consider such a possibility," Katheryn said, trying to sound breezy. "According to Eric's letters, all Garrett talks about is getting home to you and Mariann. He'll be here when the baby's born."

"You must think I'm a whimpering ninny," Jacqueline said. "All this morbid talk when there's so much to be thankful for. I feel like such a fool."

Katheryn slipped her arm through Jacqueline's. "Nonsense. Under similar circumstances, I'd feel the same way."

They reached the Bund and were approaching the Kai-Sing Department store. Katheryn turned toward the display window and caught sight of the darkly-clad figure. Was it her imagination or was the man staring at their rickshaw? *Probably one of Watchman Choy's men.* Katheryn's eyes followed the man to the corner of the department store. Her heart constricted when she saw Mr. Jones emerge from the shadows. The giant glanced at their rickshaw then began speaking to the man who had been following them.

*   *   *

ALEX Bartrum felt the urge to kill. For the better part of an hour, he'd been listening to Philip recount the details of Eric Gradek's partnership with Garrett Botha. Alex stared at the stone fireplace. Amidst orange and blue flames, he could see those damned opal eyes and arrogant half-smile.

Played for a fool --- again.

Alex remembered his shock when Garrett Botha arrived and moved his office to the Gradek International building. What business did they have together? he'd asked himself. Botha was a geologist and Gradek a silk exporter. Their only link was oil drums Gradek produced for Trident Industries. And that was a remote connection. Or, was it? As a precautionary measure, Alex began monitoring Garrett's activities. The only thing he learned was Garrett intended to stay in Shanghai. Why else would he build a house near the Bund?

Rumors soon began circulating that Garrett had teamed up with Eric to export rubber from Malaysia. Then, they both disappeared. Suspicious, Alex had Mr. Jones start following Katheryn and Jacqueline. The two women had become inseparable friends, attending social functions together. But that didn't matter, did it? Now he knew the truth.

"Storage facilities......"

Philip looked up. "Eh?"

"Storage facilities," Alex repeated. "That explains why Gradek's godcursed dwarf has been buying prime dock frontage all over Asia."

Philip's fists tightened. "Purchased with our money."

Alex finished a brandy. "No wonder Gradek's going after the dredging contract. His tankers will have no problem docking and he'll make a pile."

"Bloody Christ." Philip poured a pair of brandies. "What are the chances Gradek will be awarded the contract?"

Alex looked at his brother. "Not much. Franklin's still under our control. We shouldn't have a problem."

"Damn his soul," Philip swore. "The rotter's been dismantling us piece by piece."

"But that's about to change," Alex said. "Mr. Gradek's prosperity will be short-lived."

Philip caught the look on his brother's face. "Alex, under no circumstances will we become directly involved. You will hire people with no linkage to take care of what needs to be done."

Alex swirled his brandy, saying nothing.

"Can we expect any assistance from Dragon Mok?"

"Since Chongming Dao, Formidable Fung has damn near

wiped Mok out," Alex said. "The Green Pang controls about ninety percent of Shanghai."

"Are you saying Mok's of no use to us?"

Alex looked up. "Hell no. Mok will do anything to get back into a position of power."

"What about Sumatra? Can he help us there?"

"Don't fret about it brother." There was an ugliness in Alex's eyes that chilled Philip. "The Orient is a violent place."

*   *   *

KATHERYN saw Jacqueline safely to the door of her house. She then returned home and went immediately for a bath. Sinking into the hot water, she put her hands on her stomach and watched tendrils of steam rise from the smooth surface. Her thoughts were of Eric and Jacqueline's unborn child. But in another part of her mind she saw Mr. Jones outside the Kai-Sing Department Store huddled with the darkly-clad man that had followed their rickshaw.

Katheryn got out of the bath and dried herself. Donning a cotton robe and a pair slippers, she returned to the house. In the kitchen she shooed the servants away and prepared a light snack that she did not eat.

Once upstairs, Katheryn changed into a nightgown and had Ah-Sook comb her hair. Then she went to the balcony and listened to the cicada and frogs sing. Night breezes rustled the banyan tree leaves and the air smelled of damp earth.

Ten minutes later, Katheryn drew the curtains and went to bed. Shadows played on the ceiling, but she did not sleep.

Nineteen

DRAGON MOK BLEW DUST FROM THE TIN CUP before filling it with brandy. He was alone in the third-floor office of a dilapidated warehouse in the French section of the city. Around his waist was a money belt with a pair of fighting knives tucked inside.

Mok surveyed the rubbish and old boxes that constituted his headquarters. Movement drew his eyes to a thumb-sized cockroach. He took a moment, regarding it fondly. After all, the bug was his brother in this last bastion under the control of the Red Pang.

Closing his eyes, Mok counted the advantages of helping Alex Bartrum. There were many. The problem was having his survival linked to a barbarian he hated. But he would deal with that later. Right now, the noose Formidable Fung had slipped around his neck was growing tighter. His once vaunted Red Pang was rife with defections and was crumbling. Only last night two more opium houses fell to the Greens. Making matters worse, his money would soon be depleted. And without money there would be no soldiers. And without soldiers.....

Mok shuddered.

The only good thing coming out of his war with Fung was slitting Ting se-Bing's belly. *May all gods defecate on his malodorous head.* The cup rose and fell. But now, with joss, he could reverse his situation. Bartrum was paying an amount that would make the Yellow Emperor blink. With such money he could buy soldiers and opium. But money alone was not enough. For the Red Pang to be resurrected, Formidable Fung had to die. And he had to wield the blade. Mok smiled grimly. Perhaps, Bartrum had provided the way.

Mok poured more brandy and reviewed his plan. The necessary contacts had been made. Appropriate cables dispatched to Sumatra. All the elements were in place. Well, all except one. Fortunately, he would not be the one making the arrangements. In this instance he would use an intermediary. Draining his cup, Mok stood, satisfied. There was plenty of time to attend to this last remaining detail before Bartrum's arrival.

A shaft of sunlight caught the cockroach's black carapace as it scurried out from under a pile of litter. In the tawny light it circled, stopped, then vanished into a wedge of paper. Mok smiled and walked to the door.

It was time for his meeting with the Beggar King, Kwok-yu.

*   *   *

KATHERYN now understood the force that drove her husband and men like him. *Power.* A potent elixir that, once tasted, could not easily be set aside. Men would lie, cheat, steal and kill to possess it. She had felt it descend like a mantle upon her shoulders while sitting behind Eric's desk. The China Trade was a smash-or-be smashed world with a blind pox on morality. Civility, or the Marquis of Queensbury rules, were alien concepts. Yet, surprisingly, Katheryn found herself loving the game. Perhaps it was because she confirmed what she'd suspected for many years. Her mind was a formidable weapon. And, in a world where women's minds were relegated to presiding over teas, she blessed Eric for the opportunity to use hers.

For the past months, Katheryn had worked closely with Tong-Po and Adair MacAlister planning future moves for Crown Petroleum and Gradek International. It didn't take long for her to realize that she had a natural talent for business. She was shrewd and insightful, capable of dissecting complicated problems into their simple components. No question, there was a heady excitement knowing she could destroy the most ruthless taipan by simply using her brain.

Katheryn thought about her meeting with Gerald Farnsworth. It had been relatively easy persuading the trade ambassador about the need to dredge a deep water channel and increase the harbor depth. The associated costs would be more than offset by revenues from increased efficiency. Of course, it hadn't hurt pointing out Richard Franklin's home to Farnsworth on their way to dinner.

"Lives on the Bund, does he?" Farnsworth observed. "Rather grand for a harbormaster's salary,"

A smile tugged at Katheryn's lips. The seed had been planted about Franklin's involvement with Bartrum & Sons. Soon she would know if it had germinated.

Such a difference now, Katheryn thought. At first Tong-Po

and Adair tolerated her because she was Eric's wife. But, now they actively sought her advice. Katheryn's eyes crinkled. She had won their respect in ways that few women were accorded. For that she was greatly pleased.

Turning in Eric's high-back leather chair, Katheryn looked out at the harbor. As much as she enjoyed the game, she realized there was a dark side. The game was about power. And power distorted people. It fed their basest instincts until altruistic concepts became lost in some dark hole. All one had to do was look at the history books. Leaders and rulers the world over, even ones with the best of intentions, were transformed into despots with godlike visions of themselves. And who suffered because of their intolerable actions? Ordinary people. Wasn't that always the case?

Now Eric was poised to become Asia's most powerful taipan. Would he be consumed? Katheryn felt a chill. Would *she?* She'd heard the siren's song behind the taipan's desk. So many prizes to be won. But were they worth your humanity?

Katheryn watched coolies stream in and out of a cargo ship. In the background, merchants hawked their wares. Much had happened since Eric left. Crown Petroleum had storage facilities in major ports. A marketing organization comprised of independent European and Chinese middlemen was in place. Gradek International would probably win the dredging concession; a contract that would serve their tanker fleet.

Tong-Po told her that for the first time, millions of people in the interior would have fuel and lighting oil. Jing-Jiang's dream seemed on the verge of reality. But there were dangers. Alex Bartrum would not be toppled without a fight. And there were the other taipan to consider. Would they rally behind Bartrum to save themselves?

Katheryn's anxiety rose. Eric's rivalry with Alex Bartrum would have dire consequences. No, she corrected herself, rivalry wasn't the right word. A lethal hatred existed. On several occasions she had questioned Eric about the *Northern Star* and his brutal treatment. Reliving Eric's horror of being in the hole with rats, bleeding from a wound inflicted by Mr. Jones' knife had served to kindle her own hatred for Alex Bartrum. They had also talked about Tong-Po, the fine man constrained in a dwarf's body. Eric explained how the gods favored dwarfs and, to some degree, Katheryn's sorrow for Tong-Po was assuaged. Gulls wheeled over the harbor. Then an image conjured of Mr. Jones stepping out from the corner of the Kai-Sing Department Store. "Dear God," Katheryn whispered. "Give me strength."

Closing her eyes, Katheryn prayed again. Only this time it was for her husband's safe return.

*   *   *

"THIS will be a difficult and expensive undertaking," Dragon Mok said to Alex Bartrum. "You must go with my eldest son to Sumatra. Wu-Fat will require a great deal of bullion for his services."

Wu-Fat was Dragon Mok's half-brother from his father's third wife. For years, his pirate band preyed on British shipping along the China coast. Until Katheryn's father became territorial governor. One of Sir Geoffrey's first acts had been to dispatch a small, well-armed fleet to seek out and destroy the lairs of coastal pirates. Wu-Fat avoided the hangman's noose and escaped to Sumatra where he regrouped and took up his old trade. Considered the scourge of the Dutch East Indies, Wu-Fat now commanded a force of more than three hundred men.

Alex Bartrum stared at Mok. The scent of burning joss sticks was irritating. Beyond that, he was pleased with the way his plan was developing. Mok was raping him financially, but he would deal with that later. "Your son will leave for Sumatra tomorrow," Bartrum said. "I'll leave the day after. He will bring Wu-Fat to me. There must be no record of me being near Sumatra." Bartrum helped himself to a brandy. "According to the steamship company's manifest, Botha and Gradek will arrive in Singapore in a month. From there they've scheduled an immediate transfer to Sumatra. It's imperative that the Wu-Fat meeting take place at my Singapore office at least four days before they arrive." Bartrum set the cup down. "Make sure your son and Wu-Fat arrive after midnight."

Mok scratched his groin. "That can be arranged. When will the Opal Eye Devil be returning to Shanghai?"

"He's ticketed to leave Sumatra a week after he visits the refinery. Botha is planning to stay on for a month." Bartrum again reached for the bottle. "Wu-Fat and his bully boys better not muck it up."

"Depends on the mood of the gods." Mok shrugged. "Perhaps they will be angry; perhaps not. Nothing is certain. Chongming Dao showed us that, *heya?*"

Bartrum's jaw tightened. "Burn some frigging incense then. For what I'm bloody well paying, the gods had better be in a good mood." He took a long drink. "Have you made contact with the Lotus Tong?"

Mok winced. For years the Qing Dynasty and various warlords had used the Lotus Tong to eliminate political opposition. Tong disciples were adept in the arts of stealth, espionage and sudden death. The mercenary society's only loyalty was money.

"Your meeting is for tonight at midnight," Mok said. "Carry only the agreed upon sum of money. No personal weapons. Go to the temple on the Street of the White Tiger. Members of the Tong will take you from there to their dragonhead." Mok lifted his cup and drank. His fear of the Lotus Tong was such that he'd hired the Beggar King, Kwok-yu, to act as an intermediary. A fact he did not mention to Bartrum.

Bartrum's eyes narrowed. "I'll be alone with them?"

"Of course, and blindfolded." Mok smiled condescendingly. "If Mr. Jones or anyone else attempts to follow, your life will be forfeited."

*   *   *

THE night was cold when Headwaiter Fong stepped out of the Teahouse of the Golden Carp. For three hours he had been entertained by a willowy fifteen year old sing-song girl. Sighing contentedly, he gazed at the heavens. A horned moon lay suspended amidst a cascade of stars.

Ayeeee, my joss is grand, he thought. Many months have passed since my sacred member was subjected to such delights. Tiger Mei's jade gate would certainly raise the stalks of the dead. Perhaps I shall return next week. Eeeee, such fire in her loins. But, then again, how often would the little strumpet be afforded the opportunity of entertaining such a potent shaft as my own?

Feeling the affects of the rice wine, Fong decided to reward his prowess with a bowl of opium. Removing the flagon of wine tucked in his belt, he took a drink and began ambling towards a warehouse district near the Ho-Ping Market. An icy wind blew down the narrow street. Beggars pressed their bodies against the sides of buildings for warmth. Others huddled in alleys with their children wrapped in thin blankets.

Fong kept to the market's perimeter to avoid the crowds. The door to a small hovel opened. A pair of grimy streetwalkers appeared and beckoned him inside. Politely, Fong declined and quickened his footsteps. He turned down a back street leading to the wharf where the opium parlor was located.

The building loomed, shorn of all artificial light. He could hear dogs foraging through rubble and waves lapping against the pier. Where was the guard who usually stood at the entrance? Tentatively, Fong climbed the steps and tried the door. Locked. *Fong-pi,* he silently cursed. He knocked several times but there was no answer. The establishment was closed. Probably a casualty of the war between Formidable Fung and Dragon Mok.

Fong removed the flagon and sat in the dark foyer. The shadows were such that he could see out but could not be seen. Minutes later, a sampan drifted alongside the pier. Fong watched two men in matte black jump onto the deck and secure the boat. These were no ordinary boat people. Their movements were fluid and light. A tall man was led from the sampan. Fong's heart stood still. The man was blindfolded, but he could clearly see it was Alex Bartrum.

"How much farther?" Bartrum asked, his abrasive voice irritable over the dogs and lapping waves.

Removing the blindfold, one of the men replied in halting English, "Small distance now." Turning to his companion, he said in Chinese, "I should slit this insolent dog's secret sac. Did he think the dragonhead of the Lotus Tong would be waiting for him on this rotting pier?"

"What did you expect from a barbarian?" the other said.

"His head is filled with turtle dung. Is it not common knowledge that the brains of foreign devils are no larger than rat droppings?"

Fong's bowels loosened. He wanted to flee, but that would bring disaster. *Be still.* Bartrum and the two tong disciples left the pier. What was *Odious Mountain of Dung* doing with assassins of the Lotus Tong? One did not deal with the Lotus Tong unless one was planning to have someone executed.

Amida. Was Alex Bartrum planning to assassinate the Opal Eye Devil?

*   *   *

ALEX Bartrum was taken to an abandoned warehouse and led to the rear of the building. It was cold, but he could feel sweat trickling down his back. One of the assassins opened a door and ushered him inside. Several candles burned on a low table. "Wait," the assassin said.

Mok's assurance that the Lotus Tong was an honorable organization that kept its contractual obligations did little to ease Bartrum's anxiety.

"This meeting was most difficult to arrange and must be conducted according to Tong rules," Mok had said. "And Tong rules say you see dragonhead alone." Mok's dark lips curled into a smile. "Not to worry, you will be quite safe. The Lotus Tong is very old and venerated organization. Never would they resort to stealing from their clients. They have simple, easy business arrangement. Pay them money and you have nothing to fear. Attempt to cheat them and you will die."

Tightening his coat, Bartrum sat on a pillow in front of the table and waited. Cheating the Lotus Tong had never been a consideration. He needed them. Once the great Opal Eye Devil --- damn that fanciful name --- was eliminated Bartrum & Sons would be resurrected. *Yes,* he thought, the future looked bright. There might even be another chance for him with Katheryn. Following a reasonable period for grieving, of course. He smiled. After all, he would not be a suspect in her husband's death. He could always say that whatever enmity existed between them was business, not personal.

"I understand you seek the services of the Lotus Tong," a voice said.

The hackles on Bartrum's neck rose. Shapes and shadows shifted. Then the dragonhead of the Lotus Tong was standing before him. Bartrum stared at the dark figure. It was as if he had manifested himself through a wall of invisibility.

The dragonhead seated himself. Tall, with angular features, he had an athletic build and slitted eyes. He wore no shoes or gloves, only a matte-black uniform made from light cotton. His breath did not escape in white puffs as Bartrum's did. It was like he had developed a body independent of the elements.

Amused at Bartrum's fear, the dragonhead said, "No need to be nervous. State the purpose of your visit."

"I thought that everything had been explained to you by Dragon --- "

"I'm not interested in what third parties have to say. Any business we may have together will be agreed upon by the two of us. In this manner there will be no room for misinterpretation. Now --- the purpose of your visit."

"There is a man I wish disposed of in a manner such that his death will appear to be the result of a pang vendetta," Bartrum said. "Perhaps you have heard of him? His name is Eric Gradek."

The slitted eyes watched him.

"I know of this man," the dragonhead said, finally. "He is revered for saving many Chinese lives during the great fire. To dispatch a man such as the Opal Eye Devil will cost a great deal."

"I was under the impression that the amount had already been agreed upon."

"I have told you, I am not interested in third party prattle. You and I will set the terms to any agreement." The dragonhead stared at Bartrum. "Great risks are involved in the business you propose. Eric Gradek is married to the territorial governor's daughter. His death will not go unnoticed by British or Chinese authorities. The public will demand retribution --- rewards will be offered."

Bartrum leaned forward. "Precisely. But if Gradek's death appears to be a pang slaying it will be Formidable Fung not the Lotus Tong whom the authorities will seek to destroy."

"I am considering that possibility." The dragonhead's voice was soft. "Formidable Fung is not some peasant with mud between his ears. How long before he determines the Lotus Tong is responsible for Gradek's death?" The slitted eyes stared into Bartrum's skull. "Being hunted by the Green Pang is unappealing. The amount will be double what is strapped to your waist."

Bartrum choked. "Double?"

"The fee is non-negotiable. My terms are half now. The remainder after the contract has been honored." The dragonhead inclined his head. "If you object to these conditions, you may leave."

Bartrum inwardly cursed at having been played like a puppet into paying double an already outrageous amount. Dragon Mok had already mercilessly gouged him, and now this. He considered walking out, but that was impossible. Destroying Gradek, Botha, and their field was vital.

"Mr. Bartrum?"

Bartrum looked into the cold eyes. "We have an agreement." He reached for the money belt. As the money left his hands, Bartrum realized that had he attempted to leave without striking a bargain, he would be dead.

Twenty

JING-JIANG LIFTED THE TEACUP TO THAT delicate level just beneath his nose and inhaled. Sipping from the blue and white cup, he glanced at Tong-Po. "The teas of Hangzhou have served me well through my life's journey."

"A divine brew, *heya?*" Tong-Po said.

Jing-Jiang sipped again. "Divine --- until consumed by barbarians, who infect it with their vile creams and sugars."

"Barbarians are barbarians." Tong-Po chuckled. "Who can account for their maddening lack of civility?"

"Unfortunately, they are necessary if we are to raise China from the abyss." Jing-Jiang stared into his teacup. "My fear is the coming upheaval will erode the traditional Chinese life that once made us great."

"China is the navel of the earth," Tong-Po replied carefully. "Have we not endured the millennium because we are first and foremost Chinese? Priests, scribes, and ritual will remind us who we are and render us timeless. The government must be wrested from the foul Manchu invaders and commerce firmly controlled by Chinese. Only then will we rise from the abyss."

Jing-Jiang refilled their cups. "You are right of course, old friend. Whatever the gods decree is better than the yoke of Manchu tyranny, *heya?*" The canny eyes crinkled. "I assume you have much to tell me."

Tong-Po worried about Jing-Jiang. The cruel winter had taken its toll on the old man. *Probably the last year of a most illustrious life,* Tong-Po thought sadly. "Eric will be returning within the month. He cabled his undying respect and wishes me to inform you that the tankers produced by Clay Shipyards are without peer. Because of their advanced design they are able to transport oil with great speed and efficiency."

Jing-Jiang nodded his pleasure. "What you are saying is that Crown Petroleum will be operating the most modern fleet on the seas."

"That is my understanding," Tong-Po said. "There are additional benefits. Besides greater load capacity and speed, the tankers are equipped with cleaning equipment that enable them to return with full loads of cargo, including foodstuffs. Profits can be reaped from such efficiency."

"When do you anticipate this business to commence?"

"Within two months we should be making our first deliveries. Throughout China and the rest of the Pacific, reaching as far south as Australia, we have a distribution network to service both Chinese and foreign markets."

"What about the loyalty of these distributors? Bartrum will stop at nothing to entice them to turn on us."

"We will have their loyalty."

"Loyalty is a slippery word, old friend." Jing-Jiang frowned.

"What makes you so confident in this matter?"

The dwarf took a breath. "I did not appoint distributors as was our original plan. Rather, I sold distribution rights to the highest bidder. In this manner we may not own their hearts, but we have their gold." Tong-Po removed a document from his sleeve. "Here are the final figures. Proceeds from these sales have already recovered our investment, plus a modest profit."

Jing-Jiang squinted at the paper. "The co-hong will be pleased when they receive word of this. Such adroitness needs to be commended."

Tong-Po shifted in the large chair. "Actually, I played but a small part in this matter. Your commendation belongs to another."

Jing-Jiang watched him over his cup. "And who might that be?"

"Eric's golden haired *tai tai,* Katheryn."

Jing-Jiang lost his composure, as much as he ever did. His teacup shook, then settled.

"For a barbarian, Katheryn is astute in matters concerning business. She possesses the cleverness of a Mandarin." *But it is her beauty that makes her shine,* Tong-Po thought. *A light that glows from within and without. Ahh, to be as tall as she makes me feel.*

Tong-Po momentarily shocked Jing-Jiang by calling her Katheryn. Saying nothing, the old general sipped his tea and waited.

"Katheryn entered into an agreement with an Australian firm, Brentwood, Stanley Heavy Equipment; an Australian firm which manufactures dredging equipment. There is a good chance that Gradek International will be awarded the concession. Then she convinced us to sell rather than award oil distributorships. It enhances our position on two fronts. The co-hong will have more confidence in a venture involving barbarians with a short-term profit. And, our distributors will aggressively market our products to recapture their investment."

"Very practical --- very Chinese," Jing-Jiang said by way of response. "Obviously, my son has taught her well. Or then again" --- he laughed --- "it might be as I've always suspected that the yin is superior to the yang."

"She is quite extraordinary."

Jing-Jiang noted Tong-Po's affection. Perhaps, before passing to the next realm he would take the opportunity of speaking with his son's golden haired *tai tai.* "Bartrum and his allies will be starting their countermoves," he said. "Have security measures been taken to protect members of my son's household?"

Tong-Po nodded. "Watchman Choy has moved to the Taipan's residence and has men stationed inside and out. Also, security has been increased around Garrett Botha's tai tai and our godown complex."

"Good," Jing-Jiang said.

They heard words in the hallway. There was a knock on the door. The majordomo entered, leading a disheveled Headwaiter Fong into the study.

*   *   *

BARON Rosenberg lifted the humidor lid on Percival D. Sutton's desk and helped himself to a cigar. "Twenty tankers are presently being loaded in Bantum. They'll be sailing within a few days." He sniffed the fine Havana. "Once the Sumatran field is buggered, Crown Petroleum will effectively be out of business. An artificial oil shortage will be created."

"And after we sever our relationship with Bartrum & Sons there will be a panic in the market," Sutton said. "Every trader in Asia will be clamoring for oil when the announcement becomes public." Sutton leaned his head back. "With twenty tankers on the water we'll consolidate new distribution agreements and get top dollar for every drop of Russian oil we can supply."

Rosenberg fired a match. "What if Alex Bartrum is unsuccessful?"

"It's best not to even contemplate that."

"But contemplate it we must," the Baron said. "Failure opens a bloody Pandora's Box."

Sutton sighed. "I know. Every would-be producer on the planet will try to imitate Botha and Gradek if we're forced to withdraw from Asia. We've already got a nightmare brewing in Texas with *Spindletop,* not to mention what's happening in Pennsylvania and Oklahoma. Our pipeline and refining monopoly won't protect us from Clay's large tankers. Wherever there's a harbor our coastal operations will be under attack." Sutton's face darkened. "Crown Petroleum must be destroyed."

The Baron stared at Sutton. "Well, Percy, we'll have to make sure that's what happens, won't we?"

* * *

FORMIDABLE Fung stared out the window, keeping his anxiety compartmentalized. Bartrum had contracted with the Lotus Tong to assassinate the Taipan. *Curse all gods.* The tong was not known to fail. *So, how to best deal with the Lotus Tong?* Even though Eric was a barbarian, Fung owed him his life. *Besides, I need his gun boats to safely transport my opium.*

"Dragon Mok knows many people, but even he could not directly arrange a meeting for Bartrum with the Lotus Tong." Fung turned from the window. "He had to use an intermediary to make such an arrangement."

Tong-Po shifted impatiently. "Why couldn't Mok have made contact?"

"The Lotus Tong has no loyalty, or creed --- except gold. A middleman is required because a client today may be a victim tomorrow." Fung picked up the teapot. "After a sufficient amount of money has been paid, the only prerequisite necessary to qualify as prey for the Lotus Tong is to be alive."

Tong-Po grasped the arm of the chair. "These assassins are only men. Surely they can be stopped."

"It will not be easy," Fung replied. "They are adept in the art of killing."

Jing-Jiang's final directive rang in Tong-Po's head. "Nothing must happen to my son. Build a wall of steel about him and fortify it with a thousand men. Do whatever is necessary to protect him. With him lies the future of China."

Fung's voice lifted Tong-Po's eyes. "There is only one man in Shanghai that could have arranged the meeting."

"Who?"

"Kwok-yu."

"The Beggar King?" Tong-Po's anxiety turned to rage. "May that lowly maggot rot in his own feces." Standing to his full forty-two inch height, he clenched his knotty fist. "I would like a few words with the lord of human misery."

"Why not seize Bartrum and bring him here?" Fung suggested. "Perhaps, we could find a way to abrogate the contract."

Tong-Po climbed up into his chair. "Impossible. He sailed for Singapore three days ago."

207

"We will make do with Kwok-yu. His cooperation will not come easily, but I know how to make his tongue wag. My men will have him here by morning." Fung looked at Tong-Po. "Do you carry a weapon?"

"Only a dagger. The need for anything more has never been necessary."

Fung removed a teak box from the bottom drawer of his desk. He took out a pearl-handled derringer and a box of ammunition. Holding the pistol to the light, he admired the workmanship. "I suggest you carry this. Like you, it is small but deadly."

*   *   *

THUNDER mixed sullenly with the clouds as they rolled in from the South China Sea. It was just past midnight and very dark when a dozen of Wu-Fat's pirates fanned out around Bartrum & Sons Singapore office.

Wu-Fat and Dragon Mok's eldest son waited until the guards were in place. When the area was secure they walked to the rear of the office. Light rain fell as Wu-Fat knocked three times. A moment later the heavy bolt slid back. Mr. Jones appeared in the doorway, freezing the two men. A revolver was in his hand --- aimed at Wu-Fat's head.

"In you come, nice and easy," Mr. Jones said. "Mr. Bartrum's a bit queasy about having weapons in his office while a meeting be going on. So, real gentle like, put your knives and any boom-boom in this here basket. I'll be searching you real careful after your pockets are emptied. I best not be finding any left over."

Wu-Fat muttered something in gutter Mandarin. He walked

inside the warehouse and deposited a small fighting hatchet and stiletto in the basket. Mok's son was carrying a razor. Jones thoroughly searched the two men, then waved the gun barrel towards the stairs. "Now that we've got that little matter attended to, it's time to see Mr. Bartrum."

"Care for a tot of brandy?" Alex Bartrum asked. Noting the murderous looks on their faces, he added, "Mr. Jones took your weapons because there's a great deal of money at stake here. Naturally, I didn't want it falling into the wrong hands." He opened a leather satchel and spilled the contents onto his desk. "Wu-Fat, I believe this is the correct down payment. Care to count it?"

Wu Fat's eyes fixed on the cash; wiped his hands down the side of his pants. "No need to count," he said. "We partners, *heya?*"

Bartrum chuckled and poured a glass of brandy for the two men. "Yes, we're partners." He glanced at the money. "Plenty more of that if you can get the job done on schedule."

Insolent dog, Wu-Fat thought. *Am I not the master of four fleets? I can burn the barbarian field at a snap of my finger.* He felt an urge to choke Bartrum for his lack of manners, but was restrained by his own want and the menacing presence of Mr. Jones. Instead, he accepted the brandy. "No worry about getting job done. My men will be ready to move."

"I'm sailing for Hong Kong, tomorrow," Bartrum said. "That's two weeks ahead of Gradek and Botha's arrival in Singapore. Should be enough time to get your men prepared, eh?" Picking up a map, he spread it across the top of his desk. "This is a detailed layout of the facilities. It's vital you memorize this map. You'll be sailing up the Balaban River at night and you can't afford mistakes." Removing a pointer from his pocket, he tapped a spot marked in red on the map. "This is the communication center next to the foreman's quarters. Over here are the well sights and the pipeline that leads to the refinery located down river, here."

Wu-Fat placed his glass over the spot Bartrum was pointing. "I memorize maps if it takes rest of night. And, I do job with no mistakes. Important question is how will I get rest of money?"

"When the field's been properly torched, send someone around to collect the balance from Mok's son, here. I'm sure Dragon Mok wouldn't mind him staying on till this nasty business has been concluded."

Wu-Fat's eyes narrowed. *Very Chinese for this barbarian to offer Mok's eldest son as guarantee. By cleverly suggesting to keep him in Singapore, he has provided a hostage to guarantee payment. Bartrum is telling me there will be no treachery on his part because he will not risk making Mok an enemy by sacrificing his son. On the other hand, he is telling me the boy will be unable to flee with the money because I will naturally have placed an invisible wall of men around him. Very clever indeed.* Wu-Fat smiled at Bartrum, his gold tooth flashing. "Yes, that will be acceptable," he said. "I suggest we drink to it."

Bartrum replenished the drinks. Raising his glass, he said, "Wu-Fat. To your success. And now that we understand each other, your bonus will be doubled when Botha's confirmed dead."

*   *   *

THE Beggar King was furious when his men awakened him before dawn. But when he learned that an emissary was waiting with an urgent summons from Formidable Fung, his desire for further sleep vanished. Shanghai's supreme dragon would not have contacted Kwok-yu at such an unseemly hour unless he wanted something important.

Eeeee, what does that fornicator, Formidable Fung, want at this hour?

Obviously, a service that only someone possessing his unique talents could supply. There would be a great deal of gold in the offing. The Beggar King dressed, pausing at the nightstand to splash water on his face.

Three soldiers of the Green Pang were waiting in the grimy anteroom, but this did not intimidate the Kwok-yu. He was a short, squat and vicious man --- supremely confident in his fighting skills. A throwing knife was in the crease of his neck --- a stiletto concealed beneath his belt. If there was a hint of treachery he would be ready.

Kwok-yu reached Formidable Fung's complex just after dawn. He was taken to a small dining room where an attractive girl was waiting to serve him food and tea.

She smiled demurely. "My master will be joining you shortly."

The Beggar King nodded, contenting himself by munching rice cakes and sipping tea.

*   *   *

HOURS later, Kwok-yu awoke. His mouth felt like dried leather and his head was pounding. Blinking, he tried to bring his eyes into focus, but the walls ballooned in. He took several deep breaths. Moments later, the spinning feeling passed and his vision cleared. He was still at Formidable Fung's headquarters. Still in the same room where the girl had served him rice cakes and tea. But that had been around dawn. Now shadows were creeping across the floor. Outside he could hear fishmongers hawking their goods.

It was evening. He had been drugged. Kwok-yu tried to lift his hands, but they would not move. Looking down, he saw he was naked and lashed to a high-back chair. His testicles dangled through a hold cut out of the chair seat. A strangled scream escaped his lips.

An hour later the door opened. Formidable Fung, Tong-Po and the girl who served him tea seated themselves at a round dining table. A small entourage of servants carrying trays of food, rice wine and hot tea followed. Kwok-yu stared at Tong-Po. His heart seemed to stop beating. Could the dwarf somehow know he had arranged a meeting between Alex Bartrum and the Lotus Tong? *Impossible,* his terrified mind said. Hadn't he contacted the Lotus Tong in secret, as Dragon Mok requested? No one else knew of his involvement. Not even Bartrum.

Formidable Fung, Tong-Po and the girl began to eat. Kwok-yu gaped at them. He had the feeling that he was participating in this nightmarish scene from outside himself. "By all gods, why have you done this?"

They continued to eat and talk among themselves. When the meal was completed the servants returned with fresh tea. After the second cup, Formidable Fung turned to Kwok-yu. "My friend and I may have need of your services. But, first you will be required to answer some questions."

The Beggar King's courage momentarily strengthened on the words, like a flame in a breeze. Fung wanted his help. "What kind of way is this to ask for my assistance?" he said. "Release me and bring my clothes. Then we talk."

Fung nodded to the girl as if Kwok-yu had not spoken. "This is Miss Li, whom you met earlier today. She possesses many talents besides administering sedatives."

The girl took a potato from her bag and set it on the table. Then from her sash she removed a short wooden dowel with a metal wire attached to each end. Kwok-yu watched her insert the potato into the wire loop and twist the dowel. A soft squish sounded as the razor wire cut through the potato's skin. The girl sensuously stroked the dowel while slowly rotating it in a clockwise motion. Droplets of water oozed through the cut, dripping onto the table. The girl gave the dowel a final turn and severed the potato into two perfect halves. Kwok-yu's mouth dried out like parchment.

Tong-Po slid his chair in front of Kwok-yu and stood on it. "A meeting has taken place between the high dragon of the Lotus Tong and Alex Bartrum. The only topic of interest at such an encounter would be assassination." The dwarf's face was very close to Kwok-yu. "You arranged the meeting, and are going to provide us with the details."

Kwok-yu's terrible dilemma was, if he talked the Lotus Tong would have his head; not talk, and the girl would have his manhood. "By my ancestors," he said. "I *don* --- don't know."

"You have no ancestors,"Tong-Po said softly. "You were spawned from turtle dung." He turned to the girl. "Miss Li, it appears that the King of Beggars has elected to change his title to King of Eunuchs."

The girl knelt beside Kwok-yu's chair. Terror seized the Beggar King as he felt the wire slip around his testicles. "You will be free to go after Miss Li has finished with you," Tong-Po said. "It might interest you to know she preserves them in jars, complete with names."

The girl twisted the ivory dowel until the wire made its first bite.

Kwok-yu shrieked.

"Your chances of surviving are minimal," Tong-Po continued. "You will bleed to death or be hacked to pieces by beggar hordes. It will not take long for word of your castration to reach them on the streets. A king without stones is no king at all, *heya?*" Tong-Po shrugged. "Either way, your death is of little import. Shanghai will be the better for it."

Miss Li twisted the dowel, causing the wire to cut deeper. Faint with fright, Kwok-yu began babbling. "It was Mok! I swear by the gods! Dragon Mok asked me to arrange meeting for Bartrum with Lotus Tong."

"Why did Bartrum want such a meeting?" Tong-Po asked.

The dowel was stilled in the petite hand.

Sweat poured from Kwok-yu's forehead. "He, he has employed the Tong to kill the Opal Eye Devil."

Tong-Po stared at the Beggar King. "Worthless dog. I should castrate you myself and be done with it."

Kwok-yu fell forward in his chair. "Mercy. Whatever you want me to do, I will obey."

"Of course you will obey," Fung said. "Or you and all of your relations will pay an unpleasant price. First, you will go to the Lotus Tong and persuade them to remove themselves from this affair. Tell them they are mistakenly involved in a personal matter between the Taipan and Bartrum."

"It will do no good for me to go to the Lotus Tong," Kwok-yu cried. "Once they accept an assignment --- the gods themselves could not call them off."

Tong-Po glared. "Castrate this maggot."

Kwok-yu jumped as the wire constricted. "Wait, wait. I will

go to the Lotus Tong. I'll pay anything to --- "

"Buy them with gold," Fung interrupted. "Beg them --- find a way!"

"Yes, yes. Whatever you say. Please..."

Formidable Fung walked over to the Beggar King and stared into his eyes. "And if the Lotus Tong cannot be dissuaded, pray to your ancestors that no harm comes to the Opal Eye Devil."

Twenty-one

JANS KESSLER, THE MAN IN CHARGE OF THE Telega said oil project, greeted Eric and Garrett outside the customs area when the two disembarked in Singapore. The Dutchman's hair was sun-bleached white and his skin a ruddy ocher. Handshakes were extended all around.

"Good to have you back," Jans said. Porters arrived and began taking bags to the waiting cutter. "Seems like you've been away six years rather than six months."

Garrett grinned. "It's good to be back."

"More than good. America is nice, but the commotion of Asia is more to my liking," Eric said. He took a breath and stared at the harbor. The water was black and still as dawn's first hues touched the horizon. Fishing boats, sampans and trawlers were heading out to sea for their morning run.

"According to your cables a lot has happened since we've been away," Garrett said.

Jans nodded. "We've had a real witch's brew on our hands. Why don't we go on board and I'll fill you in?"

*   *   *

NAVIGATING through the strange flotilla of house boats and fishing boats clogging the harbor was tricky. Gulls circled lazily overhead, their screeching co-mingling with the sounds of crying boat children waiting for morning meals.

Reaching open water the skipper set a northeast course towards Sumatra. When they reached the Balaban River they would sail upstream to the refinery sight. The cutter picked up speed, rising and falling nicely with the swell.

"Grand day to be at sea, eh?" Eric said.

The three men were standing on the afterdeck, a fine spray of sea and salt blowing through their hair. A swath of gold slashed the emerald water as the sun lifted above the horizon.

Garrett inhaled, relishing the sun on his face. "That damned cruise ship was getting a bit claustrophobic," he said. "Christ, it's good to be back."

Thick black coffee, rolls and croissants were served as the men grouped around a table. Eric picked up a roll and applied marmalade. Munching, he turned to Jans. "Tell us what's been going on."

"Aside from our normal complement of problems, we had one frightening situation," the Dutchman replied. "Four months ago we found salt water in several of the tanks. Scared the hell out of me, but it turned out to be a blessing."

Garrett's eyebrow lifted. "Salt water? You never cabled about that."

"No need." Jans sipped his coffee. "Turned out the problem

was confined to several outlying wells. For confirmation, I sank a dozen new holes in and around the area. Came up with nine producers. The other three gushed salt water. The good news was they were all located in the same small tract of land with the other problem wells." The Dutchman took out a cigar. "*Telega Said* is more prolific than ever." He fired a match. "But, you haven't heard the best."

Eric and Garrett leaned forward as the cutter rode an ocean swell.

"Word reached the Sultan that *Telega Said* was possibly compromised. A week after I'd completed the test wells the old boy arrived with a retinue that would shame the Queen's court." Jan's eyes held a hint of amusement. "He demanded I provide proof that we were capable of producing oil instead of water. Naturally, that required activating the pipeline. I was nervous I can tell you. Since our system hadn't been fully tested, a thousand things could have gone wrong. I told him it would be best to wait until after the two of you returned. Said you planned a celebration marking the arrival of his namesake, the *Sultan of Langkat*. I figured that would put the old boy off from any immediate demonstration." Jans paused to refill his cup.

"And?" Garrett said.

"The Sultan wouldn't have any of it. Official ceremonies could take place as scheduled, but he wanted a demonstration then. Nothing I could do but oblige."

"God's blood," Eric breathed.

"I assembled our crew, along with the Sultan and his retainers, and opened the valve," Jans said. "Even the jungle seemed to be waiting when I finished turning the wheel. I had to fight to keep my hands from shaking. The waiting was the hard part. Minutes passed and no oil. Meanwhile, the look on the Sultan's face was none too friendly. It was not a pleasant situation," Jans said drily, helping himself to a croissant.

"And...?" Garrett and Eric said at the same time.

"More time passes. Nothing. Furious, the Sultan starts to leave. He gets a dozen steps then the whole frigging earth begins shaking. Oil's roaring through the pipeline with the force of a monsoon. It was a beautiful sound." Jans smiled. "Everyone started cheering and throwing their hats in the air. We even raised the Sultan's banner and the Dutch flag."

Eric sighed. "Thank God."

A mischievous grin appeared on Jans face. "The Sultan called me aside and said he wanted me to visit his nephew, the Rajah of Perlak. Said the waters were covered with the same paraffin."

Garrett's excitement grew. "So, that's why the Sultan wanted the demonstration."

"Beside augmenting his oil revenues, the Sultan wants to help his nephew, who's got a native rebellion on his hands. Anyway, I took a crew up to Perlak, about eighty miles upriver, and snooped around a bit." Jans's face split into a wide grin. "It's another *Telega Said.* Perlak's floating on a sea of oil."

"Sweet Jesus," Garrett whistled. "Crown Petroleum just doubled in size."

"Fantastic news, Jans," Eric said. "Timing couldn't be better. Gasoline's the fuel of the future. In a few years it'll be a hundred times bigger market than lighting oil. We're going to need all the extra production capacity we can find."

Jans' smile was cautious. "Perlak has limitations. A pipeline will have to be laid through eighty miles of jungle. That won't be easy considering that the local inhabitants are bloody head-hunters. We'll need to import a boatload of coolies."

"Tong-Po can arrange for the best Chinese workers in Shanghai. One thing" --- Eric's jaw tightened --- "we pay them decently and provide proper food and housing. The additional wages will more than be made up in time and efficiency."

"It'll be worth it if Perlak turns out like *Telega Said,*" Garrett said. "We should have enough time to slip up and visit the Rajah before you head back to Shanghai."

Eric lit a cheroot. "That would be nice. Even better if we hammered out a formal agreement with him and the Sultan before I left." Standing, he fixed his gaze starboard. Greatly enjoying the wind, sea and salt, he could see the outline of Sumatra. The lush island rose out of the water like a hump-backed whale. Farther on, the green gave way to a sapphire sea and the sea to infinity.

It'll be good to get home, he thought. Home to Kate. What a job she and Tong-Po have done. We've got the best tankers, unlimited production, a refinery, warehouses, storage facilities and distribution. All within six months. Incredible. Everything is nicely in place.

Except, Bartrum will have heard about the tankers and Telega Said by now. What mischief will he be up to? And, don't forget, he reminded himself, Sutton and Rosenberg will be coming at us with a vengeance.

Bloody hell.

*   *   *

"YOU LOOK SMASHING," THE AUSTRALIAN DREDG-ING EXPERT, MORGAN Stanley said.

"Thank you, kind sir." Katheryn was wearing an emerald green gown with a single strand of pearls. Her hair was styled in the latest European fashion, falling in soft, golden ringlets over her shoulders.

Feeling a hundred pair of eyes on her, Katheryn took Stanley's arm. She guided him through the crowd gathered at the reception. Music lilted in the background. Out of the corner of her eye, Katheryn caught Lillian Havershire and Mary Pendleton following her movements.

Biddies discussing my scandalous behavior, Katheryn chuckled to herself.

Gerald Farnsworth was talking with Pierce Stafford near the orchestra when he saw Katheryn approaching. The Ambassador gave a short bow. "Mrs. Gradek. You look lovely."

Pierce Stafford moved forward quickly. "I echo the Ambassador's observation."

"Thank you, gentlemen," Katheryn said. "Meet my associate, Morgan Stanley." She gestured first to Farnsworth, then Stafford. "Our guest of honor, Ambassador Gerald Farnsworth. And this gentleman is Mr. Pierce Stafford, president of the Commonwealth-Shanghai Bank."

After handshakes, Katheryn turned to Stafford. "If you have a moment, there are a few matters I'd like to discuss."

Knowing he was being removed, Stafford glanced at Farnsworth and Stanley, already deep in conversation. Smiling wryly, the Banker said, "Of course, Katheryn. I fancy a chat with you over shop talk any day."

From the far side of the room, Andrew Pendleton nudged Ian Havershire as Katheryn accepted a glass of champagne from a liveried waiter. "Look at that. Champagne in public. Before long, she'll be wanting to join us for cigars and brandy."

Havershire twirled his mustache, eyeing Farnsworth and

Stanley. "Come now, Andrew. If nothing else, Katheryn's a breath of fresh air. I understand she's handled matters at Gradek Internationally splendidly while Eric's been away. Rumor has it she filed a bid for the dredging contract."

Pendleton sipped his brandy. "Balderdash. She may have filed a bid, but nothing will come of it. Bartrum & Sons have had the concession in their pocket for years along with our simpleton Harbormaster."

Havershire looked up just as Philip and Alex entered. "But, things always seem to have a way of changing, don't they? I dare say you've underestimated Gradek again. Fifty pounds says you're wrong."

Pendleton smiled and extended his hand. "It's your money, dear chap."

*   *   *

"PITY Eric couldn't be here for Farnsworth's reception," Stafford was saying. "When do you expect him back?"

Katheryn took a sip of champagne, enjoying the social ripples and raised eyebrows brought about by her drinking at a social gathering. "He should be returning within the week. Meanwhile, I'd like to have documents on the new warehouse drawn for his approval."

"I'll have my clerk start on them Monday." The bank president regarded Katheryn thoughtfully. "Your stewardship of Gradek International during Eric's absence has been quite remarkable. Most unusual to find a lady so skilled in business."

"Thank you, Pierce. I've had some fine people, including your good self, to help me along."

Stafford stifled his reply as Alex Bartrum walked up.

"Good evening, Pierce," Alex said, extending a hand. Facing Katheryn, he felt his heart twist. "Mrs. Gradek, you look positively stunning." Always captivated by her beauty, he found himself coveting her more now than ever. Katheryn would be standing by his side if Eric Gradek had not come along. The man's joss was undeserved and too much.

Katheryn examined her fan, moving it a trifle. "Good evening, Mr. Bartrum."

Philip appeared with a brandy in each hand. After handing one to Alex, he looked at Katheryn. "I understand Gradek International has put in a bid for the dredging concession."

"Not a bid, Mr. Bartrum. A renovation proposal."

Philip smiled thinly. "From what I understand, a very expensive proposal."

Katheryn's gaze passed from Philip to Alex, her eyes challenging. "Expensive, but necessary." She set her champagne glass on a passing waiter's tray. "Now, if you gentlemen will excuse me."

The three men's eyes followed Katheryn as she walked away. "Fascinating woman," Pierce Stafford remarked.

"Fascinating, but naive," Philip said. "The Harbormaster's office will never go along with her plan. The associated costs are prohibitive."

Stafford accepted a fresh brandy and smiled. "We'll find out soon enough, won't we?" The banker watched as Richard Franklin and Ambassador Farnsworth approached the podium.

Franklin tapped the lectern and the crowd quieted. "Ladies and gentlemen, as you know every five years our office awards the dredging concession on a bid basis. This year we are pleased to have His Majesty's Royal Trade Ambassador, Mr. Gerald Farnsworth, with us to present the award."

The crowd applauded politely. Franklin handed a bound document to Farnsworth. "And now Mr. Ambassador, if you will do the honors."

Farnsworth stepped forward, scanned the document, then closed it. "On behalf of His Majesty's Government, I'm pleased to say that a determination has been made to transform Shanghai's harbor into a deep water port. Increasing freight demands make this undertaking an imperative that current dredging operations cannot accomplish."

Franklin moved next to Farnsworth. "This is most inappropriate, Mr. Ambassador," he whispered. "The concession falls under the responsibility of my office."

A palpable silence descended over the room as the two men stared at one another.

"Quite right, Mr. Franklin," the Ambassador said loudly. "Under normal circumstances responsibility for the dredging concession falls under the jurisdiction of your office. But these are not normal circumstances, are they? I am forthwith relieving you of that responsibility."

Franklin gaped incredulously at the Ambassador. "There must be some kind of misunderstanding."

"No misunderstanding, Mr. Franklin. Your services are no longer required." Farnsworth turned back to the subdued audience. "The contract to convert Shanghai into a deep water port is hereby awarded to Gradek International."

Franklin's mouth opened as he stared at Farnsworth. Then the silence broke. Adair MacAlister let out a cheer and slapped Morgan Stanley on the back. Katheryn smiled, accepting congratulations from well-wishers. But her real satisfaction came from watching Alex and Philip Bartrum walk out, defeated.

* * *

AFTER a week long stay in Sumatra, Eric took the cutter back to Singapore. Garrett would follow within the month. Things had gone amazingly well during their absence. Pipeline and refinery systems were all working perfectly. Storage stills had been topped off and there was enough refined kerosene to fill Crown Petroleum's new tankers when they began arriving next week. More importantly, he and Garrett wrapped up the Perlak concession with the Sultan and his cousin, the Rajah. A major windfall. With the additional resources, Crown Petroleum's ability to challenge Trident Industries for dominance in Asia was enhanced. That was the good news. The bad news was a price would be exacted for their actions. There always was when one engaged in war, commercial or otherwise. And just what that price might be began to weigh heavily. As a precaution, security was doubled around the refinery and additional guards stationed at the drilling sites.

Eric stood at the bow, a cheroot clenched between his teeth. A brisk north wind was blowing over the choppy sea. The swell was deep and spray bathed the deck around him. Once he reached Singapore, he would sail on the evening tide for Shanghai. The thought ignited the now familiar ache. Kate. One more week and he would be home. *Seven days.* It felt like an eternity.

For the next hour Eric stared at the sea, his thoughts focused on the problems awaiting him. No question, there would still be obstacles to overcome, but nothing insurmountable. His one hope now was to make Jing-Jiang's dream a reality while there was still time for the old warlord to see it.

Eric looked up and watched the distant outline of Singapore

materialize out of a shroud of mist. Cumulus were forming along the horizon. Licking his finger, he tasted the wind. Precipitation, but no nimbus.

Only rain for now.

*   *   *

IN London the air was sunny, crisp and cold --- the city covered by a dome of blue sky. Baron Albert Rosenberg took advantage of the respite from fog and rain by strolling through Regent's Park.

Near King's Road he sat on an empty bench and lit a cigar. For some time he watched people moving along the streets. Most were walking, others rode in horse-drawn carriages --- a lucky few traveled by motorcar.

Ah, the motorcar.

This marvelous machine, with its internal combustion engine, had opened the door to making the world totally oil-dependent. Soon the world's gasoline markets would blossom. People would no longer walk through streets spotted with horse manure to reach destinations. Instead, they would drive. The Baron smiled. And, for a modest profit, Trident Industries would be there to provide them with the necessary petrol.

The future was vividly painted on the canvas in Baron Rosenberg's mind. Oil and its derivatives were about to become woven into the fabric of civilization. The *Industrial Revolution* was about to shift into high gear. And who would be there directing mankind's entry into the twentieth century? It was a thrilling thought to think that he and Percival D. Sutton would be standing at the helm of this great social transfiguration, ready to take their places in history.

The Baron sighed. Yes, the future looked as bright as the

blue skies. Wealth and power beckoned from beyond his wildest imagination. Motor-cars were allowing people to travel considerable distances, eliminating the need to live in the city. Land prices would rise as people moved away and new, outlying towns began popping up. That meant increased demand for building materials and, of course, there would have to be networks of petrol retail outlets along commuter routes. Other opportunities in industries such as railroads and banking abounded, as well.

Opportunities ripe for taking, the patriarch of Europe's most powerful family thought, each built upon another into a veritable chain of profits.

But, the Baron reminded himself that twenty tankers had passed through the Suez canal and were steaming toward Asian ports. *Trident Industries versus Crown Petroleum,* he thought. Classic David and Goliath, wasn't it? Except, on that occasion, the giant had lost.

Baron Rosenberg shivered. It was getting colder, obliging him to sink deeper into his overcoat. He and Sutton were engaged in a dangerous game: regardless of the outcome, there were risks. If they succeeded in destroying Garrett Botha and Eric Gradek, powerful enemies like Queen Wilhelmina and her foreign ambassador, Janvillem van de Botha, would be made. Two people the Baron would rather have on the friendship side of the ledger. Then again, failure to destroy Crown Petroleum would be perceived by opportunists as weakness. And a chink in the armor of Trident Industries was something they could ill-afford. Already there were ominous rumblings from wildcatters out of Texas and Oklahoma, plus the Czar Nicholas' government was teetering. There were other problems as well. Clay Shipyards' refusal to sell them their new oil-powered tanker limited Trident's capacity to efficiently move product from one port to another. The list of possible pitfalls went on and on. And the more the Baron contemplated the matter the more he felt like it was he with his finger in the dike.

A horse drawn carriage moved against the curb as a motor-car clattered by. In retrospect, it was easy to see the mistake in allowing Alex Bartrum to fire Garrett Botha. It had been a decision that he and Sutton had opposed. Nevertheless, they had acquiesced to the Bartrum brothers because Asia was their sphere of influence. Hardly an acceptable excuse. No question, he and Percy had been fools. If Garrett Botha instead of Alex Bartrum was still on board, Trident wouldn't be in the muck. The Sumatran oil concessions would be under Trident's control, along with the monopoly on Clay Shipyards' new large tankers.

If...?

The Baron heaved himself off the bench. There was nothing to be done about it now, was there? Flicking a speck of dust from his lapel, he started back through the park. All told, it had been a bloody rotten day to have taken a walk in the first place.

Twenty-two

A T THE BOTHA'S HOUSE, MARIANNA WAS pleading with her amah. "Tell sleepy me another story, Ah-Ping. I'm not sleepy. *Pleeese,* just one more."

The amah fluffed Marianna's pillows. "*Eeeee,* go on with you, little missee. Mistress Botha will send your old mother to the streets if you not in bed on time." Ah-Ping was the half-sister of Ah-Sook, Katheryn's amah, and had been with the Bothas since they arrived in Shanghai. With the work associated with the new house and a new baby due in three months, Jacqueline considered Ah-Ping a godsend.

"One more story and then I'll go to sleep." Marianna's doe-like eyes danced, sensing victory.

Ah-Ping glanced at the clock on the table. Five minutes until ten. Her bones were aching after a long day. *Well, perhaps one more tale for little empress,* the old woman thought. "Is that promise, little missee?"

Marianna beamed. "Promise." She crooked her little finger and locked it with Ah-Ping's.

Ah-Ping dimmed the oil lamp. "Very well," she said, loving the child greatly. "One more, then it's off to bed with you."

* * *

JACQUELINE was in the bedroom preparing to put on her nightgown when the clock chimed a tenth time. Laying her clothes on the bed, she studied her body in the mirror. The reflection was not unkind. She radiated that special kind of beauty only a woman with child can possess. Her eyes strayed to her breasts, which were full and hard. Cupping them, she felt the dull ache caused by added weight. Even so, it was a sensation she rather enjoyed. Next, she focused on her rounded stomach, which was hard to the touch. She smiled. "Now where was it that my belly-button used to be?" She examined herself in profile. No stretch marks or unsightly veins.

Jacqueline tilted her head in coquettish fashion. *All in all, good for six months along.*

Donning her nightgown, Jacqueline sat at the vanity and began brushing her black hair.

Upstairs, Ah-Ping extinguished the oil lamp and tucked Marianna in for the night.

* * *

AIDED by low clouds, Mr. Jones, Dragon Mok and a half dozen Red Pang soldiers converged on Jacqueline's house. By ten fifteen the three guards posted by Watchman Choy to protect Jacqueline and Marianne were dead. Two died by garrote, the third from a knife. This last victim did not go easily, and managed to carve a three inch gash along Dragon Mok's left shoulder.

Minutes later a crash followed by sounds of shattering glass froze Jacqueline at her vanity seat. A second later she realized the back door had been forcibly broken open.

Dear God. Marianne.

Dropping her brush, Jacqueline rushed out of the bedroom and into the arms of a nightmare.

"Going somewhere, Mrs. Botha?" Mr. Jones said. "We was hoping you might invite us in for a spot of tea."

Jacqueline desperately fought to escape, but the giant's grip played with her.

"Come now, Mrs. Botha --- is that a proper way to be treating your house guest?"

"*Wh* --- what's the meaning of this intrusion? You've no right to be barging --- "

Mok held a bandanna on his bleeding shoulder. "Enough talk. Stick the cow and be done with it."

Jacqueline stared at the stocky Chinese. *Stick the cow and be done with it.* They were going to kill her. *Dear God in Heaven.* She looked beyond Mok to the two Red soldiers at the front door. Others would be stationed in the back. Trapped. But she had to get Marianne to safety. "I've done you no harm," she said quietly, forcing down her fear. "Take whatever you want and go."

"Don't mind if I do, Mrs. Botha." Jones' eyes moved to her breasts. Jacqueline's gown was ripped away.

"Please don't, I'm pregnant," she said, using her only weapons of calm, reason and decency. Jacqueline tried to cover herself.

Jones laughed. "That little condition won't stand in the way."

Mok barked, grabbed Jones's wrist. "Fool. Have you no eyes? I'm bleeding like a stuck pig!"

Jones knew that Mok was right, but he had crossed the threshold. His eyes plundered Jacqueline's pregnant body. She was incredibly beautiful, especially with her domed stomach. Just like his sister had looked all those years ago.

Mok's grip tightened. "Finish her now."

"Button up Chinaman. First I'm gonna have my way with this creamy skinned woman. Look at that skin, just look at it."

Lifting his fighting hatchet, Mok advanced towards Jacqueline. "If you won't finish her, I will."

Jones' knife appeared in his right hand. "Another step and you're a dead man.'

Jacqueline's mind disintegrated. Screaming, she bit Jones' wrist and tore off a piece of flesh. The blood was warm in her mouth.

"Godcursed bitch!" Jones hilted his knife in her stomach and ripped upwards.

Just before the darkness, Jacqueline stared into his grotesque face. At least she had denied him what he wanted.

*   *   *

AWAKENED by Jacqueline's screams, Ah-Ping rushed from her room and found Marianne on the landing by the stairway. The child's eyes were bright with fear. Her tiny hands gripped the stairway dowels.

Ah-Ping peered over the railing. Jacqueline lay in a ripped, bloody nightgown, her eyes open but unseeing. Many times Ah-Ping had looked into such eyes that peered back from the next realm. A barbarian giant and a squat Chinese stood over Jacqueline but they did not see Ah-Ping.

Ah-Ping sank to the floor. Terrified, she saw Marianne was about to scream. She clamped her hand around the child's mouth and trapped the sound. Then, she carried Marianne to the attic and bolted the door.

Enveloped by darkness, Ah-Ping rocked the strickened child back and forth as the tiny mouth fought her hand.

*   *   *

IN Sumatra, Wu-Fat's junk fleet of three hundred pirates entered the Balaban River from the Strait of Malacca. All were heavily armed and dressed in black pantaloons and shirts. Sails filled by a leisurely wind, the fleet would reach the refinery at *Telega Said* around midnight. From there Wu-Fat would divide his men into two assault forces. One group would attack the refinery and general offices, while the other concentrated on the wells and housing quarters. The pirate leader had decided to command the first group himself, while his most trusted lieutenant, Li-Pung, would lead the second.

*   *   *

JUST before midnight two men darted out of the jungle and across the open space that led to *Telega Said's* production area. Their faces, darkened with sepia dye, were streaked by perspiration when they reached the well site. One of the men shoved a packet of dynamite beneath a wooden joist, while the other cupped a match and lit the fuse. They sprinted back to the jungle. Moments later, the explosion shook the earth. Gobbits of wood, metal, and fire arced skyward as the frame around the well disintegrated.

The Sumatran night blossomed with flame.

Wu-Fat's pirate band was now attacking workers around the well sites and refinery area.

Gunshots, coming in ragged volleys, carombed against billowing flames when Garrett ran out of his bungalow. He grabbed a nearby man. "Help get weapons passed around." The man raced off, but fell to a pirate bullet. Drawing his revolver, Garrett sidestepped a cutlass wielding pirate and shot him between the eyes. Jans cut down another attacker at Garrett's back with a knife to the heart.

"Jans, get over to the wells," Garrett shouted. "I'll handle things here."

The Dutchman raced off.

More explosions. Garrett whirled to see the supply depot and offices consumed by flame. "God's blood!"

The smoke and fumes were suffocating, but the fires enabled defenders to see the pirates. From tower platforms Garrett's men began picking them off. By the time Jans arrived the surviving pirates had scattered back into the jungle. Several were wounded, writhing on the ground. Among them was Wu-Fat's chief lieutenant, Li-Pung.

Garrett's shot fragmented the skull of a pirate placing a charge against the pipeline, but not before the fuse was lit. Falling, the pirate landed on top of the charge and disappeared in the blast. Sounds of twisting metal. Garrett knew the pipeline was damaged. Defenders gathered at the refinery repulsing attack after attack until the ground was littered with dead and wounded pirates.

Silence fell, save for low moans from bloodied shapes

Garrett went to examine the damage to the pipeline. His heart sank at the sight of twisted metal. An entire section obliterated. It would take months to fix. And their tankers were on the water.

Shit.

Sensing another presence, Garrett whirled and found himself staring into the face of Wu-Fat.

"Barbarian dog." The pirate plunged his knife into Garrett's belly.

Only a brief burning pain, then numbness. Garrett sank to the ground.

*   *   *

AT KATHERYN'S HOUSE AH-SOOK RUSHED UP THE STAIRS into the bedroom and awakened her. "MISSEE, you come quick."

Katheryn's eyes opened, glazed from sleep. "What is it?"

"Plenty big trouble. Ah-Ping is downstairs with Marianne."

Katheryn struggled upright, shoving aside bedclothes. "The baby? Mrs. Jacqueline?"

Ah-Sook's face was a mask of pain. "Please, you hurry."

Katheryn put on her robe and hurried downstairs. Watchman Choy and several guards were standing around a sobbing Ah-Ping. Marianne trembled inside a blanket, staring at nothing.

"What happened?" Katheryn said.

"Missee deaded," Ah-Ping cried. "She deaded."

Katheryn knelt beside Ah-Ping and took Marianne into her arms. "What do you mean, Missee deaded?"

"Men come and....." Unable to continue, Ah-Ping fainted.

Katheryn shook Ah-Ping's shoulder. Nothing.

Damnit, think, she told herself. Don't give in to the fear.

Katheryn got up and handed Marianne to Ah-Sook. "Take care of her. Perhaps some warm milk and a bath will help." Then she turned to Watchman Choy. "Get some men ready. You're going to take me to Mrs. Jacqueline's house."

Choy gaped at Katheryn. "Missee, far too dangerous. Best for you to wait here."

Katheryn was already on her way upstairs to change. "I said get some men ready. Have them here by the time I return."

* * *

IT was one in the morning when Katheryn reached Jacqueline's darkened house. "Choy, go inside and light the lamps."

A few minutes later Choy returned and blocked the door. "Missee, you please stay away. *Weeery* bad here."

Katheryn fought down the first thin edge of hysteria. "Step aside Choy, I have to go in." She entered the house and felt a part of herself die. Disemboweled and naked, Jacqueline now lay in a pool of blood on the floor. Katheryn grasp a table, doubled over and retched. "Choy," she managed. "Choy."

Watchman Choy stepped in front of her. "Missee, no good for you to see."

"Out of my way." Katheryn shoved at him. "I've got to cover Mrs. Jacqueline."

Choy stepped aside.

Katheryn took several steps and froze. The baby's small head was protruding from Jacqueline's open womb. The sight branded itself on Katheryn's soul. *Dear Father in Heaven.....* Sinking to her knees, Katheryn crawled over to Jacqueline's body and covered it with the torn nightgown.

Watchman Choy touched her shoulder. "Missee, you come with me. This place no good."

Katheryn stared at her bloody hands. She had just been baptized into the world of man. *What kind of fiend could commit such an act?* But, she knew who was responsible for this baptism. There could be only one, for not even his brother, Philip, could have wrought this. The image of Alex Bartrum appeared behind her eyes.

With an icy calm, Katheryn got up. She walked over to the desk and inked out a note. "Send a man round to fetch Tong-Po, then take this paper to my father."

*   *   *

AFTER seeing that Jacqueline's body was properly attended, Katheryn went upstairs to Marianne's room. The bed was unmade, a stuffed bear with a red ribbon around its neck lay on the pillow. Katheryn went to the window and stared down at the dark courtyard. She could see Tong-Po, in the shadows, issuing instructions to the men. She turned, her eyes taking in the room.

A child's room, with Jacqueline's loving touches everywhere.

Toys, books, drawings and stuffed animals filled the shelves. Katheryn sat on the bed and picked up the bear. A small envelope was tucked beneath the bear's arm.

Katheryn opened the envelope and removed the card.

For my little princess.

I love you,

Daddy.

Katheryn slipped the card back inside and stared at the darkness outside the window. There were no tears. They would come later. Or never.

Twenty-three

TONG-PO WAITED FOR ERIC'S SHIP FROM Singapore to dock. Dozens of guards milled inconspicuously in the crowds. Still, he was very uneasy. The quay was a madhouse. Workers in tattered pants rolled up to their knees scurried about unloading crates and foodstuffs. Barked orders by overseers mingled with the din of street-sellers hawking their wares.

The dwarf patted the derringer inside his sash. Thanks to Formidable Fung he was now a proficient shot at close range. Tong-Po had his driver park where he could study the crowd. Coolies and vendors swarmed. Everything appeared normal, but somewhere out there a Lotus Tong assassin was waiting to strike Eric down.

Eric emerged from customs, the look on Tong-Po's face telling him there was serious trouble. "What's the problem, old friend?"

"We have suffered great misfortune, Taipan."

Eric's eyes flashed. "Nothing to do with Katheryn or Jing-Jiang, I trust?"

"Not to worry --- *tai tai* and Jing-Jiang are in good health," Tong-Po replied. "Too many eyes and ears here to discuss our problems. We go to my house, then talk."

Eric stared at Tong-Po. "It will have to be quick. I'm anxious to see Katheryn."

Tong-Po signaled for the porters to get the baggage loaded.

Eric waited silently, his tension building, as the smells and sounds of Shanghai washed over him. For the moment, he was greatly relieved the problems did not involve Katheryn or Jing-Jiang.

Tong-Po pointed to a waiting sedan chair. "This way, Taipan."

* * *

KWOK-YU'S number three son burst into his office. "Father, the Opal Eye Devil is back in Shanghai. He arrived on the morning ship from Singapore."

The Beggar King's stomach twisted. Despite his generous financial offering to the Lotus Tong, he had been unable to persuade the dragonhead to cancel Alex Bartrum's contract on Eric Gradek. Making matters worse was contending with Formidable Fung if the Opal Eye Devil died. The mere thought of how Formidable Fung and Tong-Po had very nearly robbed him of his manhood caused his secret sac to shrivel.

Kwok-yu glared at his son. "Fornicate unnaturally all dwarfs and foreign devils with opal eyes. I have wasted enough gold on this barbarian to last ten lifetimes. And still the gods decree that I must protect his miserable life." Coughing up phlegm, he spat into a nearby basket. "Put out a message that he is to be watched at all times. If so much as one hair on his head is misplaced there will be much pain."

*   *   *

ERIC accepted a brandy and stared at Tong-Po, waiting.

The dwarf handed him a decoded cable from Jans Kessler. He would not tell Eric about the Lotus Tong until after Formidable Fung arrived.

Eric unrolled the paper.

Dear Eric: With the deepest sense of personal loss and sorrow, I must inform you that Garrett has been killed by pirates led by Wu-Fat. I shall miss him greatly as he was my friend and one of the best men I have ever known.

We were attacked early morning by a substantial force and suffered many casualties. As a consequence, Telega Said has been rendered inoperable. A section of our pipeline and a number of drilling sites were damaged by dynamite. After receiving the necessary supplies, I estimate it will require a minimum of three months to repair. Another problem is our tankers will begin arriving next week. What shall I instruct them to do since they cannot be loaded in the foreseeable future?

Li-Pung, Wu-Fat's chief lieutenant, was captured. He is badly wounded, but should recover. I will question him about this attack and the motives behind it. If he harbors information it will soon be ours.

Please express my heartfelt sympathy when you notify Garrett's wife and father. Until then I shall await your instructions. Yours faithfully, Jans Kessler.

Eric stared at the cable. "Garrett's dead." After a long

silence, he turned to Tong-Po. "I'll have to tell Jacqueline straight-a-way. No telling how this will effect her pregnancy. And, dear God, what about Marianne...?"

Tong-Po laid his hand on Eric's arm. "Garrett's *tai tai* is dead, Taipan. Murdered the same night as the pirate attack."

Eric's insides coiled, but his outer calm was frightening. "Who did it?"

Tong-Po retreated under Eric's opal stare. "Ah-Ping was upstairs with Marianne. She did not see their faces, but from her description we can assume it was Jones and Mok. Marianne saw the murder." Tong-Po's eyes closed. "Ever since, she has locked herself into a world of silence."

"I see." Eric walked over to the decanter and filled his glass, breaking his predatory spell. He stared out the window at nothing, his sadness absolute. Only killing Alex Bartrum could assuage it.

*   *   *

FORMIDABLE Fung arrived and told Eric about Alex Bartrum's meeting with the Lotus Tong. "This is not a matter to be taken lightly, Taipan," Fung said. "It is essential you not go anywhere unless heavily guarded."

"I agree, Taipan," Tong-Po said. "Lotus Tong assassins are highly skilled."

Eric's eyes hardened. "I'll not conduct my business surrounded by guards." With that, he turned and walked outside to the waiting rickshaw. The fact that he had been marked for death was pushed aside. His sole concern now was for the safety of Katheryn and Marianne. They must be protected at all costs until he faced Bartrum.

*   *   *

BEFORE going home, Eric stopped to cable Ambassador Botha and Jans Kessler. After sending the messages, he returned to the rickshaw and gave the runner directions to his house.

Along the Bund people were crowded into rows of stalls to purchase food and wares. Many stood with their bowls and chopsticks, shoveling rice into their anxious mouths. The eternal cries of China welled in Eric's head, numbing him further.

Many eyes followed Eric's progress home. Jing-Jiang's men and soldiers of Formidable Fung's Green Pang blended with the crowds. There were scores of Kwok-yu's beggars, lepers and other untouchables charged with protecting the Opal Eye Devil. And there was another pair of eyes watching Eric's rickshaw pass. They belonged to a man whose left arm bore the tattoo of a lotus unfurling.

Eric forced his mind to work. Crown Petroleum was out of business. Without refined kerosene to load his tankers there would be no money to pay for them, much less to repair the damage done to the pipeline and drilling sites. Mikolits would cancel their financing the moment he learned about the attack on *Telega Said.* Crown Petroleum and Jing-Jiang's dream for a better China were in a rubble heap.

And then there was Bartrum.

*   *   *

KATHERYN was in their bedroom when Eric arrived. The drapes had been drawn, casting her profile in relief.

"Kate?"

Then she was across the room and in his arms, clinging to

him in despairing silence. "Jacqueline has been --- "

"Shhh, I know, sweetheart," Eric whispered. He wanted to wrap her in his arms forever, but she needed to hear the rest of the horror. To delay telling her would make the shock worse. Gently, he pushed her back and looked into her eyes. "They killed Garrett as well."

*　　*　　*

ALEX Bartrum walked into Philip's office. "He's back."

Philip looked up. "When did he arrive?"

"This morning, on the Singapore ship." Alex poured a brandy. "Within the week he'll be out of our hair forever."

"We'll be suspected if Gradek dies right after he gets back."

Alex smiled. "Suspicion is one thing --- proving it is quite another. We will have solid alibis. The only thing for certain is Garrett Botha was the unfortunate victim of a pirate attack. On the same night, his poor wife was murdered by a killer while her house was being robbed. All terribly tragic, but not the least bit related. Bad joss wouldn't you say?"

"When Gradek dies there will be trouble," Philip said uneasily.

Alex took a drink. "Nonsense. When Gradek's body is discovered it will look like the work of the Green Pang. Rumors will be circulated that he and Fung are having at it over opium money. Katheryn's father, Sir Geoffrey, will have no choice but to send the army after Fung." Alex snapped his fingers. "Poof, all of our problems will be removed."

*　　*　　*

THE water was very hot when Katheryn and Eric stepped

inside the bathhouse. Overwhelming need had engulfed them earlier in a frantic love-making session, some primal affirmation of life. Now they were sated, their souls healing. Slipping off their robes, they sank into the steaming water. As the heat took them, neither could know that Eric's seed had been planted. The child Katheryn so desperately wanted was now growing in her womb.

Eric studied his wife through half-closed eyes. Katheryn had changed since he'd been gone. *Much stronger.* But there was a ghostly countenance about her. The horror of that night would have a lasting effect. In what ways he could not say, but she was possessed by an eerie calmness and it troubled him.

"He must die for what he's done," Katheryn said softly.

"That he does. Philip, Jones and Mok as well."

Katheryn stared across the tub. "They all must die, but you don't have to be the executioner. Let the authorities handle it. Father says --- "

"The authorities can't handle it." Eric watched her. "Ah-Ping saw the backs of the killers, not their faces. Her description fits Jones and Mok, but without positive identification the authorities won't pick them up. And they'll not touch the Bartrums. Alex and Philip were on board a ship coming from Hong Kong when it happened."

"I don't want to lose you." The hardness in Katheryn's eyes matched his. "There's already been more than a lifetime of suffering."

Eric moved through the water and took her hands. "Kate, you can bet Bartrum's got plans for us as well. We can't stay in here forever. Besides, this is something I have to do. Someone's got to stop that black-hearted bastard."

244

"But it's more than that, isn't it, darling?"

"More?"

"The Northern Star. That seventeen year old boy from another lifetime so long ago?"

Eric was quiet for a long time. Finally, he said, "If I don't try, I'll never be able to look Marianne in the eyes again, nor remember Garrett and Jacqueline with any sense of honor, or what is right."

Katheryn saw the fire in Eric's eyes. She touched his cheek. "Just swear that you'll keep Watchman Choy nearby."

Eric took her in his arms. "I swear." And for the first time, he contemplated the Lotus Tong assassin stalking him.

* * *

MARIANNE was sitting by the window looking at the moon when Eric and Katheryn returned from the bathhouse. Images of her parents floated in the air, speaking to her. She moved her lips to say something, but no words would come. Marianne wanted to cry, but there were no more tears. She sat in the silence, her terror locked away in some dark hole in her mind.

Twenty-four

"DREADFUL NEWS ABOUT JACQUELINE AND Garrett. Terrible that such fine, vibrant people be cut down in the prime of their lives." Franz Mikolits shook his head. "I pray the responsible parties are brought to justice."

"The guilty will pay, but it is small compensation for the loss," Ambassador Botha said. "But for now, I must serve my son's interests." He slid a document across the desk. "The damage report from *Telega Said*."

Mikolits scanned the paper. *Telega Said* was shut down --- out of business. At best, it would be three months before the refinery could be operational. That meant Crown Petroleum would be unable to make payments on the tanker fleet the Banque de Swisse Credit had leased to them. But that didn't particulary bother Mikolits. Kaiser Wilhelm's government was ready to pay a premium for the prized fleet. The bank's profit would be doubled. Putting the paper aside, Mikolits looked up.

"Terrible what these pirates have done."

"Many people died." Ambassador Botha steepled his fingers, working the problem. "We are told three months, perhaps longer, to get *Telega Said* back into operation. That is a long time for the world's most expensive tanker fleet to languish."

Mikolits nodded. "Too long, I'm afraid. It will be difficult for Mr. Gradek to meet his obligations." The banker's palm turned up. "Banque de Swisse Credit has millions of francs invested."

"True," Ambassador Botha acknowledged. "You have been steadfast in your friendship, Franz. Now I'm afraid it will be necessary for you to temporarily wave Crown Petroleum's payments and extend additional financing to cover repair costs associated with *Telega Said.*"

"I would be delighted to be of service." Mikolits' smile was benign. "Provided Mr. Gradek is able to meet current obligations and collateralize additional loans. However" --- he lifted a slim forefinger --- "if memory serves, Crown Petroleum's asset base is inadequate to cover existing notes, much less increased financing. I'm afraid without oil from *Telega Said* to fill their tankers Crown Petroleum is dead."

The Ambassador watched him across steepled fingers. "That is your position?"

Mikolits nodded. "I wish there were another way."

"I wish there were another way as well, Franz." Ambassador Botha looked at the Banker. "If you withdraw financing from my son's company then I will be forced to initiate actions against you and the Banque de Swisse Credit." .

Mikolits removed his wire-rim glasses. Janvillem was one of Europe's most powerful men, and not a person given to making idle threats. But what action could he take? Outside of the

Telega Said oil concession which was shut down, the only value was the tanker fleet. And the Banque de Swisse Credit held the paper. The banker's eyes met the Ambassador's. "If Crown Petroleum can produce assets to back up additional loans my bank will be accommodating. But, without assets......"

"Certain friends in the diplomatic community have informed me about your intentions to sell tankers and technology to Prussia. Perhaps you are planning to sell my son's fleet to Kaiser Wilhelm to further his demented dreams of power, yes?" The Ambassador leaned forward. "Aside from the inbred idiot Hapsburgs of Austria, there are few governments who want Europe turned into a graveyard. Any individual, institution or government directly or indirectly assisting Wilhelm to succeed in that effort would be viewed by the rest of the world most unfavorably."

Mikolits' blood chilled. How could the Ambassador know about his discussions with the Prussian Government? But that didn't really matter now, did it? He was clearly threatening Switzerland with diplomatic reprisals because of his actions. Still, there was the possibility that Janvillem was bluffing. "I am Swiss and quite beyond the internal politics of others."

"I need little reminding of your neutrality, Herr Mikolits. But, be advised not to take my words lightly. It would not be considered a neutral act if you sold tankers and technology to a country that would use them for purposes of war." Ambassador Botha regarded Mikolits disdainfully. "However, the purpose of my visit is not to apply political pressure, it is to insure the continued financing of Crown Petroleum. *Telega Said's* reserves should be sufficient collateral for any financing needs, I should think."

Mikolits gaped at the frail diplomat. "Reserves! Surely, you jest. Unrefined oil beneath the earth's surface that may or may not see the light of day is not collateral. Give me gold or something tangible to hold on to, then we can talk. Meanwhile, I expect Crown Petroleum to make their lease payments on a timely basis or I shall --- "

"You've made your point, Herr Mikolits," the Ambassador interrupted. "Now I shall make mine. The tanker fleet you're leasing Crown Petroleum is worth double what you've extended. I'm certain your Prussian bedmates have indicated they would pay such an amount, or more. But before that transaction can take place it will be necessary for you to take possession of the fleet. A fleet currently on the other side of the world in Dutch territory." Janvillem smiled an icy smile. "The weather in Sumatra is unpredictable this time of the year. I trust you're fully insured?"

A vein began pulsing on Mikolits's right temple. "What exactly are you implying, Janvillem?"

"My dear fellow, I'm merely saying that disaster is all around us. Perhaps the weather, or unforeseen mechanical malfunction, or another pirate attack will send your tankers to the bottom of the sea." Janvillem shrugged. "Who can say? We live in troublesome times, yes? If such a catastrophe occurred, Prussia would not get their tankers. And, from what I understand, Kaiser Wilhelm is an unforgiving sort." The Ambassador stared across the desk. "On the other hand, if diplomatic representatives from governments opposed to Prussian expansionism were to learn that you had planned to assist a man they consider to be an international criminal......."

Mikolits thought it through. Experience taught him every situation had a negative and positive side. Obviously, Janvillem was serious about sinking the fleet. That left him little negotiating room. His Prussian trump card would be rusting on the ocean floor. More disturbing, Janvillem would see Switzerland denounced by the international community because of his collaboration with the Kaiser's government. And, if Switzerland were ostracized, the stage would be set for the Prussian army to invade. That was the bad news. The good news was that the Ambassador needed him for *Telega Said* to succeed. In truth, oil reserves ranked right up there with bullion as collateral. There were world markets for both commodities, making them easily disposable. The only problem was that oil couldn't be stored in a bank vault. But, it could be stored in underground repositories. The bank could turn its collateral into cash as it was drawn upon and sold. With luck, Mikolits might persuade Janvillem to get Queen Wilhelmina's government to guarantee his legal access to the reserves. That would portray him as a friend to governments nervous about Prussian saber rattling. At the same time, he could quietly approach Clay Shipyards about providing the Kaiser with modern tankers. If Clay refused --- well, it would not be because he had not tried. Switzerland's neutral relationship with Prussia would not be compromised. Matters could be a lot worse.

Still, it was a bitter pill knowing Janvillem had played him so well.

"Franz," the Ambassador said, "this petty bickering is not for us. I'm merely suggesting you reconsider using the reserves as additional collateral. Oil is about to transform the world and become an irresistible force unto itself. Mankind will become dependent on it. On that point we are in total agreement, yes? And as this new change is ushered in there will be a great deal of money to be had. More than we ever dreamed of making with *Telega Said.* Would you be interested in my telling you how?"

Mikolits leaned forward.

*   *   *

ERIC FINISHED HIS BRANDY AND STARED AT THE
FIRE. A SHOWER OF orange sparks erupted from the fresh
logs. It was past midnight and the house was quiet. Since
returning from Sumatra, he had isolated himself at home, leaving day to day operations to Tong-Po and Adair MacAlister.
His world was disintegrating and he needed to get a grip on it.

Closing his eyes to the crackling fire, grief doubled back on
him. Hatred and guilt were the only emotions left. Garrett and
Jacqueline murdered; Katheryn and Marianne traumatized;
Crown Petroleum out of business; Jing-Jiang's dream shredded.
All because of the grim life's game he played with Alex
Bartrum. There was now a bloodscape of ruined lives.

Complicating matters was the emotional damage done to
Marianne. The child, withdrawn and silent, was cloistered
away somewhere in her mind. And then there was Katheryn.
She was very pale, and until earlier that evening possessed with
that eerie calm he found so unnerving. Eric's concern for her
safety had become so great that he'd given her a small caliber
handgun.

"Tomorrow, Watchman Choy is going to teach you how to
use this. I want it with you at all times until I've dealt with
Bartrum and Jones. If someone so much as blinks the wrong
way, shoot first and devil the consequences. I'll not have the
same thing happening to you as did Jacqueline."

Katheryn accepted the gun, cradling it in her palm. Looking
at him, she said, "I would relish being the one to take their

251

lives."

Eric had been stunned. "What did you say?"

"Don't look so shocked," Katheryn said. "I said I'd enjoy killing them. Their kind of evil is beyond my capacity to forgive. I saw Jacqueline and her unborn child. It was a scene too awful to describe, even though I can see every detail quite clearly." Katheryn began shaking. "Dear God, look what they've done to our lives. And we've become just like them."

Eric reached for her. Katheryn's body trembled against him and Eric cursed Alex Bartrum for grubbing his dirty hands across the soul of the woman he loved. He opened his mouth to speak, to provide soothing words, but thought better of it. Words at this point would be useless. But he was worried at her changes: in the bath she had talked of the authorities, now she was ready to kill. She was becoming unstable.

The logs in the fire hissed, heralding another shower of orange sparks. Eric poured another brandy. Katheryn was not going to be able to hold on much longer. Not with Alex Bartrum strutting about unscathed, untouched. Safe. So, how was he going to deal with him? Officially, Bartrum wasn't a suspect. If Eric killed him he would be the one at the end of a hangman's rope. The best way would be to bait him in front of witnesses. Force Bartrum to openly challenge him. *But where, and when?*

The fire crackled and a plan began to form. Eric sipped his brandy. Thus far the game was being played according to Bartrum's rules. He had initiated the assault. Well, that was about to change.

Sensing he was not alone, Eric turned from the fireplace and found Marianne standing in the doorway. Exuding the silent serenity of one who had witnessed the unspeakable, Marianne was so still she could have been a doll.

Eric extended his hand. "Come here child."

Watching the small figure pad noiselessly across the room, Eric wondered if the light of a happy little girl would ever appear in her eyes again. Then she was in his lap with his arms wrapped around her, protecting her. Loving her greatly, he cradled her head on his chest. "No one will ever harm you again, lass. I promise."

*   *   *

AMBASSADOR Janvillem Botha arrived in London three days after meeting with Franz Mikolits. He was now seated on a divan in Baron Rosenberg's office. The Dutch Ambassador had just finished having lunch with Baron Rosenberg and Percival D. Sutton. It had been an unpleasant affair --- one where he'd been obliged to endure a litany of condolences over the deaths of Garrett and Jacqueline. It had been daunting for him to mask his hatred, convinced as he was that they were culpable parties in his son's death. The fact that he was unable to prove their complicity only heightened his hatred.

"Cigar?" The Baron offered a humidor.

"Yes. Thank you." Janvillem selected a fine Havana and let his diplomat side take control. After lighting the cigar, he let his gaze pass from Baron Rosenberg to Percival D. Sutton. No discernible emotion on their faces as they stared back at him. Not that Janvillem had expected any. After all, he was dealing with a pair of elite predators.

"I understand twenty of your tankers are on their way to Asia," Janvillem said. "Quite a coincidence that such a vast quantity of oil would be on the water at the same time my son's field was razed."

Sutton smiled. "Not a coincidence, Janvillem. A calculated business decision to protect our interests in the event Crown Petroleum had notions of engaging us in a price war."

Ambassador Botha puffed on his cigar. "There will be no price war if you pull out of Asia immediately and agree to certain other concessions."

"Really?" Baron Rosenberg's gaze was bland. "Why should we pull out of Asia, much less agree to concessions?"

"Janvillem, your logic is a bit hard to follow," Sutton added. "There can be no price war when the field in Sumatra is not operative. Trident Industries is the only supplier capable of servicing the Asian market."

The Ambassador cast the two men the kind of withering look teachers reserve for inept students. "The damage caused by the pirate attack will be repaired within a matter of months, a mere ninty days," he replied. "In the short run, you might supply Asia with oil, but that situation will change. Despite efforts by your pirate mercenaries they only inflicted minor damage to the pipeline. The refinery and drilling sites remained largely intact."

Sutton's jaw tightened. "That accusation is slanderous and ill-advised."

Janvillem put his cigar in the ashtray. "Is it?" He took a cable from his pocket that Eric had sent the previous day and placed it in front of Sutton. "Fortunately, the pirates suffered losses in Sumatra as well. Wu-Fat's second in command was captured. A despicable character named Li-Pung. He confessed. I suggest you read what he had to say."

Sutton picked the cable up and read the details of Wu-Fat's meeting with Alex Bartrum in Singapore. He stared at the

Ambassador. "Why should I put any faith in the insane babbling of some Chinese cutthroat? A man who probably confessed under torture." Sutton passed the paper to Baron
Rosenberg.

After the Baron finished reading, he put a hand on Sutton's
arm. "You've touched a nerve here, Janvillem. The truth is this
document might be accurate. It's possible Alex Bartrum
entered into an alliance with this pirate, Wu-Fat. I wouldn't put
anything past the man. However"--- the Baron lifted a finger -
-- "we are innocent of complicity. When Percy and I received
word about these monstrous acts we severed our relationship
with Bartrum & Sons. As of yesterday, the Bartrums are no
longer part of Trident Industries. Cables have already been sent
to the *London Times and Economist.* We're sitting on the same
side of the fence on this issue."

"Since you've disassociated yourselves with Bartrum &
Sons, I'm certain you'd have no objection selling the oil currently en route to Asia to Crown Petroleum." The Ambassador
frowned thoughtfully. "Say thirty percent below market."

Sutton stared at the aging diplomat. "What you're suggesting is preposterous. If anything there's currently a shortage of
oil in Asia. We should be considering raising the price, not low-
ering it."

"I caution you to reconsider." Janvillem's voice was soft. "If
you refuse to withdraw from Asia and abide by certain conditions there will be consequences."

"Conditions, consequences. What kind of gibberish is this?"
Sutton replied. "You are in no position to dictate to us."

The Baron put down his cigar. "What are your conditions,
Janvillem?" .

"First, Trident Industries will cease operations in Asia.

Second, Crown Petroleum will become the exclusive shipping agent for Trident's bulk product between Europe and the United States." Janvillem smiled thinly. "Of course, Crown Petroleum's exclusive agency will be extended to any subsidiaries of Trident Industries."

"Ridiculous," Sutton said. "You've taken leave of your --- "

"And, the consequences, if we do not agree?" the Baron asked.

"If you stay in Asia, Crown Petroleum will reduce prices. It will be costly, but we have funding from my government and a consortium of banks. And because of Crown Petroleum's ability to minimize shipping costs, Sumatran oil will be shipped into U.S. and European markets. Already exclusive shipping agreements have been negotiated with groups in Texas, Oklahoma and Pennsylvania. These companies will no longer be dependent on your pipelines to get their product to market. And lastly" --- Janvillem paused --- "I'll expose the holding companies you've used to monopolize the oil industry to interested governments. That information and your association with Bartrum & Sons link you to the deaths of my son, his wife and the attack on Crown Petroleum's field --- a property located on sovereign Dutch territory. With the right attorneys you might escape conviction in a court of law." Janvillem shrugged. "Who can say? Either way, you will be convicted by the court of international public opinion and subject to ruin."

The air in the Baron's office crystallized. The three men stared in stony silence. "Mr. Ambassador," Sutton said, "the court of public opinion is a province where we enjoy good standing The Baron and I have established numerous foundations that endow museums, libraries, hospitals and universities. Our reputations will not be easily sullied by innuendo." Sutton removed a cigar. "Your threats are nothing but speculation, and speculation doesn't hold a drop of water in a court of law. And, as far as engaging us in a price war......" He laughed. "Well, we've been down that road before."

Baron Rosenberg felt the first signs of a migrain. "Janvillem, surely you don't expect us to agree to the demands as you've laid them out. On the other hand, I see the need for some kind of accommodation to avoid harm inflicted on both sides. What is the *quid pro quo?*"

"It's all rather simple," Janvillem said. "Withdraw from Asia and give Crown Petroleum exclusive shipping rights for Trident's bulk transport. Once that is done, Sumatran oil will not be shipped east of Suez. Your *quid pro quo* is that Trident will remain unchallenged in Europe, plus you will enjoy reduced transportation costs. Naturally, you will loose the Asian market --- as you so richly deserve."

Sutton's palm hit the the table. "*Quid pro quo* in a pig's eye. What you propose is unacceptable."

"Percy," the Baron said, "I think we need to talk about that."

Twenty-five

ERIC WAS FINISHING BREAKFAST WHEN A messenger from the Dutch Consulate came to tell him a cable from Ambassador Botha had arrived.

"Why not take Marianne?" Katheryn suggested. "I'm quite sure getting out of the house will do her a world of good."

Eric gulped the last of his coffee. "Why not?"

Ah-Sook alerted Watchman Choy, who dispatched a man to fetch a rickshaw. More men, dressed as coolies, were ordered to take up positions along the route leading from the house to the consulate.

Eric and Marianne were greeted by a glorious day as they climbed into the rickshaw. Gulls hovered overhead against a cloudless sky, and, for the moment, their spirits were lifted.

Approaching the business district, Eric pointed out flags from the nations of the world streaming above the cargo ships. Junks and sampans glided through shipping lanes as piquant odors of steaming fish, soups, and spice fused with the scents of sea and sweat. Coolies swarmed over gangplanks, their haunting chant of *hai-yo, hai-yo* omnipresent. Marianne watched, but she did not speak. And Eric watched her. When the consulate came into view, he took her tiny gloved hand in his.

They were ushered into an anteroom by a buxon Dutch lady. After seeing they were seated comfortably she returned with a pot of tea for Eric and chilled orange juice for Marianne.

Minuted later, the Dainish consul, Johann Specz arrived. The bearded, beefy man handed Eric a diplomatic pouch. "Ambassador Botha instructed me not to trust this to a messenger." Taking Eric aside, Specz said, "The Ambassador mentioned by separate cable you would need a place to decode his message. I trust these facilities will serve. However, if there are any other services we at the consulate can render, please do not hesitate to ask. Those responsible for these terrible crimes must be brought to a swift and final justice, *ja?*"

Eric glanced at Marianne, who was silently standing on the other side of the room. "I appreciate your assistance."

The Danish counsul was unnerved at the fire in Eric's eyes.

*　　*　　*

PHILIP'S clothes were disheveled after his being up all night. "I've sent cables to London and New York without an answer. The bastards have dropped us flat. We'll be lucky to escape the hangman's noose."

Alex turned from the fireplace. "Shut-up. The only way we'll see the end of a hangman's noose is if you keep up your godcursed sniveling."

Philip glared back. "You don't understand, little brother.

We're frigging broke and Sutton and Rosenberg have severed their relationship with us. Why? Because you sent Jones and Mok after Garrett's wife. Your insane need for revenge has taken us over the line. Now there's no way out from under this muck-heap. Every bank from here to London will be out for our blood."

"It's you who doesn't understand, brother. There's no way we can be linked to Garrett or his --- "

"Maybe not directly," Philip interrupted. "But what the hell are people going to think now that we've been kicked out of Trident Industries? Rosenberg and Sutton might just as well have painted "*Guilty!*" down our backs. Since Chongming Dao they knew we would be pressed to make the final payment. Then up pops Garrett's Sumatran field and Trident's Asian market is at risk. Sutton and Rosenberg had to get rid of Gradek and Botha. So they sent me off to Shanghai with money and empty promises. And now that we've done their dirty work they walk away." Philip rubbed his hand through his hair. "Christ, it makes me sick to my stomach."

"Sutton and Rosenberg initiated and financed this action," Alex said. "Plus we know about the interlocking corporations making up Trident Industries. There's more than a few governments who'd be interested in how they've monopolized and manipulated the oil market. Once Eric Gradek's dead, I'd say we'd certainly be in a position to strike a deal that would resurrect Bartrum & Sons. They'll be wanting to slip into Sumatra and we could bugger their plans if they refuse to negotiate. What we need is a little liquidity to keep us afloat."

"How do you expect us to raise money? We're papered to the hilt."

"That's your department, brother. I'm quite sure you'll think of something. We still have a few days before anyone learns about our fallout with Sutton and Rosenberg. I'd suggest you begin by going to the bank."

"Twenty tankers full of kerosene will be arriving early next week. No one knows about our situation with Trident" Philip massaged his chin. "I might persuade the bank to lend against our normal share of the shipment."

"Jolly good, brother," Alex clapped. "Jolly good."

*   *   *

AFTER decoding Janvillem's cable, Eric lit a cheroot and reread the message.

Dear Eric:

My anguish over the obscene deaths of Jacqueline and Garrett is without limit. However, I take a measure of solace knowing that Garrett's legacy will live on. In that spirit, I'm happy to report my meetings have born fruit. Crown Petroleum is now positioned to become strong.

This cable will provide a summary of my dealings with Franz Mikolits, Baron Rosenberg and Percival Sutton. Meanwhile, I have mailed you a detailed report, along with dossiers on each of the individual parties by diplomatic pouch. There are a number of other politically sensitive documents that should prove useful to you as well.

Mikolits has agreed to suspend Crown Petroleum's lease payments until Telega Said is operational. Additionally, he has established a credit line in your name with the Commonwealth-Shanghai Bank to purchase the consignment of lighting oil on Trident's twenty tankers at thirty percent below market. A recalcitrant concession by Sutton and Rosenberg, but one that should start things off nicely for you.

After reading Li-Pung's confession, Rosenberg and Sutton agreed to cease their operations in Asia, for guarantees you will not compete against them in the European market, unless dictated by a state of war. Furthermore, in return for a 'Most Favored' rate schedule, they will contractually appoint Crown Petroleum as the exclusive shipping agent for Trident's bulk products. More importantly, Sutton and Rosenberg capitulated to our demand that they sell Trident's tanker fleet to Crown Petroleum at current market value. Mikolits enthusiastically agreed to finance the fleet and associated modernization costs once I presented him drafts of shipping contracts from Trident and the Texas and Oklahoma groups. Matthew Clay assured me the ships can be upgraded with marine boilers at considerable savings over new models. Any attempt by Sutton or Rosenberg to abrogate these agreements would result in Li-Pung's confession and other materials related to their illegal monopolistic practices being distributed to the world press.

It sickens me they cannot be prosecuted as co-conspirators for murder, but I realize evidence against them is not conclusive. Still, it is something that they would be damned by the court of public opinion and subject to a lifetime of disgrace. For them that would be a fate worse than death, so I expect no trouble from their quarter. Fortunately, we have other options available to deal with the Bartrums.

You will be pleased to learn my government has agreed to limit development of Dutch oil holdings in Asia to Crown Petroleum. Naturally, time and quantity provisos will be attached, so I advise you to immediately hire the necessary geological talent to find and develop oil elsewhere in the Indies. Gasoline will soon become an indispensable commodity and you will need additional reserves to fill the demand.

Do you recall our conversation in Boston about secretly purchasing shares in the Commonwealth-Shanghai Bank? After due consideration, I believe this to be integral to your long-term strategy as it would free you from dependency on lending institutions. Mikolits would be a good choice as a nominee to purchase blocks of stock on your behalf. Swiss Banks maintain the confidentially of their client's transactions. Plus, as an additional precaution, you will have the dossier I prepared on Mikolits. It contains enough damning material to dissuade him from any form of treachery.

The ramifications of what has so recently transpired are enormous. Crown Petroleum is poised to dominate transportation and distribution of oil products. Work closely with Clay Shipyards as they will support your efforts. Maintaining a state of the art tanker fleet will be your salvation. The world is about to be transformed and mankind will demand its oil.

Eric, you are destined to become a man of power. This saddens me greatly, because your life will be changed. How? I cannot say, except that in some way you will be irrevocably altered. The best advice I can offer is remember the use of power is not a sin. The transgression is being consumed by it. History is littered with despots who started as well-intentioned people. So, in dealing with friends and foes, I caution you to wield power judiciously. Alas, you will never be loved by all, but you will be respected.

Now, there is the matter of Marianne. There is nothing more I would rather do than to devote my life to raising her but, the disease eating my insides has left me precious time. Therefore, I'm trusting her to your good care. I do so with a clear conscious as I know this is what Jacqueline and Garrett would

want. A copy of my Last Will and Testament is being sent to you for safekeeping. Love her and cherish her as I know you will. Your faithful servant,
Janvillem van de Botha

Eric stared at the cable. Janvillem, the consummate diplomat, had not only saved Crown Petroleum, but enhanced its position. Garrett's work would continue, which meant Jing-Jiang's dream for a better China remained alive and well. Sutton and Rosenberg's dream of monopolizing the world's oil had been smashed.

A rustle of fabric caused Eric to look up. Turning his head, he saw Marianne silently staring at him from the other side of the room.

Solemn eyes spoke of pain too great to bear.

*   *   *

PAULINE Han was filing reports when Eric arrived with Marianne. "Good morning, Taipan. I see you have brought little Missee with you."

"Morning, Pauline. Take a moment and locate Adair and Tong-Po for me."

"Yes, Taipan."

Minutes later the two men were sitting in front of Eric. Pauline followed with a pot of hot tea and rice cakes. Marianne sat on the sofa staring out the window at the harbor.

"Good news," Eric said after Pauline had left. "Crown Petroleum is out from under the muck-heap and is stronger than ever."

Tong-Po reacted first. To everyone's surprise, the normally stoic dwarf jumped up and twirled to a sailor's jig. Addie

MacAlister followed with several steps from a highland cotillion.

"*Eeeee,* by all gods, Taipan, how did you manage such a feat?" Tong-Po asked.

"We can thank Ambassador Botha," Eric said. "I had bloody little to do with it." He then spent the next hour filling them in on the details of Janvillem's cable and answering questions.

Eric looked at Tong-Po. "Make sure our distributors are ready to move. By weeks end we'll off-load twenty tankers of kerosene Trident Industries was going to use to destroy us."

"Such bloody irony," Adair said. "Still, we can expect trouble from the other taipan when they learn they'll not be receiving their monthly allotment from Trident."

"I've considered that," Eric said. "With Bartrum out of the picture, our best course of action will be to continue supplying them at competitive prices. They'll face more competition from our distributors and the Chinese handling sales to the interior. Havershire, Pendleton and the others will be smarting, but that will change when we pick up the syndicate's financial obligations for the tanker fleet."

Addie tugged the end of his handlebar mustache. "Aye, that should bring a smile to their lips. The tankers, in their present state, are worthless. Plus, Bartrum has been bleeding them for years with ballooned payments."

Eric checked his watch. He was anxious to see Pierce Stafford's successor as the Commonwealth-Shanghai Bank's president, Clifford Avery, before lunch. Silently, Eric blessed his joss he'd played an instrumental role in getting Avery the appointment.

"Addie, I need a few words with Tong-Po," Eric said. "Afterwards, you and I are going to the bank. Bring the files on any outstanding notes."

The Scot grunted and headed for the door.

"By the way," Eric said. "I expect your resignation on my desk by weeks end."

"What?" MacAlister's jaw dropped.

Eric grinned. "I have a feeling you'll be going into a new line of work."

Twenty-six

"**Q**UITE FRANKLY, I'D RATHER SEE MY successor, Clifford Avery, making a loan of this sort," Pierce Stafford said. The banker placed the loan request on his desk and stared at Philip Bartrum. "Perhaps you're not aware of it, but I'm due to retire by months end."

"Yes, yes, I'd heard," Philip replied. "But if I'm to pick up the Malaysian sugar and rubber options I need the loan approved now. Our share of the kerosene is worth twice what I'm asking and the fleet is fully insured against general loss."

Stafford held his glasses up to the light and breathed on the lenses. "True." He removed a pocket handkerchief and began wiping away the fog. "Still, it seems a bit improper for me to approve a loan of this size then go dashing off to England, what?"

"Poppycock," Philip said. "I can ill-afford to wait for Avery to take over. The loan needs approval today. You are still bank

---

president and the only one with authority to authorize a transaction this size. Besides, my collateral is more than sufficient." Philip leaned forward. "Bartrum & Sons has been your primary customer for the past forty years. By withholding the funds, you will cost our company tens of thousands. And that, sir, I will not countenance." He eyed Stafford coldly. "Refuse my request and I'll make my feelings known in London about the damage done to our hong. I dare say your retirement benefits will be nipped right smartly by the time I'm finished with you."

Stafford's palms went damp. He hated being intimidated by someone like Philip, but the last thing he needed at the moment was someone mucking up his neatly planned retirement to the English countryside. The banker adjusted his glasses. "No need to get testy, Philip. The Bank has always stood by valued customers. If timing is so critical then perhaps I can make an accommodation. Shall we say twelve months at eight percent?"

"Pierce, if I wasn't so pressed for time I'd take issue with you over the interest rate. But since you've got me over a bloody barrel twelve months at eight percent it is."

Stafford scanned the information a last time. Everything seemed to be in order. Well, almost everything. There were two disturbing aspects about this transaction. One was the size of the shipment. In all of his years in Asia, Stafford could not recall a time when twenty tankers were scheduled to arrive simultaneously. And why was Philip willing to pay such an outlandish interest rate? The elder Bartrum had always enjoyed the lowest allowable rates. The questions rose in Stafford's throat, but he cut them off. *Retirement,* he reminded himself, was just around the corner. Besides, how could the bank be at risk holding such a vast quantity of kerosene as collateral? After all, people had to have lighting oil, didn't they?

Grunting, Stafford stood. "Let's go outside and I'll have my clerk prepare the documents. Shouldn't be a problem completing the paperwork by late this afternoon. First thing tomorrow morning we can execute the agreement, *eh?*"

* * *

ERIC finished opening the line of credit Franz Mikolits had arranged toward the purchase Trident's kerosene. He was in the bank's conference room with Adair MacAlister, Marianne and the incoming bank president, Clifford Avery. The room was appointed with deep-cushioned suede sofas and Chinese silk carpets on hardwood floors. Around the rosewood table were a dozen tooled leather wingback chairs. On the walls were oils of past presidents and defining moments in the bank's history.

"Don't believe I've ever seen a credit line to equal this," Avery said. "You'll be purchasing enough kerosene to keep Asia alight for quite some time."

Enough to where I can instruct Mikolits to start buying the bank stock. Now to get my man MacAlister a position of authority. Eric smiled. "Should hold us nicely until Crown Petroleum is back on line."

Avery shook his head. "Still don't know how you pulled it off. Last year, after the fire, I thought you were finished. Bartrum had you in a bloody vice, but you wriggled free and came back stronger than ever."

"Things have a way of sorting themselves out," Eric said softly.

Avery looked at Eric. "Yes. They do, don't they?" Glancing at the documents a final time, he applied the bank's chop and handed Eric his copy. "Everything seems to be in order.

269

Naturally, it will be necessary to provide us with vessel names, discharge dates, and locations before drawing down."

"Of course. I'll have a detailed report on your desk in a few days."

Avery nodded. "Meanwhile, don't hesitate to call on me if there is any service the bank can render."

Eric poured a fresh cup of tea. "Actually, there is a small matter. Addie has had his fill of trading and wants to get back into banking. I'll stand for his character. He was with the Royal Bank of Scotland before coming over and working for me."

The future president of the Commonwealth-Shanghai Bank smiled. "Your recommendation couldn't have come at a better time, Eric. With Pierce Stafford retiring, and the other changes at the bank, I'll be needing a good man."

*   *   *

IN the lobby, Eric saw Pierce Stafford leading Philip Bartrum from his office. He left Marianne with Adair and walked over to the two men, arriving when Stafford was about to hand the file containing Bartrum & Sons loan request to his clerk.

"Morning Pierce. I trust we'll be seeing you at Sir Geoffrey's for dinner on Friday evening?" Philip stiffened when Eric's eyes fell on him. He and Alex had been excluded from the guest list.

"Eric. Nice to see you," Stafford said. He grasped the extended hand. "My wife and I will be there. Wouldn't miss Sir Geoffrey's annual dinner party for the world." The Banker was smarting over having been intimidated by Philip earlier and so twisted the knife. "Half of Shanghai will be there, what?"

Eric nodded. "Should be quite an occasion."

"Dreadful this business about Jacqueline and Garrett," Stafford said. "A terrible tragedy to lose such fine young people. I pray the guilty parties are rooted out and dealt with swiftly."

Eric's gaze rested on Philip. "Oh, the guilty will pay."

The silence became palpable.

"One positive development is that Garrett's legacy will live on," Eric said, turning to Stafford. "Repair work has begun on the damaged pipeline and should be completed in a manner of months. Actually, Crown Petroleum's in a stronger position than before. I've opened a line of credit with the bank to purchase Trident Industries' entire Asian inventory of kerosene."

Stafford's eyes widened. "The entire inventory?"

Eric lit a cheroot. "Just completed the paperwork with Avery. We'll be picking up where Bartrum & Sons left off, now that they are no longer connected with Trident Industries."

Stafford turned to Philip. "Why didn't you mention anything about this sale? You were going to use that inventory as collateral for a loan."

Philip was sweating, he caught the rank wetness of it. How could Gradek afford such a purchase? *Bloody impossible!* But what seemed impossible was apparently fact. Gradek had wrecked his last chance at living a comfortable life. He'd been caught like a common criminal trying to embezzle from the bank. It was beyond nightmare. The only thing Philip had left was denial. "He's a bloody liar. Trident would never sell kerosene to ---"

Eric faced Philip, freezing his words in mid-sentence. The lobby of the bank had become eerily silent. "I'll attribute that last remark to ignorance, Philip. If it happens again I'll horsewhip you through the streets of Shanghai."

Philip's face conjested with blood.

Eric kept staring at Philip. *Pity Alex isn't present.* But that was acceptable, he told himself. It would soon be the talk of Shanghai that the Bartrums had lost everything because of him. That would bring Alex and Jones out of their hole. Alex would come for him now. After all, he had nothing left to lose. Eric smiled grimly. Except his life.

Eric removed a document from the folder he was carrying and handed it to Stafford. "Here's a copy of the terms and conditions of Trident's kerosene sale to Crown Petroleum. You'll notice that we won't begin discharging product until the first of next week."

The Banker's hands trembled, partly from excitement, partly from fear as took the document. *God's blood,* Stafford thought, *if I were the Bartrum's I'd be getting the hell out of Shanghai.*

"I'll have a list of vessel names and discharge dates for the bank in several days." Eric exhaled a stream of smoke. "I won't receive confirmation cables for dock times until tomorrow evening. Looks like I'll be working most of the night getting the paperwork in order."

Stafford glared at Philip. "Leave before I have the guards throw you out."

*   *   *

MARIANNA, Eric and Addie MacAlister walked outside, greeted by a crisp southerly wind.

"Still can't believe I'm going to work for the bank," Addie said. "You're certain that's what you mean for me to do?"

"If things go according to plan it'll be the best move you've ever made," Eric replied. Pausing on the landing, he buttoned

Marianna's coat. "When you get back to the office have Pauline send invitations for lunch day after tomorrow at the Commerce Club to the tiapan participating in Trident's tanker syndicate. With Bartrum & Sons out, I think it's a proper time to let them know they'll be able to purchase kerosene from us at fair prices in the future. As a matter of fact, have an invitation sent around to Alex."

"Good idea," MacAlister replied. "Should tickle their fancy to learn they're out from under the tanker financial responsibilities. That bit of news should earn us a few friends, eh?"

"We'll be needing all the support we can muster." Eric gave MacAlister several other instructions, one of which was for Tong-Po to arrange a meeting with Formidable Fung for the next morning. Afterwards, he hailed an approaching rickshaw to take him and Marianne home.

An elderly runner trotted up. "*Hola,* Taipan," he said. A single tooth protruded from his lower gum. "Where-*ah* you want go-*ah?* I take plenty chop, chop."

Eric gave the old man his address. He began helping Marianne up when she went rigid.

Stunned by her expression, Eric knelt and took her hand. "What is it, lass?"

Marianne stared across the street.

Eric followed her gaze. Alex Bartrum and Mr. Jones were climbing out of a rickshaw across from them.

When they started across the street Marianne flew into Eric's arms, grabbing insanely, terrified. "There's the bad man who hurt mommy."

MacAlister put a hand on Eric's shoulder. "Now's not the time, man. All you'll accomplish is winding up in jail yourself. Just be thankful for now the lassie can talk again. She's going to be all right."

Eric choked down the blood lust. MacAlister was right. Now wasn't the time. Eric willed himself to climb into the rickshaw while still holding Marianne. "You're safe now, sweetheart. And I want you to keep talking to me. Talking is good, do you understand?"

"Yes." The trembling died away.

*　*　*

THE Lotus Tong assassin was invisible in the shadowed rafters of Eric's bathhouse. Cloaked in matte-black, he might have been mistaken for a giant bat as he watched the house servants light candles and begin filling the huge tub with hot water.

How easy it had been to get inside the heavily guarded premises. Breaching the wall surrounding Eric's house just before three in the morning, minutes before the guards changed shifts, had not been difficult. Experience taught him that men anxious to be relieved were lax in their duties. Looking down, he saw that the servants had finished filling the tub. He smiled into the darkness. His prey would soon be arriving.

Now all he had to do was wait.

*　*　*

AH-SOOK went upstairs to the sitting room, large white towels bulky over her arm. "Bath ready."

Eric and Katheryn were in front of the fire discussing the incident at the bank with Marianne. "Ready?" he said, taking his wife's hand.

Cherishing him, Katheryn found herself comforted knowing

that the bathhouse originally constructed for his private pleasure now belonged to them both. She managed a smile. "I should think a hot bath will do us a world of good."

They changed into robes and sandals. Katheryn unpinned her hair, seated herself in front of the vanity and called for Ah-Sook. Turning to Eric, she said, "You go ahead and make things comfy. I'll be along after I get these tangles brushed out."

*   *   *

THE assassin's pulse quickened. Eric had just stepped inside the bathhouse with a male servant. Through the steam, he watched his prey remove his robe and sandals. The legendary barbarian known as the Opal Eye Devil, seated himself on a wooden stool while the servant scrubbed his body with pumice and soapy water. In spite of himself, the assassin could not help but admire the fact that a foreign devil appreciated civilized ways. But the fleeting admiration did not keep his jaw from tightening. After being hidden in the ceiling rafters for sixteen hours, he was anxious to get his assignment over with.

Eric slipped into the bath. Tired after the long day, he laid his head back on a rolled towel, closed his eyes and surrendered to the beguiling wet heat.

*   *   *

"QUIT dawdling, Ah-Sook. The Taipan is waiting." Katheryn's voice was sharp, though she was inwardly pleased with her amah's results.

The amah continued to brush with long even strokes as if she hadn't spoken. In a land of brunettes, she took great pleasure in tending Katheryn's golden hair. And, despite Katheryn's admonition, she made several additional strokes before laying the brush down. "There," she said, admiring the lustrous sheen. "Taipan strong man, but even his mighty knees buckle in the face of such beauty."

Katheryn picked up her bag and went downstairs.

*   *   *

TENSION in Eric's body melted away, but his mind was on Marianne. The trauma of seeing Jones had brought her voice back, and that was something to be grateful for, considering the nightmare she'd endured.

Yet, despite the horror, she's held up. Not many adults could have done as well.

Eric shifted position and readjusted the towel behind his head. Now that Marianne had confirmed Jones as Jacqueline's killer he could have the police pick him up. It would be easy enough to establish that Bartrum gave the orders. Then they would be tried in a court of law and most probably hanged. Bui that would be the easy way.

The assassin uncoiled and dropped silently to a spot on the floor about ten paces behind Eric. He crouched and froze. Eric's head did not move. The assassin removed a thin-bladed knife and crept forward.

Eric would never know if it was the slightest rustle of fabric or some primal sense that made him turn around. His eyes locked with the assassin's, then he was being attacked. Candlelight glinted off polished steel, but Eric was already moving as the knife whistled through the air. Razor steel sliced his shoulder as he pushed himself to the other side of the tub.

The assassin leapt in after him. Eric whirled to meet the onrush. The knife arced again, only this time Eric stepped in with an upward thrust of his forearm, blocking the blow. Twisting his hand, he locked onto the assailant's wrist. Anticipating such a defense, the assassin stiffened his fingers, striking at Eric's mid-section. Eric fell winded to the edge of the tub, but somehow maintained his grip on the assassin's wrist. The aberration loomed above him, the knife at his eye.

Relentless downward pressure propelled the blade forward. Soft laughter behind the mask. "Soon now."

Eric knew he was about to die. Visions of Katheryn and Marianne, then Bartrum surged in his mind. Rage took him. With a mighty effort, he pushed the knife point away as it cut into the fleshy area between his right eye and cheek. It was useless. The man's power was unbelievable.

An ear-shattering report rocked the room. There was a shower of blood as the assassin's hood flew off.

Eric looked up and saw Katheryn framed against the door. The stink of gunpowder was strong. Her pistol was still aimed at the lifeless form floating beside him.

Leaping from the tub, Eric grabbed his robe and took the gun from her hand. He held her close. "Thank God, Kate. You saved my life."

Katheryn's body shook. Killing another human being was an act she had not dreamt possible. But she felt no remorse. She would kill again and again, a thousand times again, if it meant protecting Eric's life. "Bartrum's responsible for this, isn't he? When in God's name will this nightmare end?"

"Shhh," Eric said. "Everything will soon be right."

"Taipan, you okay-*ah?*" Watchman Choy panted as he raced into the room. Several other guards followed close behind.

Eric glared at Watchman Choy, then at the guards. "I am, but no thanks to you and these sleeping dogs you call guards." Eric deliberately spoke back-street Mandarin. "Had it not been for *tai tai* I would be visiting my ancestors as we speak. I should replace you with a woman, perhaps? In fact, that's an idea I'm going to give serious consideration. Meanwhile, you're docked a month's pay."

The guards kowtowed in fright, while Watchman Choy hung his head. *Oh ko,* he thought, *terrible joss that the Taipan was nearly killed on my watch.* Cheeks flaming with shame, he promised himself to thumbscrew every guard that had been posted during the past two day's watch. If he managed to escape the Taipan's wrath.

"Well, don't just stand there," Eric roared. "Get that piece of turtle dung out of here. In fact, tear out the entire godrotten tub and have it rebuilt."

The guards converged around the body. A great deal of excited chatter erupted when one rolled the assassin's right sleeve up and exposed the dreaded Lotus Tong tattoo.

"Please don't shout at Choy," Katheryn said.

Eric looked at his wife. She was still pale, her words not coming easily. "I don't blame Choy for what happened," he said softly. "That devil would have slipped in through a mosquito net. The tongue lashing was necessary to save his face. Had I not given Choy a bit of hell, he would have been diminished in front of his men. For the Chinese no discipline means no order. As it stands now he'll wreak havoc with the other guards. I sure as hell wouldn't want to be in their shoes when he's done with them."

"Where you want us to take body, Taipan?" Watchman Choy's head remained bowed.

Katheryn slipped out of Eric's arms. "Don't bury it. Take it to Bartrum & Sons and tie it to the front gate."

Twenty-seven

AT DAWN THE CORPSE OF THE LOTUS TONG assassin was discovered impaled on the iron gate fronting the godown complex of Bartrum & Sons. News of the discovery blew through the Chinese community. As the news spread, the face of the Opal Eye Devil's beautiful golden-haired tai tai, Katheryn, who bathed as a civilized person, and put the bullet through the assassin's head, soared. Conversely, Alex Bartrum's face was diminished to the level of a sewer rat. Every man capable of wielding a meat cleaver fantasized that he might be the one to cut down Odious Mountain of Dung, who had for so long plagued the illustrious Opal Eye Devil.

*   *   *

AFTER a sleepless night, Eric left the house for his meeting aboard Tong-Po's junk. There he would tell Formidable Fung and Tong-Po about the events surrounding the assassination attempt and of his meeting at the bank with Philip Bartrum. Afterwards, a plan would be devised to deal with Bartrum and Jones.

The rickshaw runner turned right onto the *Bund.* Vendors were cleaning their stalls as the great street of commerce came alive. Elsewhere, in the shadows, clusters of people were gathered around charcoal braziers to drink tea. Feeling their eyes on him, Eric smiled grimly. He knew word had spread about the dead Tong assassin on the gate in front of Bartrum & Sons. A vision of Katheryn holding her pistol after she shot the assassin conjured itself. *Kate, Kate, Kate..... What would I do without you? Wife, lover, best friend, master strategist, fighter. Bloody brilliant to have the Tong assassin planted in front of Bartrum & Sons. What face Alex had left is destroyed. That should go a long way in winning the other taipan over tomorrow.* Leaning back, he lit a cheroot and blessed his joss for Katheryn's courage and wisdom.

The morning sky was streaked with gray when Eric passed one of Shanghai's city parks. He could see shadows within shadows flowing gracefully in concert with one another. Old people moving through the rhythms of Tai Chi Chuan. Eric had once tried to master the ancient breathing and temple boxing techniques, but found he lacked the temperament.

Beyond the park, the marble columns of the Commonwealth-Shanghai Bank came into view. Eric's pulse quickened. After settling with Bartrum, he'd have the devious Swiss banker, Mikolits start buying shares. It would be his investment in the future. *The future of Asia.* Janvillem was right about maintaining a tanker fleet to distribute bulk petroleum on a contract basis. Especially with signed contracts from

Trident Industries and the Texas and Oklahoma groups.

Just a matter of time and Crown Petroleum's tankers will be delivering oil to major ports around the world. His spirits buoyed. Yep, owning a bank will have it's advantages. I'll be in a position to finance my own ships without being dependent on others.

Eric stared at the harbor. As always, the sight thrilled him. *Yes,* the future looked grand. But Bartrum would have no place in it.

*   *   *

PHILIP took several deep breaths to trying to control his shaking. Finding the assassin's corpse hanging from their front gate had terrified him. "Gradek stared at me with those godcursed eyes of his at the bank. He's the bloody devil incarnate." Philip ran his fingers through his hair. "It won't be long before all of us are rotting in a pine boxes."

Alex glared at his brother. "Shut-up with your incessant sniveling. Gradek's godrotten joss has been good. We've still got a chance out of this muck-heap. But, first he must die."

Philip's fear turned belligerent. "Easy enough to say. Have you forgotten what was hanging outside --- "

"I said shut-up damn you." Alex balled his fists, then walked to the bar and poured a brandy. "There are ways of getting him."

Mr. Jones was standing against the wall, stropping his knife, watching the brothers. The giant slapped the blade back and forth against the leather. Sitting nearby, a bemused expression on his face, was Dragon Mok.

Eeeee, by the Eight Immortals how did I ever become

involved with such simpletons as these? Bartrum & Sons is finished, and they stand around arguing like Dowager Court dunces. Didn't the fools see that in a matter of days they would be in jail, or run out of China forever? Mok pleasantly scratched his groin at the vision of Alex Bartrum getting frog-marched through the streets and to the gallows. *Still,* he mused, about one thing *Odious Mountain of Dung* was right. Gradek must die, and Mok had to be the one to see it come about. Without the Opal Eye Devil by his side, Formidable Fung would be left without his most important ally. Then Mok could rebuild the Red Pang.

Mok thought about how life's gifts and hardships were given and taken at the whim of the gods. Perhaps, ushering Gradek into the grave would lessen his hardships and speed the gift-giving along. His excitement grew. There would be a period of chaos once the Opal Eye Devil was dead. Sir Geoffrey would send the British army against the Green Pang. But then, when Fung was at his most vulnerable, with joss and a wink from the gods, Mok could slip in and destroy him.

Alex drained his brandy and poured another. "You're sure Gradek told Stafford that he would be working late tonight?"

Philip looked up wearily. "That's what he said."

Alex glanced at Mok and Jones. "Tonight would be a good time to pay Mr. Gradek a little visit, don't you think?"

"I'll bring my best men," Mok said.

"We can't afford a bloody street battle," Alex said. "This has to be done quietly and made to look like a pang killing."

Jones continued to strop his knife. "Consider him dead, Mr. Bartrum."

*   *   *

JUST before midnight Eric completed the paperwork for the bank. Stretching, he put his pen down and poured a fresh cup of tea. Then he moved to the window and looked out. The moon was high in a cloudless sky. In the distance, he could see outlines of ships docked along the quay. Oil lights flickered on junks and sampans as they nodded on the water. Most were nighttime pleasure boats where one could eat, drink and indulge one's wildest sexual fantasies.

Sipping his tea, Eric watched the street below. Were Bartrum and Jones waiting for him? Excitement welled. He was perched on the edge between life and the abyss. Enemies were nearby, and the danger of it surrounded him --- intoxicating him like a heady draught.

*   *   *

"ANYTHING of interest?" Watchman Choy had been on the roof for the past five hours when Eric crept up beside him.

"The crows are out, but in this light they cannot hide." Choy glanced at Eric. "I have counted seven. Three in the alleyway and two at each end of the street."

"A gauntlet, *eh?*" Eric leaned over and studied the length of empty street. Nothing moved. Firecrackers sounded in the distance, and closer in dogs growled as they rooted through detritus in search of a meal. The sounds and smells of the night seemed normal. *Normal, except for the seven men waiting to put a knife through my heart,* he reminded himself. "Have you spotted Bartrum or Jones?"

Choy pointed at a darkened warehouse. "Bartrum is not here, but his running dogs, Jones and Mok, are behind the godown on the corner. The men in the alley and at the opposite end of the street are Chinese."

Eric counted the muffled chimes coming from inside the office. Midnight. He checked his watch. So, Fung had been right. At their meeting, he'd predicted Mok would be on hand.

"Mok views your death as his last chance to topple the Green Pang," Fung had said. "But I will be there to personally slit his belly."

Bloody fine with me, Eric thought. He touched the derringer inside his belt. Fine, so long as I have the pleasure of putting a bullet through Jones's heart.

At one a.m. they left the roof and returned to the office. Eric stood in front of the window and lit an oil lamp. Adjusting the wick, he set the lamp on his desk, waited several minutes, then extinguished the flame and led Choy downstairs into the basement.

They emerged at the rear of the building through a trapdoor that Choy had camouflaged by surrounding it with stacks of wooden crates. "I'll draw them out," Eric said. "When they're on the street come in from the rear with Fung and his men."

"Taipan, you be plenty careful, *heya?*"

Grasping Choy's shoulder, Eric slipped out from behind the crates. At the corner, he turned onto the street fronting his office. Standing there a moment, he watched shadows shift, felt the cool brush of wind against his cheek. Every nerve taught, he moved towards Jones and Mok's hiding place. His ears caught the sounds of the night; water lapping against the pier, cats hissing as they fought for food and sex.

Eric kept to the middle of the street, expecting an attack at any moment. After walking a short distance, he became aware of a new sound. Barely distinguishable at first, but little by little becoming defined. Soft padding sounds. Glancing over his shoulder, Eric saw the Chinese men that had been hidden in the alley. He began trotting up the street. Like a pride of lions, the five Red Pang soldiers spread out and came after him.

Eric was about twenty-five yards from where Jones and Mok were hidden when the commotion broke out behind him. Palming his knife, he turned and saw Fung, several Greens and Watchman Choy fighting with the five Chinese. He rushed into the fray and was immediately attacked by an ax-wielding Red.

Eric's blade went into the Red's ribcage. Nearby, Fung slashed another Chinese, while Watchman Choy attacked a third with his cleaver.

Keeping to the shadows, Dragon Mok darted down the side of the street. Stopping behind a post, he withdrew a hatchet and waited until Eric's back was to him. The opportunity came and he threw the weapon with great accuracy. Watchman Choy never looked in Mok's direction. He had no idea death was flying through the air. He simply stepped in front of the whirling blade's path, dying instantly when the ax buried itself in the side of his head.

A part of Eric died with him. He watched the figure running down the street. *Mok!* Blood roared in his head. Ridding the world of Jones and Mok was all that mattered. Eric hurtled over a fallen Green and rushed into the night.

Suddenly, Fung was by his side, matching him stride for stride. "Remember, Mok is mine," he said. "The motherless dogs will be behind the godown."

They raced around the corner and came to an abrupt halt. Moonlight was obscured by the three story godown. Darker here. Faint shadows spilled over the narrow street. Eric stood stockstill. He was vaguely aware of a cargo ship's low boom coming from somewhere in the harbor. The only other sounds were his pounding heart and the slapping of surf against the pier.

Eric watched Jones and Mok step out of the shadows.

Jones held his great knife and Mok was armed with a hatchet. "Would've been a simple thing to kill you from a distance," Jones said. "But then I wouldn't have had the pleasure of watching you die up close."

Fung withdrew his own fighting ax and took a step in Mok's direction, his voice a hiss on the night air. "Cowardly dog, now we shall settle our differences."

"We shall see who is a cowardly dog." Mok raised his weapon and stepped into the middle of the street. "All gods bear witness how I have longed for this --- " Before the sentence was finished, Fung attacked and the two men began hacking at each other.

Eric glared into Jones' eyes and withdrew his knife. "Murderer of women and children, let's see how you stand up to someone who can fight back."

Jones lunged, slashing viciously. The tip of the knife whizzed by Eric's eyes. Eric countered, but the giant side-stepped. They began circling each other.

A blow came in. Eric parried it then twisted out of range. Blinded by rage, Jones slashed wildly. His carelessness left his midsection exposed. The giant raised his knife, but Eric was faster. He hilted his blade in Jones' abdomen. There was a sudden expulsion of air, followed by an animal cry. Dropping his knife, Jones staggered, falling trying to stem the spurting blood.

Seeing that Fung had dispatched Dragon Mok, Eric picked up Jones' knife and tossed it away. "Bowels burning?" he asked, bending down, making sure Jones could see him. "Bleeding to death with your insides hanging out? Just like me on the *Northern Star.*"

Jones thrashed on his side, before managing to sit in a gout of blood. "*Northern Star?*"

Eric walked away.

*   *   *

DESPITE his own wounds, Formidable Fung exulted over killing Dragon Mok. It had been a hard fought victory, but he had prevailed. *Shanghai is mine.* He looked about for Eric. But, along with Watchman Choy's body, the Opal Eye Devil was gone.

Fung signaled for the two surviving Greens. "Take Mok's head and plant it on a stake at the market. Then bury his body beneath the Red Pang soldiers. Tomorrow, Shanghai will know the Green Pang is the ultimate power."

After completing their work, Fung and his men moved off.

Mr. Jones lasted another hour before the rats came.

Twenty-eight

'TAIPAN!'

Ah-Sook's eyes widened. Eric was at the front door, his face ravaged and pale.

Following his fight with Jones, he had taken Watchman Choy's body back to the office. Rage helped him carry the dead weight. After wrapping his friend in canvas, he went to Tong-Po's junk and arranged for the body to be transported to Hangzhou for burial. "Make sure it's a grand funeral with many mourners, bells, and drums," he ordered.

"It will be done, Taipan," Tong-Po said.

The dwarf was distraught but at once relieved that no harm had befallen Eric. Later that morning, Tong-Po planned to burn joss sticks at a nearby temple. The gods in their infinite wisdom needed praise for extinguishing one so miserable as Mr. Jones, while, at the same time, having the foresight to preserve one so exalted as the Opal Eye Devil.

Composing herself, Ah-Sook took charge of the house. "We can't have you standing there like beggar man, Taipan. Come in and I fix food and tea." Then she imperiously called for Ah-Ping, who appeared instantly. "Are you deaf, dumb and blind, old woman? Bath and fresh clothes for the Taipan, plenty quick!"

Ah-Ping scurried away.

"Thank God you're home." Ignoring his bloody clothes, Katheryn wrapped him in her arms. "I've been frantic."

"Watchman Choy is --- "

"Shhhh." Katheryn put her finger to his lips. "Let's talk after we get you fed and cleaned up."

*   *   *

ERIC felt more human after bathing and a meal, but the burden of death weighed heavily on his shoulders. He looked at Katheryn. "Mok's ax was meant for me. If Choy hadn't stepped in the way --- " He went to the window and stared out.

"Jones is dead, and I'm glad," Katheryn said. "But, his death will not resurrect Garrett or Jacqueline or Watchman Choy, will it?" She moved to the window and touched his arm. "Why not put an end to the carnage now? Turn Li-Pung's confession over to father and let the authorities deal with the Bartrums. There's enough damning information in it to send them to the gallows."

"Give the confession to your father?" Eric turned and stared at her. "Do you think I'd risk those sods going free?"

Katheryn clenched a fist. "Why would they go free? The confession is original, duly signed by the Dutch Counsel General in Sumatra. What more could you want?"

Eric turned back to the window. "Let the police have Philip, but I'll deal with Alex. That's the least I can do for Marianne."

"Eric, there's too much killing. Look at you, look at us. In the past two nights, you've nearly been killed twice yourself and still you're bent on revenge. Please. Think about Marianne and me. Next time you might not make it back home....." A sob rocked her.

"Kate." Eric turned and reached for her.

"Don't touch me." Katheryn twisted away. "I thought my hate could carry me through this nightmare, but I was wrong. God, I was wrong. Now, all I want is for things to go back to the way they were."

"They will, as soon as I've dealt with Bartrum."

"Will they? Or will it be just that much more blood staining your hands? Our hands?" Katheryn turned and began moving toward the door.

Catching his wife, Eric put his arms around her. "I'll do as you ask, Kate," he said. "All I ask is that you don't take Li-Pung's confession to your father before noon today. If I haven't settled with Bartrum by then the authorities can take over."

Katheryn looked at him. "All your life it's been Alex Bartrum."

"I love you, Kate."

Eric put his arms around his wife and she allowed him to hold her.

*   *   *

ERIC and Katheryn paused on the upstairs landing. It was time for him to go to the Commerce Club. Below, Tong-Po was play-acting with Marianne. The child was still withdrawn, but

291

there were moments of warmth that boded well for her.

"Pretend we're at a ball, and that you're my escort," she said.

"*Eeeee,* how the gods have smiled upon me." Tong-Po laughed and looked around the room. "I have most beautiful lady of all." He stood in front of her and bowed at the waist.

Marianne giggled, then curtseyed.

"I've never seen Tong-Po so taken," Katheryn said. "He loves her a great deal."

"Yes, we all do." Eric faced her. "Kate, I'll be going now. Tong-Po will stay until I return."

"I don't like this. I don't like what you're doing."

"I know."

"But I can't fight it, can I? This is beyond who I am, it goes back to a seventeen year old boy and who he was."

Eric stared into Katheryn's eyes. "And to who I am now."

Katheryn hugged him fiercely. "Be home for dinner."

"I promise." Eric smiled gently. Then he was gone.

*   *   *

THE Commerce Club was bedlam when Eric arrived just before noon.

Headwaiter Fong met him at the front door. "All important taipan waiting for you," he said hurriedly. "Much brandy and ale consumed."

Eric saw Ian Havershire and Andrew Pendleton in the dining room huddled with a group of taipan. *Laying bets, no doubt.* At the bar, another noisy group.

Eric let Fong help him with his coat. "I shouldn't worry about it," he said. "What I've got to say should calm them down nicely."

*   *   *

ALEX Bartrum was brooding in his study. In his hand, the engraved invitation Eric had sent him for the Commerce Club meeting. On the table next to him was an uneaten sandwich and a half-full brandy snifter. Gradek was hammering the final nail into his coffin. How the godrotten bastard must be laughing.

The door to the study opened. "Now what do you propose, little brother?" Philip said. "Jones and Mok are dead and Gradek is meeting with the other taipan as we speak. It's over."

Alex crumbled the invitation and threw it in the fire.

Philip was haggard, a panicked expression scored into his face. "It's the bloody gallows for us. We've no money, no friends, nowhere to turn. We're down the shitter because of your obsession with Eric Gradek. He didn't steal Katheryn from you." Philip's voice was a lash. "He didn't have to. She hated your guts from the beginning."

"Liar!" Alex threw his brandy glass at Philip. "Shut-up, godrot your soul." He was out of his chair and flying across the room. Yanking his brother up by the collar, Alex backhanded him viciously across the face. "I might be going down, but not before taking that bloody shit with me."

Philip held his face. "Go ahead and try. You'll only wind up dead like all the others."

Alex shoved his brother onto the sofa. "A pox on you and your sniveling. Alex walked to a nearby cabinet and opened a velvet-lined teak box. He stared at the inlayed dueling pistols. After choosing one of the weapons, he checked the load, then walked out of the room.

Philip lay on the shattered sofa. He watched a pair of house-cats converge on Alex's sandwich.

* * *

CAPTAIN Albert Jamison arrived at Bartrum & Sons just past noon and found the offices empty. He immediately ordered the lock on the front door to be broken and a full-scale search of the premises.

Philip Bartrum was discovered several minutes later sprawled on the couch in Alex's study. A dueling pistol lay on the floor near his outstretched hand.

The other brother, the younger one, Alex, was nowhere to be found. Sir Geoffrey had been especially interested in having him brought in. *Nevermind,* Jamison told himself. *He's probably be at the Commerce Club with the other taipan.*

Jamison signaled to his adjutant. "Wrap the body and take it to the morgue. I'll be going to the Commerce Club." Before leaving, the young captain lingered, marveling at the fine porcelains and rugs and paintings that graced one of China's most famous hongs. Any one of the items would cost more than a lifetime of service in the army. Jamison shook his head. Pity to have so much and lose it. More pity still that, at the end, none of it did a bit of good.

* * *

ERIC'S news about the demise of Bartrum & Sons rocked the assembled taipan. Now, the question that crept into the back of every trader's mind was, *Who would be next to fall before the powerful Opal Eye Devil, now that he had smashed the once invincible hong of Bartrum & Sons?*

Alcohol flowed and the meeting deteriorated into a shouting match. "I told every last one of you pig-headed bastards what would happen if we backed that godrotten tanker fleet," one disgruntled trader shouted.

"Stop belly-aching," the man next to him snapped. "You're part of the syndicate along with the rest of us. The question is what in the hell do we do now?"

"Another thing," said another, "what will make the situation improve now that Crown Petroleum's controlling the bloody oil supply instead of Bartrum? We could be jumping from the frying pan into the fire."

Nursing a glass of ale, Eric listened as a new roster of future enemies and allies began to materialize.

"Quiet down," Ian Havershire roared. "We're shooting off our mouths when we'd best be listening."

"I bloody well agree," Andrew Pendleton added. "If you want answers, we should be hearing what Eric has to say."

*   *   *

THE mood changed appreciably by the time Eric finished laying out his proposals. He would continue supplying the assembled taipan with refined oil products, while relieving them of their financial obligations to Trident's tanker fleet. When he stepped away from the podium there were many toasts and much talk about the demise of Bartrum & Sons. Overall, the traders, who had been adroitly led by Havershire and Pendleton, seemed quite pleased with the new order.

Eric was pleased, as well. He had won them over. Well, at least for the time being, and as much as such men could ever be won over.

At the bar, Havershire and Pendleton led another round of toasts.

Eric raised his tankard and smiled.

Tomorrow, they'll curse me to hell and rise up. Only this time, by God, I'll not be caught unprepared. Just remember, old chum, adversaries are always waiting to slip in from the night.

Havershire slapped Eric on the back. "When will we get to see one of those giant tankers of yours? From what I've read in the *Economist,* I understand ---"

"Gradek."

Alex Bartrum's voice had blood in it, the timbre of a trapped and dangerous man.

Eric turned slowly and put down his tankard. He looked at the dueling pistol aimed at his heart.

"Godcursed bastard. I'll see you in hell before you take everything I have."

Bartrum pulled the trigger at the same moment Eric dived. Rolling forward, Eric felt a searing pain as the bullet scored his back. In the next moment, he was on his feet, a knife in his hand.

Bartrum threw the pistol. Eric sidestepped and moved forward.

Several taipan started to intervene, but were restrained by Havershire. "This clash has been brewing a lifetime. It has to be."

Bartrum palmed his own knife. The two men circled, feinting. For them, the world had ceased to exist. Hatred, hardened by time, pumped their blood. They slashed and tore at one another. For years they had been fighting a war, but until now the battle had always raged in their minds and over conference tables.

"Thirteen years ago you had your chance to kill me, and failed," Eric said. "Remember *Northern Star?* You had your man, Jones, gut a snot-nosed seaman, then leave him to die in the stinking hole. I was that boy, Bartrum. And now I'm going to send you to bloody hell."

"You...."

Bartrum's head pounded, Eric Gradek, the brash seaman who'd helped the cursed dwarf, Tong-Po those many years ago? It didn't seem possible, but he knew it was true. Gradek was an aberration that had to die. Bartrum's self-control snapped. Sound ceased, and the whole of his world was consumed by a terrible urge to kill.

Coming together, they crashed into a table, locked in mortal combat. Crystal and china flew as the two tumbled to the floor in a spray of glass. So personal was this struggle that their eyes never wavered --- never blinked as they rolled over and over fighting for a final advantage. The physical and mental strain of the battle turned minutes into eternity. Veins popped on their foreheads. Knives moved within inches of their throats. But neither man would yield.

Slowly, Eric rolled on top of Bartrum. Mere centimeters between the tip of his knife and delivering death to the man responsible for having Garrett, Jacqueline, and Choy murdered. Marianne's and Katheryn's suffering steeled his arm.

Eric cursed Bartrum to hell. Then, with a mighty effort, he smashed his fist into Bartrum's face. Bones cracked, blood spurted. Standing, Eric stared at the man who'd haunted his dreams. But all he heard was Katheryn's voice.

*   *   *

CAPTAIN Jamison arrived minutes after the fight and arrested Alex Bartrum. Already, scores of Chinese had gathered in the street. Word about the Opal Eye Devil's great victory over *Odious Mountain of Dung* had been sent down by Headwaiter Fong. The news flew from mouth to mouth and the crowd swelled.

Eric emerged hours later to a huge roar of approval. Such an emotional outpouring was uncommon, especially when bestowed upon a barbarian. But, had the gods not favored the Opal Eye Devil with fantastic joss? Therefore, it was only prudent that a proper showing of respect be accorded one so blessed. Perhaps, the gods would see fit to pass a portion of the Taipan's good fortune their way.

Wearily, Eric climbed into a waiting rickshaw and ordered the driver to take him home. People lined the street to watch him pass, but he ignored them. The important thing was that he'd won. At least for today. But was the victory worth the price? Alex Bartrum was going to hang, but that wouldn't bring Garrett, Jacqueline, and Watchman Choy back.

No, they won't be coming back, but Jing-Jiang's dream of a better China will take a step closer to reality.

Off to his right, he saw one of the tankers he'd purchased from Trident Industries. The sight buoyed his spirits. Kerosene would soon be finding its way into the heartland, bringing new light to millions. Amongst all the blood and murder, surely that was good.

Eric lifted his face skyward. Gulls circled as the sun dropped to the west. Excitement welled. He was close to home. *Home.* The word now held new meaning.

The rickshaw runner turned off the *Bund* onto Eric's street. He could see the gate fronting his house. Home had never looked so good.

A servant posted out front jumped up and disappeared inside.

Moments later, Tong-Po and Marianne appeared, waving excitedly. Then Katheryn was there and he was filled with the sight of her. There were things to work out between them, things that had to heal. But their love was bedrock.

"Made it home for dinner just like I promised, Kate."

For the first time in his life, the man known as the Opal Eye Devil was at peace.

If you enjoyed Opal Eye Devil, you won't want to miss John Hamilton Lewis' newest, most provocative thriller.

BASHA

Turn the page for an excerpt from this captivating new novel. Coming fromDurban House in the spring of 2001.

Prologue

T el Aviv, 1978

EVERY DAY THE BOY WAS THERE AT THE FENCE.

Afternoons found this five year old Palestinian staring at the green courts and modern training facilities beyond the partition surrounding the tennis center. For six months he had arrived with dedicated regularity to watch Israel's most celebrated tennis coach take the university team through practice sessions. From the moment Amon Weizman appeared on court the boy's dark eyes focused on the man with the burn-scarred face.

*   *   *

DESPITE best efforts by the country's finest plastic surgeons, the burn on Amon's face remained painfully evident. Beginning at the hairline an elongated red patch of flesh covered his right cheek, fading above the upper lip like a birthmark. Much of his body was the same, though miraculously the fire had not injured his arms and hands.

Three years before the fire, Amon had been an enormously popular tennis professional. He had broken into the top ten after winning the Italian Open. By season's end, he had four tournament victories and was ranked number five in the world. The only Jew ever to achieve such greatness on the tour.

Ascending to the number one ranking seemed preordained, but destiny's script had deemed otherwise. Amon's hopes of challenging for the top spot were dashed inside smoldering wreckage. The metronome of eternity had required but a few ticks. More than enough time to transform his bright world into a private hell.

Amon had been returning to Tel Aviv from Hafia with his fiancée, Esther. Her fingers were stroking the back of his head. "I love you, Amon," she whispered.

Turning, Amon kissed her. "I love you too, sweetness." When he looked up, a school bus filled with terrified young faces was on the highway directly in front of his car. They went off the road at sixty with Esther's hand digging into his shoulder. Concrete pilings gleamed in the sun, then the sounds of tortured metal.

Days later, after regaining consciousness, Amon learned that the sun's angle had momentarily blinded the bus driver when he drove the bus onto the center lane. But the question that ate at Amon's sanity was why had he not been watching the road? He could still feel Esther's caress and hear her words. *I love you, Amon.* She was always there, in the darkness of his soul, casting no blame.

Now, three years later and midway through his second season at Tel Aviv University, Amon's depression had grown worse. He had thought that taking the position of head tennis coach would resurrect his shattered life. Of course, he could never play the game again, but having two good hands and arms would enable him to coach. Well, at least, for as long as his damaged lungs held out. And that was better than nothing, wasn't it?

How wrong he'd been. At night, Amon felt Esther's caress, heard her voice. "Not you darling, it wasn't you." Then the nightmares would begin. Suicide beckoned like an intimate friend. Morning's light found Amon staring at his scars.

Making matters worse was coaching college students who didn't give a damn about the game Amon so loved. They would rather be at Kikkar Atarim on surf boards, or hitting the bars on Ha-Yarkon Street. It was rather like they were equipping themselves with a social grace. *Tennis anyone?* Amon watched the team practice. Nothing there. A little technique, but no killer instinct --- no commitment to win. They should have taken up bridge.

Easy enough to end it all, a now familiar inner voice whispered.

To the steady whack of tennis balls and occasional laughter, Amon considered what he had.

A life that was no life.

Closing his eyes, Amon let it go.

"Enough for today." Amon clapped his hands sharply. "We'll pick it up again tomorrow."

There were smiles of appreciation as the players scrambled off.

Amon watched them trot toward the locker room At that moment, he felt the young boy watching him. His eyes were passionate, clear and intelligent. Palestinian and tall for a boy of five years. Thin. Wavy brown hair over a high forehead. Amon stared at him, catching his hidden desire. Something in the eyes he had seen many times across a net. The boy had an olive complexion, good jaw, and straight nose. Had Amon not known better, he would have placed him as Mediterranean --- Northern Italy or, perhaps, Spain.

"The team should be so dedicated," Amon muttered, the Jewish inflection heavy in his words. He began picking up his racquets and was about to walk away, but changed his mind.

"Come over here, son," Amon yelled. "Want to hit a few balls?"

The boy's head bobbed. He jogged to the gate, a pair of frayed black high-tops on his feet.

"Got a name?" Amon asked, offering a racquet.

The young Palestinian grasp the handle in a Western forehand grip. "Ahmed --- Ahmed Naji."

"You come with the gardeners?"

"Yes, sir. My father and uncle."

"You here all the time."

"Yes, sir."

"Ever play tennis, Ahmed Naji?"

"No, but I know how."

Amon smiled at the boy's confidence. "And how's that?"

"Inside here." Ahmed pointed at the side of his head. "I see myself playing in here. Many times, I hear you talk to players about *visua,* vis..........."

A hairless piece of scar tissue, once Amon's eyebrow, arched. "Visualization, preparation, and reaction."

Ahmed smiled for the first time. "My visualization is very good."

"Let's see what you've got."

Thirty minutes later the word *prodigy* entered Amon's mind. His jaw tightened. The young Palestinian was covering the court with the fluidity of a greyhound. Ahmed Naji had never played tennis, but possessed the speed and power of someone with years of experience. Effortlessly, he chased down all manner of shots.

Strong and fast --- great form. Damn right. His visualization was excellent.

Amon's own blood coursed, his skills focusing. He served a ball to the deuce court. Ahmed whipped a topspin backhand down the line for a winner.

Dear God!

With proper coaching and training, Amon knew Ahmed could make the top ten by the time he was twenty. Perhaps higher. *Maybe even....*

Suddenly, Amon's spirit rallied --- his long dormant champion's heart thumped against a scarred chest. This scruffy little Palestinian with the wavy hair and winner's eyes could be his legacy. More, he could be his redemption.

This Palestinian boy could be the player I never was, the man I used to be.

Ahmed Naji smiled from across the net.

BOOK ONE

Revenge is a kind of wild justice.
                          Francis Bacon

One

N ew York, Present

A PERFECT OVERHEAD LOB. BEN WEIZMAN KNEW IT
the moment the ball left his racquet. Top-seeded Jon Thorenson
raced for the baseline, but the ball had already dropped scant
inches inside the corner of the ad court, bouncing high and
away. No chance. A clean point.

"Advantage Weizman."

Bending backward, Ben pumped his fists. "Yes." One more
point and the semifinal match would be his.

The roar from the crowd at Center Court was like nothing
Ben had ever experienced before. His body burned with primal
fire. Wimbledon and the French were exciting, but not like this.
The U.S. Open was blood and guts tennis. Ben loved it, and the
fans loved him. They loved his gut-wrenching fight for every
point, while his Mediterranean good looks stirred the women.

It was sweltering at the Arthur Ashe Stadium in Flushing Meadows. Beneath a relentless sun, court temperatures had sailed to one hundred ten degrees. Jets from La Guardia thundered overhead. But, far below their silver wings the players were singularly focused. Victory was all that mattered. For five grueling hours two of the world's best had dazzled the crowd with brilliant tennis. Now, it was down to this. The score was 7-5, 5-7, 5-7, 7-5, 5-6. Advantage Weizman in the fifth and final set. But Thorenson had the serve.

"Quiet please," a warning from the announcer.

Toweling off the handle of his racquet, Thorenson walked up to the baseline. The crowd quieted, jets faded. A wild silence settled over Center Court.

The Swede glanced stoically across the net.

Ben looked back. *Bastard's got ice water for blood,* he thought, readying himself.

Thorenson bounced the ball, once, twice. Torso forward, sweat soaked, Ben danced from side to side. After the third bounce Thorenson would make his toss.

"Concentrate on the toss. Take the ball on the rise." Ben's adopted father, Amon, had drilled this endlessly into his head. "A good return kills the serve. It gives you time to get into the point."

The Swede's left hand lifted, his arm straightening in model form over his head. Ben's eyes riveted on the ball. It drifted up through the humid air as Thorenson's back arched, his racquet cocked. The ball started its descent.

Flat serve down the middle.

Ben danced on his toes, side to side.

A one hundred seventeen miles an hour serve exploded off the catgut, but Ben was positioned and ripped a blistering forehand cross court. Thorenson was already up on his toes and running. The Swede lunged, barely getting his racquet behind the ball. Any other player would have missed completely, but Jon Thorenson, ranked number one in the world, wasn't any other player. It was a great *get.* Ben rushed forward, his eyes never leaving the yellow ball as it floated over the net. Not waiting for a bounce, he smashed a fierce overhead to the far corner. A perfect put-a-way.

Game, set, and match --- Weizman.

Bedlam. Thunderous applause caromed around the stands. Ben sank to his knees and kissed his racquet, a moment of release and celebration. Then he focused on the next step --- the Final.

"For you, Father," Ben whispered. Now he would need to phone the hospital.

*   *   *

REPORTERS and cameramen crowded around Ben outside the men's locker room.

"Ben, you've just beaten the number one player in the world in the U.S. Open. How does it feel?" a well-known sports columnist asked.

"Fantastic," Ben said. He smiled across note pads, and recorders held towards him. "I've trained hard for this moment."

"In the finals you'll be facing either Ryerson or Ivonavic. Which one would you rather play?" a network reporter asked.

"It really doesn't matter." Ben shrugged. "At this point, I'm just happy to be here. Now if you will excuse me." Turning, Ben moved toward the door. That was when he caught sight of his business manager signaling.

"Bad news, Ben," a worried Michael Dern said, once they were inside the locker room. "The doctors say Amon's not doing well. He's probably holding on for you."

The sweat on Ben's body turned cold. His father had been at the Johns Hopkins Cancer Center in Baltimore for three months. "Make reservations on the first flight," he told Dern.

"What about the final?"

"Fuck the final."

*   *   *

AMON Weizman could not move, but he could hear. And, he could see the crystal droplets rolling down the I.V. into his wasted arm. Three months in Johns Hopkins and he'd gone from one hundred eighty pounds to seventy-two. Perched on the threshold dividing life and death, Amon was about to pass over. *Into what?* The possibilities were terrifying. His God, the God of Abraham, was a vengeful God, and his sins were great. And killing was a mortal sin, wasn't it? Of course, he had not killed deliberately. There had been the bus driver blinded by the sun. But Esther was nonetheless dead. Except in his restless dreams. Even cancer could not eat those away. A blinding sun had found a bus driver's eyes, but Amon had not been watching the road. It was a sore on his soul that would not heal.

And he had stolen. Stolen a life.

Amon stirred, his lungs protesting. He remembered the day he'd first asked the Palestinian boy to come out onto the court and play. So fast and strong for his five years. Such God-given talent.

Stolen.

A talent Amon had exploited --- used to mold an innocent boy into an image of himself. But that wasn't enough, was it? Then Amon had stripped Ahmed of his heritage by stealing his name. Yes, he had stolen everything. Ahmed Naji had become Ben Weizman.

My clone. My blood and dreams.

A pain unrelated to the cancer settled inside Amon's stomach. Nineteen years had passed since Ben Weizman emerged from his chrysalis, his rebirth.

A haze of morphine gave him back that day. The day Amon met Ahmed's father.....

*　　*　　*

"AHMED. Come, we will miss the bus."

"Yes, papa."

Amon looked at the worn down grounds keeper, then the boy was walking towards him. *God, he's going to return the racquet.*

"Is that your father?" Amon asked.

Nodding, Ahmed handed him the racquet.

"Think he'd mind if you stayed a bit longer? I'll see to dinner and getting you home safely. In between, I could show you a few film clips of some well-known players. Studying the great ones helps develop technique."

Ahmed's eyes brightened.

The Palestinian approached the Jew. Deep lines scored the man's dark face, giving him the appearance of someone much older. His beard was white, peppered with black. Like most émigrés he had exchanged his loose cotton robe for trousers and shirt. Perhaps, because they had seen too much suffering in this war-torn land, his eyes were dull and sunken.

"Mr. Naji, I'm Amon Weizman."

"The tennis coach."

"Yes. I've been watching your son, Ahmed, play. He's really quite gifted, you know."

The Palestinian lit a cigarette. "That's not really surprising, since hitting that yellow ball over the net is all he thinks about."

"Would you have any objections if he stayed a little longer? I will personally see to his evening meal and make sure he is returned home safely."

The dull eyes regarded him. "For what purpose, Mr. Weizman? Already, the boy's head is in the clouds. Our life is hard. Why offer him more disappointment?"

Amon struggled to find the right words. His own life probably counted on them. "Look at my face, Mr. Naji. I know about disappointment every time I look in the mirror. I ask only to evaluate his abilities."

"And if his abilities are great?"

"Then, perhaps, I could be of assistance," Amon said. "There are possibilities. We could discuss them."

Ahmed's father watched the cigarette smoke drift upward, dissipating into nothing. "A famous Jew interested in helping a poor Palestinian boy. A most improbable circumstance, don't you think, Mr. Weizman?"

"We are discussing gifts, undeveloped hidden talents. This is not about religion or politics."

The Palestinian's eyes surveyed the landscape. He saw some bushes that needed more trimming. "Everything's about religion and politics," he said finally. "But I understand what you say. Talent and gifts come from God, Mr. Weizman. It would be a sin to waste them."

*   *   *

AMON began coaching Ahmed on a daily basis. Nothing seemed too difficult for the boy to master. There was a magnificent combination of power and touch in his play. At the net his volleys were sharp and crisp. On the baseline, he could hit the ball with looping topspin, underspin, or blistering flat returns. Ahmed's reactions and foot speed enabled him to save points that would be lost to others. Above all, he had a fighting spirit.

Three months passed and Amon was convinced Ahmed could become one of the greats of the game. One of the greats like he should have been. The question now was what to do about it? By this time a deep emotional bond had developed. During quiet times after intense practice, Amon would show the boy Tel Aviv University's academic buildings and modernistic sculpture. They would walk across the central lawn as bordering palm trees moved on sea breezes. Ahmed, shy at first, began to talk about his first home in the village, with its winking campfires at night. About the straw mat on which he slept after an evening meal of maize and how the shepherds guarded their sheep. He often said he preferred life in the city, but that living in shanty towns of mud and tin was hard.

Ahmed's life expanded as his skills increased. And Amon was reborn through nurturing the talent of his protege. But a shot at greatness required that Ahmed have the best. The best facilities, the best financial backing, the best of everything. As a Palestinian he would be denied that in Israel. Amon had to get him out.

Take him to Florida. You've arranged the documentation to get him into the United States. Why wait? Do it now.

Several days later, Amon disguised himself as an Arab and went to Ahmed's home. It took several hours to locate the tiny hovel stuck in the honeycomb streets that made up the Palestinian section of Tel Aviv.

Ahmed's mother, a tall handsome woman with the same Mediterranean features as her son, answered the door. She was wearing a *hijab,* the traditional headscarf worn by Muslim women. Mrs. Naji did not trust this Jewish man with the scarred face hidden beneath an Arab *keffiyeh,* but kept her suspicions to herself. "Come in. Ahmed is off playing with friends."

Amon seated himself at a small wooden table across from Ahmed's father. There was no running water or electricity, but the Naji household was neat and inviting.

"This is my older son, Ali," the father said, glancing at the youth standing beside him. Tall and wiry, about ten years Ahmed's senior, Ali's coloring favored his father.

"How are you, Ali? I'm Amon Weizman."

"Why does a Jew dress like an Arab?" Ali asked.

"Be quiet, boy," Mr. Naji said. "Use your head, not your mouth."

Ali stepped back into the shadows, a brooding presence.

Mrs. Naji served the customary freshly brewed coffee. Amon turned to the father. "Mr. Naji, I believe Ahmed could become a great champion. He has all the necessary skills --- speed, power, willingness to learn, and most importantly an indomitable will to win."

Mr. Naji sipped his coffee.

Amon's palms were moist. He grasped his cup, feeling its

heat. "Ahmed needs full-time training at the best training and educational facilities. Those things are denied him in Israel."

Mr. Naji set his coffee cup down. "What exactly are you suggesting, Mr. Weizman?"

"Taking Ahmed to the United States." A thick silence descended. "I will personally see to it that he receives the finest training and best education. The United States offers so much. There, he will be free of the war and conflict we have here. He can concentrate on his profession while advancing his education."

Ali stepped forward. "Education in the ways of Satan? No Zionist will --- "

"Silence!" Mr. Naji glared at his son. "This matter is of no concern to you." Ali retreated, staring incredulously at his father.

Mr. Naji stared at his coffee, considering the madness of war. Already, he had lost three brothers and a sister. Once again, Israeli warplanes and tanks were attacking Palestinian bases in Lebanon. With this new fighting, he would be forced to move his family. *So much suffering,* he thought. *But perhaps Ahmed can be spared. Yes,* the ways of Allah were strange. Perhaps, in His infinite wisdom, he had sent this Jew to save him?

"Forgive Ali's manners," Mr. Naji said at last. "The war has left a bloody mark."

Amon lowered his gaze. "We have all suffered."

Mrs. Naji stood beside her husband. "What about Ahmed's religion and Palestinian heritage?"

Amon looked into her suspicious eyes. "As I explained, my interest in Ahmed is not religious or political. I have no desire to separate you from your son. In the United States his teachings of Islam will continue, according to your wishes. And, I will see that he returns here to visit at least twice a year."

Mrs. Naji adjusted her *hijab* and stared at Amon. For a terrifying moment, he imagined she could see the lie inside him. "And, what will you get out of this, Mr. Weizman?"

"Redemption, Mrs. Naji. Redemption."

*   *   *

AMON opened his eyes. His breathing rasped under the oxygen mask. Crystal droplets continued to drip down the I.V., but the plastic bag was shriveled, nearly empty. Like his life, it too was about to run out. Amon tried to remember the exact moment when he sacrificed his soul. Perhaps, it was the first time he had seen the young Ahmed hit the ball. An innocent boy exploited to salvage his own ravaged life. Dear God! Adopting Ahmed and changing his name to Ben Weizman had been crime enough. But, introducing him to Judaism and, years later, when his memory of Palestine began to fade, planting lies that his Jewish birth family had been killed by Palestinian terrorists...... An abomination.

To make the transformation complete, he even had Ahmed circumcised. Then, with the help of an Israeli Embassy contact in Washington, legally adopted him. After that, with the passage of time, Amon's lies became Ben's reality. Amon carefully constructed the young boy'sworld. To produce the perfect clone, he became Ben's father, savior, coach, and friend.

Amon's eyes were terribly heavy. The shriveled fluid bag jogged on its hook. *So many lies,* he thought. *God's punishment will be vast.*

*   *   *

AMON was slipping away when he heard the familiar voice, but faint, so faint. "Amon. Can you hear me, Amon?"

I should go now, face my God.

"Amon." Gentle pressure on his hand drew him back.

Ben. Is that you, Ben?

Amon's eyelids fluttered. Ben was there. He opened his mouth to speak. But a lifetime of lies could not be spoken on collapsing lungs.

"Don't try to talk," Ben whispered. "I'm here with you."

Ben sat on the side of the bed and took Amon's hand. "I beat Thorenson today," he said. "It was a tough match, but I pulled it out in the fifth."

Amon watched the darkness pearling around him like soft velvet. His last thought was about the vastness of God's punishment.

Check out these other fine titles by
Durban House at your local book store.

Exceptional Books
by
Exceptional Writers

TUNNEL RUNNER by Richard Sand.

Tunnel Runner is a fast, deadly espionage thriller peopled with quirky and most times vicious characters. It tells of a dark world where murder is committed and no one is brought to account; where loyalties exist side by side with lies and extreme violence.

Ashman "the hunter, the hero, the killer" is a denizen of that world who awakens to find himself paralyzed in a mental hospital. He escapes and seeks vengeance, confronting this old friends, the Pentagon, the Mafia, and a mysterious general who is covering up the attack on TWA Flight 800.

People begin to die. There are shoot-outs and assassinations. A woman is blown up in her bathtub.

Ashman is cunning and ruthless as he moves through the labyrinth of deceit, violence, and suspicion. He is a tunnel runner, a ferret in the hole, who needs the danger to survive and hates them who have made him so.

It is this peculiar combination of ruthlessness and vulnerability that redeems Ashman as he goes for those who want him dead. Join him.

ROADHOUSE BLUES by Baron Birtcher.

From the sun-drenched sand of Santa Catalina Island to the smoky night clubs and back alleys of West Hollywood, Roadhouse Blues is a taut noir thriller that evokes images both surreal and disturbing.

Newly retired Homicide detective Mike Travis is torn from

comfort of his chartered yacht business and into the dark, bizarre underbelly of LA's music scene by a grisly string of murders.

A handsome, drug-addled psychopath has reemerged from an ancient Dionysean cult leaving a bloody trail of seemingly unrelated victims in his wake. Despite departmental rivalries that threaten to tear the investigation apart, Travis and his former partner reunite in an all-out effort to prevent more innocent blood from spilling into the unforgiving streets of the City of Angels.

MR. IRRELEVANT by Jerry Marshall.

Sports writer Paul Tenkiller and pro-football player Chesty Hake have been roommates for eight career seasons. Paul's Choctaw background of poverty and his gambling on sports, and Hake's dark memories of his mother being killed are the forces which will make their friendship go horribly wrong.

Chesty Hake, the last man chosen in the draft, has been dubbed Mr. Irrelevant. By every yardstick, he should not be playing pro football. But, because of his heart and high threshold for pain, he preservers.

Paul Tenkiller has been on a gravy train because of Hake's generosity. Gleaning information vital to gambling on football, his relationship with Hake is at once loyal and deceitful.

Then during his eighth and final season, Hake slides into paranoia and Tenkiller is caught up in the dilemma. But Paul is behind the curve, and events spiral out of his control, until the bloody end comes in murder and betrayal.